THE GREATER TRUMPS

THE GREATER TRUMPS

by

CHARLES WILLIAMS

WILLIAM B. EERDMANS PUBLISHING COMPANY

Printing History

First published in 1932 by Victor Gollancz
Limited. New edition published in 1954
by Faber and Faber Limited, London. This
American paperback edition published in
1976 by Wm. B. Eerdmans Publishing Co.,
Grand Rapids, Michigan 49502

Reprinted, May 1984

Library of Congress Cataloging in Publication Data

Williams, Charles, 1886-1945.
    The greater trumps.

    Reprint of the 1954 ed. published by Faber &
Faber, London.
    I.   Title.
PZ3.W67144Gr8   (PR6045.I5)   823'.9'12   76-18873
ISBN 0-8028-1649-5

CONTENTS

Chapter One

THE LEGACY

". . . perfect Babel," Mr. Coningsby said peevishly, threw himself into a chair, and took up the evening paper. "But Babel never was perfect, was it?" Nancy said to her brother in a low voice, yet not so low that her father could not hear if he chose. He did not choose, because at the moment he could not think of a sufficiently short sentence; a minute afterwards it occurred to him that he might have said, "Then it's perfect now." But it didn't matter; Nancy would only have been rude again, and her brother too. Children were. He looked at his sister, who was reading on the other side of the fire. She looked comfortable and interested, so he naturally decided to disturb her.

"And what have you been doing to-day, Sybil?" he asked, with an insincere good will, and as she looked up he thought angrily, "Her skin's getting clearer every day."

"Why, nothing very much," Sybil Coningsby said. "I did some shopping, and I made a cake, and went for a walk and changed the library books. And since tea I've been reading."

"Nice day," Mr. Coningsby answered, between a question and a sneer, wishing it hadn't been, though he was aware that if it hadn't been . . . but then it was certain to have been. Sybil always seemed to have nice days. He looked at his paper again. "I see the Government are putting a fresh duty on dried fruits," he snorted.

Sybil tried to say something, and failed. She was getting stupid, she thought, or (more probably) lazy. There ought to be something to say about the Government putting a duty on dried fruits. Nancy spoke instead.

7

"You're slow, auntie," she said. "The correct answer is: 'I suppose that means that the price will go up!' The reply to that is, 'Everything goes up under this accursed Government!'"

"Will you please let me do my own talking, Nancy?" her father snapped at her.

"Then I wish you'd talk something livelier than the Dead March in *Saul*," Nancy said.

"You're out of date again, Nancy," jeered her brother. "Nobody plays that old thing nowadays."

"Go to hell!" said Nancy.

Mr. Coningsby immediately stood up. "Nancy, you shall not use such language in this house," he called out.

"O, very well," Nancy said, walked to the window, opened it, put her head out, and said to the world, but (it annoyed her to feel) in a more subdued voice, "Go to hell." She pulled in her head and shut the window. "There, father," she said, "that wasn't in the house."

Sybil Coningsby said equally, "Nancy, you're in a bad temper."

"And suppose I am?" Nancy answered. "Who began it?"

"Don't answer your aunt back," said Mr. Coningsby, still loudly. "She at least is a lady."

"She's more," said Nancy. "She's a saint. And I'm a worm and the child of . . ."

She abandoned the sentence too late. Her father picked up his paper, walked to the door, turned his head, uttered, "If I am wanted, Sybil, I shall be in my study," and went out. Ralph grinned at Nancy; their aunt looked at them both with a wise irony.

"What energy!" she murmured, and Nancy looked back at her, half in anger, half in admiration.

"Doesn't father *ever* annoy you, auntie?" she asked.

"No, my dear," Miss Coningsby said.

"Don't we ever annoy you?" Nancy asked again.

"No, my dear," Miss Coningsby said.

8

"Doesn't anyone ever annoy you, aunt?" Ralph took up the chant.

"Hardly at all," Miss Coningsby said. "What extraordinary ideas you children have! Why should anyone annoy me?"

"Well, we annoy father all right," Nancy remarked, "and I never mean to when I begin. But Ralph and I weren't making all that noise—and anyhow Babel wasn't perfect."

Sybil Coningsby picked up her book again. "My dear Nancy, you never do begin; you just happen along," she said, and dropped her eyes so resolutely to her page that Nancy hesitated to ask her what she meant.

The room was settling back into the quiet which had filled it before Mr. Coningsby's arrival, when the bell of the front door rang. Nancy sprang to her feet and ran into the hall. "Right, Agnes," she sang: "I'll see to it."

"That'll be Henry," Ralph said as she disappeared. "Wasn't he coming to dinner?"

"Yes," his aunt murmured without looking up. One of the things about Sybil Coningsby that occasionally annoyed other people—Ralph among them—was her capacity for saying, quite simply, "Yes" or "No", and stopping there, rather as if at times she were literally following Christ's maxim about conversation. She would talk socially, if necessary, and sociably, if the chance arose, but she seemed to be able to manage without saying a lot of usual things. There was thus, to her acquaintances, a kind of blank about her; the world for a moment seemed with a shock to disappear and they were left in a distasteful void.

"Your aunt", Mr. Coningsby had once said, "has no small-talk. It's a pity." Ralph had agreed: Nancy had not, and there had been one of those continual small rows which at once annoyed and appeased their father. Annoyed him—for they hurt his dignity; appeased him—for they at least gave him a dignity to be hurt. He was somebody then for a few minutes; he was not merely a curiously festering consciousness. It was true he was also a legal officer of standing—a Warden in Lunacy. But—his emotions worried him with a question which his intellect refused to define—what, what exactly was the satisfaction of being a Warden in Lunacy? Fifty-eight; fifty-nine. But Sybil was older; she was over sixty. Perhaps in a few years this gnawing would pass. She was contented: no doubt time would put him also at peace.

He was not thinking of this while he sat in the room they called his study, looking at the evening paper and waiting for dinner. He was thinking how shameful Nancy's behaviour had been. She lacked respect, she lacked modesty, she almost lacked decency. All that he had done . . . no doubt her engagement to—her understanding with—whatever it was she had along with this young Henry Lee fellow—had hardened her. There had been a rather vague confidence, a ring had appeared, so had Henry quite often. But to what the engagement was tending or of what the understanding was capable—that Mr. Coningsby could not or had not been allowed to grasp. He sat thinking of it, consoling himself with the reflection that one day she'd be sorry. She wasn't . . . she was . . . confused; all confused . . . confusion confounded . . . yes. . . . Suddenly Nancy was in the room—"Look here, old thing"—no, he wasn't asleep; she was saying it. He hated to be discovered asleep just before dinner; perhaps she hadn't noticed—"and all that. Come and talk to Henry a minute before we eat."

If her father had been quite clear how far the apology had gone, he would have known whether he might reasonably accept it. But he wasn't, and he didn't want to argue because of not having been asleep. So he made a noise in his throat and got up, adding with a princely magnanimity, "But don't be rude to your aunt: I won't tolerate *that*."

Nancy, glowing with her past brief conversation with Henry, and looking forward to the immediate future with zest, subdued an inclination to point out that it was she who had called Sybil a saint, and they both returned to the drawing-room.

The Legacy

Although Mr. Coningsby had known his daughter's *fiancé*—if indeed he were that—for some months now, he still felt a slight shock at seeing him. For to him Henry Lee, in spite of being a barrister—a young, a briefless barrister, but a barrister—was so obviously a gipsy that his profession seemed as if it must be assumed for a sinister purpose. He was fairly tall and dark-haired and dark-skinned, and his eyes were bright and darting; and his soft collar looked almost like a handkerchief coiled round his throat, only straighter, and his long fingers, with their quick secret movements—"Hen-roosts", Mr. Coningsby thought, as he had thought before. A nice thing for Nancy to be tramping the roads—and Nancy was a gipsy name. That was her mother's fault. Names had for him a horrid attraction, largely owing to his own, which was Lothair. That disastrous name had to do with his father's godmother, a rich old lady with a passionate admiration for Lord Beaconsfield. To please that admiration her godson's first child had been named Sybil; the second Lothair. It might have been Tancred or Alroy; it might even have been Endymion. Mr. Coningsby himself allowed that Endymion Coningsby would have been worse. The other titles would no doubt have been allocated in turn, but for two facts; first, that the godmother abandoned politics for religion and spent large sums of money on Anglican sisterhoods; second, that there were no more children. But the younger was at once there, and there too soon to benefit by the conversion which would have saved others. Lothair—always, through a document-signing, bank-corresponding, cheque-drawing, letter-writing, form-filling, addressed, directoried, and important life, always Lothair Coningsby. If only he could have been called Henry Lee!

He thought so once more as they settled to dinner. He thought so through the soup. Something had always been unfair to him, luck or fate or something. Some people were like that, beaten through no fault of their own, wounded before the battle began; not everybody would have done so well as he had. But how it dogged him—that ghastly luck! Even in the last month Duncannon (and everyone knew that Duncannon was well off) had left him . . . no honest, useful, sincere legacy, but a collection of playing-cards, with a request that it should be preserved intact by his old friend, the legatee, Lothair Coningsby, and a further request that at the said legatee's death the collection should be presented to the British Museum. About that the legatee refused to think; some of the packs were, he believed, rather valuable. But for a couple of years or so, or anyhow for a year, nothing could be done: too many people knew of it. There had even been a paragraph in one of the papers. He couldn't sell them—Mr. Coningsby flinched as the word struck him for the first time—not yet awhile anyhow.

"Father," Nancy said, "will you show us Mr. Duncannon's playing-cards after dinner?" Mr. Coningsby just checked a vicious sneer. "Henry", Nancy went on, "saw about them in the papers." Mr. Coningsby saw a gipsy reading torn scraps of newspapers under a hedge. "And he knows something about cards. What a lot you *do* know, Henry!" Yes, in a fair, cheating yokels out of their pennies by tricks or fortune-telling: which card is the pea under? Something like that, anyhow. Bah!

"My dear," he said, "it's rather a painful business. Duncannon was my dear friend."

"Still, father, if you would. . . . He'd have loved people to be interested."

Mr. Coningsby, looking up suddenly, caught a swift, tender smile on Sybil's face, and wondered what she was grinning at. Nancy had hit on the one undeniable fact about the late Mr. Duncannon, and he couldn't think of any way of getting round it. But why should Sybil be amused?

"I'd be very grateful if you would, sir," the young man said. "I do find them interesting—it's in my blood, I suppose," he added, laughing at Nancy.

"And can you tell fortunes? Can you tell mine?" she answered joyously.

"Some by cards and some by hands," he said, "and some by the stars."

"O, I can tell some by hands," she answered. "I've told father's and auntie's. Only I can't understand father's line of life—it seems to stop at about forty, yet here he is still alive." Mr. Coningsby, feeling more like a death's head than a living Warden in Lunacy, looked down again.

"And Miss Coningsby's?" Henry asked, bowing towards her.

"O, auntie's goes on for ever, as far as I can see," Nancy answered, "right round under the finger."

Henry for a moment looked at Sybil a little oddly, but he said nothing, and the chatter about palmistry was lost in Ralph's dominating the conversation with an announcement that those things, like Spiritualism, were all great rubbish. "How can you tell from the palm of my hand whether I'm going to be ill at fifty or have a fortune left me at sixty or go to Zanzibar at seventy?"

"Hands are strange things," Henry said. "Nobody knows very much about them yet."

"Eh?" said Ralph, surprised.

"Auntie's got the loveliest hands I ever saw," Nancy said, sending a side-glance at Henry, and meeting the quick astonishment of his eyebrows. This being what he was meant to show—because she did think she had good hands, the rest of her being tolerable but unnoticeable, hair, face, figure, and everything—she allowed her own hand for a moment to touch his, and added, "Look at them."

They all looked, even Sybil herself, who said softly, "They are rather nice, aren't they?"

Her brother thought privately that this remark was in execrable taste; one didn't praise one's own belongings, still less oneself. What would people think if he said his face was "rather nice"?

"They're dears," said Nancy.

"Jolly good," said Ralph.

"They're extremely beautiful," said Henry.

"There's a very striking hand in the British Museum", Mr. Coningsby said, feeling the time had come for him to break silence, "belonging to an Egyptian king or something. Just a giant head and then in front of it a great arm with the fist closed—so." He illustrated.

"I know it, sir," Henry said, "the hand of the image of Rameses: it is a hand of power."

"The hand of power! I thought that was something to do with murderers; no, of course, that was glory," Nancy said, adding immediately, "And now, father, do let's look at the cards while we have coffee."

Mr. Coningsby, seeing no easy way out, gloomily assented. "Where did you have them put, Sybil?" he asked as the whole party rose.

"In the chest in your study," she answered. "The catalogue's with them."

"Catalogue?" Ralph said. "He did it in style, didn't he? Fancy me making a catalogue of my old tennis racquets."

"These cards", Mr. Coningsby said with considerable restraint, "were not worn-out toys. They are a very valuable and curious collection of remarkable cards, gathered together with considerable difficulty and in some sense, I believe, priceless."

Nancy pinched Henry's arm as they followed their father from the dining-room. "The dear!" she said. "I've heard him say the same thing himself, before they belonged to him."

Ralph was whistling. "O, but I say now, priceless?" he said. "That'd be pretty valuable, wouldn't it?"

"I don't know exactly what the value would be to collectors, but considerable," Mr. Coningsby said as he opened the large wooden chest, and then, thinking of the British Museum, added in a more sullen voice, "Considerable."

Sybil took from the chest a fat writing-book. "Well, shall

I read the descriptions?" she asked. "If someone will call out
the numbers." For each pack was contained in a special little
leather cover, with a place on it for a white slip containing a
number.

"Right ho!" Ralph said. "I'll call out the numbers. Are
they in order? It doesn't look like it. Number ninety-four."

"I think I will read, Sybil," Mr. Coningsby said. "I've
heard Duncannon talk of them often and it's more suitable.
Perhaps you'd pick them up and call the numbers out. And
then the young people can look at them."

"Give me that chair, then, if you will, Henry," Sybil assented. Her brother sat down on the other side of a small table,
and "the young people" thronged round it.

"Number——," Sybil began and paused. "Ralph, if you
wouldn't mind going on the same side as Nancy and Henry,
I could see too."

Ralph obeyed, unaware that this movement, while removing an obstacle from his aunt's gaze, also removed his own
from the two lovers. Sybil, having achieved the maximum of
effort, said again, "Number——"

"I didn't think you'd be very interested, aunt," Ralph, with
a belated sense of apology, threw in.

Sybil smiled at him and said again, "Number——"

"I have never known your aunt *not* be interested in anything,
my boy," Mr. Coningsby said severely, looking up, but more
at Sybil than at Ralph, as if he were inclined to add, "and
how the devil she does it I can't think!"

"Darling," said Nancy, "aunt's a perfect miracle, but can't
we leave her for now and get on with the cards?"

"We are on the point of 'getting on' with them, as you
call it, Nancy," her father answered. "I wish you'd remember this is something of an ordeal to me, and treat it more
seriously."

Nancy's hand, under the table, squeezed its impatience into
Henry's and relieved her tongue. When the momentary silence

had achieved seriousness but had not reached self-conscious-ness, Sybil's voice collected and, as it were, concluded it with the words, "Number ninety-four".

"Ninety-four," Mr. Coningsby read out, " 'French; *circa* 1789. Supposed to have been designed by David. A special Revolutionary symbolism. In this pack the Knaves are painted as a peasant, a beggar, an *aubergiste*, and a *sansculotte* respectively; the Queens (Marie Antoinette) have each a red line round the neck, as if guillotined; the Kings are reversed; over the ace is the red cap of liberty. Round the edge of each card is the legend, *La République, une, libre, indivisible.*' "

"Number nine," Sybil said, and put down another pack.

"Nine," read Mr. Coningsby. " 'Spanish pack, eighteenth century. The Court cards are ecclesiastical—cardinals, bishops, and priests. It is unlikely that this pack was ever used for play-ing; probably it was painted as an act of devotion or thanks-giving. See Appendix for possible portraits.' "

"Number three hundred and forty-one," Sybil said.

" 'Most rare'," Mr. Coningsby read. " 'Very early pack of Tarot cards. I have not been able to trace the origin of these; they have some resemblances to a fifteenth-century pack now in the Louvre, but would seem to be even earlier. The material of which they are made is unusual—? papyrus. The four suits are, as usual, sceptres, swords, cups, and coins; the Greater Trumps are in the following order (numbered at the foot in Roman): (i) The Juggler, (ii) The Empress, (iii) The High Priestess, or Woman Pope——' "

"The what?" Nancy exclaimed. "What! Pope Joan? Sorry, father, I didn't mean to interrupt."

" '(iv) The Pope—or Hierophant, (v) The Emperor—or Ruler, (vi) The Chariot, (vii) The Lovers, (viii) The Hermit, (ix) Temperance, (x) Fortitude, (xi) Justice, (xii) The Wheel of Fortune, (xiii) The Hanged Man.' "

"Jolly game of bridge we could have with these," Ralph remarked. "I lead the Hanged Man."

The Legacy

There was a tremendous pause. "Ralph, if you can only make fun——" Mr. Coningsby began, and stopped.

"Do go on," Sybil Coningsby's voice implored. "I should have had to say something silly if Ralph hadn't. It's so exciting."

Mr. Coningsby gave a suppressed grunt, fortunately missed Nancy's low-breathed comment on it—"The Hanged Man!"—and proceeded.

" '(xiv) Death, (xv) The Devil, (xvi) The Falling Tower, (xvii) The Star, (xviii) The Moon, (xix) The Sun, (xx) The Last Judgement——' "

Mr. Coningsby paused to shift his eyeglasses; in a perfect silence the others waited.

" '(xxi) The Universe, (o) The Fool.' "

"Nought usually comes at the beginning," Ralph said.

"Not necessarily," said Sybil. "It might come anywhere. Nought isn't a number at all. It's the opposite of number."

Nancy looked up from the cards. "Got you, aunt," she said. "What about ten? Nought's a number there—it's part of ten."

"Quite right, Nancy," Mr. Coningsby said with something like pleasure. "I think the child has you, Sybil."

"Well, if you say that any mathematical arrangement of one and nought really makes ten——" Sybil smiled. "Can it possibly be more than a way of representing ten?"

"It doesn't matter, anyhow," Nancy hastily said. "Aren't they fascinating? But why are they? And what do they all mean? Henry, why are you looking at them like that?"

Henry indeed was examining the first card, the Juggler, with close attention, as if investigating the smallest detail. It was a man in a white tunic, but the face, tilted back, was fore-shortened, and darkened by the brim of some black cap that he wore: a cap so black that something of night itself seemed to have been used in the painting. The heavy shadow and the short pointed beard hid the face from the observer. On the breast of the tunic were three embroidered circles—the first

made of swords and staffs and cups and coins, balanced one
on the other from the coin at the bottom to the apex of two
pointing swords at the top; and within this was a circle, so
far as Nancy could see, made up of rounded representations
of twenty of the superior cards each in its own round; and
within that was a circle containing one figure, but that was so
small she couldn't make out what it was. The man was apparently supposed to be juggling; one hand was up in the air,
one was low and open towards the ground, and between them,
in an arch, as if tossed and caught and tossed again, were
innumerable shining balls. In the top left-hand corner of the
card was a complex device of curiously interwoven lines.

Henry put it down slowly as Nancy spoke and turned his
eyes to her. But hers, as they looked to plunge into that other
depth—ocean pouring into ocean and itself receiving ocean—
found themselves thwarted. Instead of oceans they saw pools,
abandoned by a tide already beyond sight: she blenched as a
bather might do in the cold wind across an empty shore.
"Henry!" she exclaimed.

It was, surely, no such great thing, only a momentary pre-
occupation. But he was already glancing again at the cards;
he had already picked up another, and was scrutinizing the
figure of the hierophantic woman. It had been drawn sitting
on an ancient throne between two heavy pillars; a cloud of
smoke rolled high above the priestly head-dress and solemn
veil that she wore, and under her feet were rivers pouring out
in falling cataracts. One hand was stretched out as if directing
the flow of those waters; the other lay on a heavy open volume,
with great clasps undone, that rested on her knees. This card
also was stamped in the top left-hand corner with an involved
figure of intermingled lines.

"Well!" said Nancy, as she stared at it.

"But, look here," Ralph asked, "does one play with them,
or what?" He peered over Henry's shoulder. "Old Maid, I
suppose; and Beggar my Neighbour with the first."

The Legacy

"They're very wonderfully done, aren't they?" Sybil Coningsby asked, and herself delicately picked up one of what her brother had called the Greater Trumps. It was the nineteenth card—that named the Sun—and was perfectly simple: the sun shone full in a clear sky, and two children—a boy and a girl—played happily below. Sybil smiled again as she contemplated them. "Aren't they the loveliest things?" she breathed, and indeed they were so vivid, so intense, so rapturous under that beneficent light, of which some sort of reflection passed into Sybil's own face while she brooded. Or so it seemed to Henry, who had put down his card when Ralph spoke and over Nancy's bent head was now watching her aunt. Sybil looked up and saw him. "Aren't they perfect, Henry?" she asked.

"They are very, very fine," Lee said, and yet seemed a little puzzled, as if he had expected something, but not quite that.

"But what—are—they—all—about?" Ralph asked. "What's the idea of it?"

"Duncannon used to tell me", Mr. Coningsby said; he had put down his catalogue now, and was standing by the table with the others; his high, bald forehead gleaming a little in the light, his thin, dissatisfied face bent towards the pack, "that the Tarot cards were an invention of the fourteenth century, though supposed by some to be Egyptian." He stopped, as if everything were explained.

"Stupendous bit of work—inventing them," Ralph said gravely. "But why did anyone bother? What I mean—it seems rather . . . rather needless, doesn't it?"

"We have a tale about them," Henry Lee began, with a cautious ease, and Mr. Coningsby said, "We?"

Ever so slightly the young man flushed. "I mean the gipsies," he answered lightly, and added to Nancy, "That's your fault, darling, for always pretending that I'm a real gipsy with a caravan, a tin kettle, and a grandmother with a black pipe."

"Wouldn't she love these cards?" Nancy said enthusiastically

"Henry, darling, do have a grandmother, so that she can tell us stories about Tarots, and perhaps even tell fortunes with—what did you call them, father?—the Greater Trumps."

"Well," said Ralph, abandoning the whole subject, "shall we look at some more?"

"At least, I've a grandfather——" Henry said to Nancy; but "O, a grandfather!" she mocked him. "But he lives in a house with electric light, doesn't he? Not in a caravan under the moon. Still, can he tell us what this is?" She picked up the last card, that numbered nought, and exhibited it. It might have needed some explanation, for it was obscure enough. It was painted with the figure of a young man, clothed in an outlandish dress of four striped colours—black and grey and silver and red; his legs and feet and arms and hands were bare, and he had over one shoulder a staff, carved into serpentine curves, that carried a round bag, not unlike the balls with which the Juggler played. The bag rested against his shoulder, so that as he stood there he supported as well as bore it. Before him a dragon-fly, or some such airy creature, danced; by his side a larger thing, a lynx or young tiger, stretched itself up to him—whether in affection or attack could not be guessed, so poised between both the beast stood. The man's eyes were very bright; he was smiling, and the smile was so intense and rapt that those looking at it felt a quick motion of contempt—no sane man could be as happy as that. He was painted as if pausing in his stride, and there was no scenic background; he and his were seen against a flatness of dull gold.

"No," said Henry, "that's the difficulty—at least, it's the unknown factor."

"The unknown factor in what?" Mr. Coningsby asked.

"In——" Henry paused a second, then he added, "in telling fortunes by the Tarots. There are different systems, you know, but none of them is quite convincing in what it does with the Fool. They all treat it as if it were to be added to the Greater Trumps—making twenty-two."

The Legacy

"So there are twenty-two," Mr. Coningsby said. "I've just read them out."

"No, sir," Henry answered, almost reluctantly, "not exactly. Strictly there are the twenty-one and the nought. As Miss Coningsby said. And you see the nought—well, it's nought—nothing, unaccountable."

"Well, shall we look at some more?" Ralph asked.

"Can you tell fortunes by them?" Nancy said eagerly, but Henry shook his head.

"Not properly," he answered; "at least, I'd rather not try. It can be done; my grandfather might know. They are very curious cards, and this is a very curious pack."

"Why are they curious cards?" Nancy went on questioning.

Henry, still staring at them, answered, "It's said that the shuffling of the cards is the earth, and the pattering of the cards is the rain, and the beating of the cards is the wind, and the pointing of the cards is the fire. That's of the four suits. But the Greater Trumps, it's said, are the meaning of all process and the measure of the everlasting dance."

"Some folk-lore survival, I suppose?" Mr. Coningsby said, wishing that his daughter hadn't got herself mixed up with a fellow very much like a folk-lore survival.

"Certainly it may be that, sir," the young man answered, "from the tales my people used to tell round their fires while they were vagabonds."

"It sounds frightfully thrilling," Nancy said. "What *is* the everlasting dance, Henry darling?"

He put his arm round her as Mr. Coningsby turned back to his chair. "Don't you know?" he whispered. "Look at the seventh card."

She obeyed; and on it, under the stamped monogram, she saw the two lovers, each aureoled, each with hands stretched out; each clad in some wild beast's skin, dancing side by side down a long road, that ran from a far-off point right down to the foreground. Her hand closed on Henry's and she smiled at him. "Just that?" she said.

"That's at least the first movement," he answered; "unless you go with the hermit."

"Sybil, I'm waiting," Mr. Coningsby said, and Sybil hastily picked up another pack, while Ralph very willingly collected and put away the Tarots.

But the interest had flagged. Henry and Nancy were pre-occupied, Mr. Coningsby and his son were beginning to be bored, and in a few minutes Sybil said pleasantly, "Don't you all think we've looked at about enough for to-night?"

"She really does know when to stop," Mr. Coningsby thought to himself, but he only said cheerfully, "Just as you like, just as you like. What do you say, Henry?"

"Eh? . . . O, just as you like," Henry agreed with a start.

"I vote we push them back then," Ralph said, even more cheerfully than his father. "Jolly good collection. But those what-you-may-call-them are the star lot."

Hours later, by the door, the sight of a single star low in the heavens brought one of the "what-you-may-call-thems" back to Nancy's mind. "O, and darling," she said, "will you teach me how to tell fortunes by those other cards—you know, the special ones?"

"The Tarots?" Henry asked her, with a touch of irony in his voice.

"If that's what you call them," she said. "I can do a bit by the ordinary ones."

"Have you got the sleight of hand for it?" he asked. "You have to feel how the cards are going, and let yourself do what they mean."

Nancy looked at her hands, and flexed them. "I don't see why not, unless you have to do it very quickly. Do try me, Henry sweet."

He took both her hands in one of his. "We'll try, darling," he answered; "we'll try what you can do with the Greater

Trumps. If it's the pack I think it is. Tell me, do you think your father would ever sell them to me?"

"Why? Do you want them?" she asked in surprise. "Henry, I believe you're a real gipsy after all! Will you disguise yourself and go to the races? O, let's, and I'll be the gipsy maiden— 'Kind sir, kind sir,' " she trilled, "and everyone'll cross my palm with pound notes because I'm so beautiful, and perhaps the King will kiss me before all the Court ladies. Would you like that? He might give me a diamond ring too, and you could show it to the judges when they came to tea. No, don't tell me they won't, because when you're a judge they will, and you'll all talk about your cases till I shall only have the diamond ring to think about and how the King of England once gave it to Nancy the little gipsy girl, before she became Lady Lee, and tried to soften her husband's hard heart for the poor prisoners the ruffians in the police brought to him. So when you see me dreaming you'll know what I'm dreaming of, and you must never, never interrupt."

"I don't really have much chance, do I?" Henry asked.

"O, cruel!" she said, "to mock your Nancy so! Will you call me a chatterbox before all the world? or shall I always talk to you on my fingers—like that?"—they gleamed before him, shaping the letters—"and tell you on them what shop I've been to each day, as if I were dumb and you were deaf?"

He caught a hand in one of his, and lightly struck the fingers of his other over its palm. "Don't flaunt your beauties," he said, "or when I'm a judge you'll be before me charged with having a proud heart, and I'll send you to spoil your hands doing laundry-work in a prison."

"Then I'll trap the governor's son, and escape," she said, "and make a ballad of a wicked judge, and how first he beat and then shut up his own true sweetheart. Darling, you must be getting on. I'll see you to-morrow, won't I? O, good night. Do go home and sleep well. Good night. Don't let anything happen to you, will you?"

"I'll stop it at once," he said. "If anything starts to happen, I'll be very angry with it."

"Do," she said, "for I don't want anything to happen ever any more. O, good night—why aren't you gone? It doesn't take you long to get home, does it? You'll be asleep by midnight."

But when she herself fell asleep Henry was driving his car out of London southward, and it was long past midnight before he stopped it at a lonely house among the Downs.

Chapter Two

THE HERMIT

An old man was sitting alone in a small room. He was at a table facing the door; behind him was another door. The walls were bare of pictures: the table was a large one, and it was almost completely covered with a set of Tarot cards. The old man was moving them very carefully from place to place, making little notes on a sheet of paper, and sometimes consulting an old manuscript book that lay by him. He was so absorbed that he did not hear the step outside, and it was not till the door opened that he looked up with a sudden exclamation. Henry Lee came lightly into the room.

"Why, Henry!" the old man said. Henry looked at the table, let his eyes run over the whole arrangement of the cards, and smiled.

"Still no nearer, grandfather?" he asked.

"Nearer? No, no, not nearer yet," his grandfather answered. "Not quite, yet awhile. But I shall do it." He sighed a little. "I keep the account very carefully," he said, "and some day I shall do it. I spend all my time on it."

Henry nodded towards the other door. "And—*they*?" he asked, lowering his voice a trifle.

"Yes," the old man said. "I watch them too. But, you know —it's too difficult. But I must do it at last. You're not . . . you're not coming back to help me, are you?"

"Why, I may even do that," Henry said, taking off his motoring-coat.

Aaron Lee got to his feet. He was certainly very old—nearly

a century, one might think, looking at the small wizened figure, dark-skinned and bald; but his movements, though slow, were not uncertain: his hands were steady as he leaned on the table, and if his voice shook a little, it was with excitement and not from senility.

"What do you mean, Henry?" he asked. "Have you found out anything? What have you heard? Have you—have you the secret?"

Henry sat down on the edge of the table, and idly fingered one of the cards. "Don't believe me too much," he said. "I don't believe myself. I don't know about the secret—no, I think we still have to find that out. But I think"—he dropped the card and looked burningly at his grandfather—"I think I have found the originals."

Aaron gave a short gasp. "It's not possible," he began, and fell into a fit of trembling so great that he dropped again into his chair. When to a degree it had passed, he said once more, "It's not possible."

"You think not?" the younger man asked.

"Tell me," Aaron exclaimed, leaning forward, "what are they? Why do you believe—how can you—that——" His voice stopped, so anxious was he, but after a moment's pause he added—"Tell me; tell me."

"It is so unlikely," Henry began, "and yet with *them* there is nothing either likely or unlikely, is there? One cannot tell how they will move to-morrow. Tell me first, grandfather, do you still watch my future every day?"

"Every day by the cards," Aaron said.

"And did yesterday promise nothing for to-day?" the young man asked.

"Nothing that I thought important," Aaron answered. "Something was to come to you, some piece of good luck; the ace of cups lay on the Wheel of Fortune—but I thought it had to do with your law. I put it by to ask you about when you came."

The Hermit

"You are old, grandfather," Henry said. "Are the cups only deniers for you to think so?"

"But what *could* I think?" Aaron protested. "It was a day's chance—I couldn't. . . . . But what is it? What have you found?"

"I have told you I am betrothed," Henry went on, using the solemn word as if deliberately, "and her father has had left him—by a friend of his who is dead—a collection of playing-cards. . . . O, the usual thing, except for a set of the symbols. He showed them to us and I tell you, grandfather, I think it is the very one original set. I've come here to-night to see."

"Have you got them?" the old one asked eagerly, but Henry shook his head.

"Time enough," he said. "Listen, among *them* is not the Chariot an Egyptian car, devised with two sphinxes, driven by a Greek, and having on it paintings of cities and islands?"

"It is just that," the other said.

"And Death—is not Death a naked peasant, with a knife in his hand, with his sandals slung at his side?"

"It is so," the other said again.

"Certainly then they are the same," Henry concluded. "But let us look at *them*, for that's why I have come."

The old man got up, and took from an inner pocket of his coat a key. He walked slowly to the inner door, and Henry followed him. He put the key in the lock, turned it, and opened the door. Within the room they were on the point of entering, and directly before them, there hung from ceiling to floor thick black curtains, and for a moment, as he laid his hand on one of these, the old man hesitated. Then he half pulled it aside, half lifted it, and went through, holding it so that his grandson might enter after him.

The place into which they came was smaller than the outer room. It was hung all round with a heavy black stuff, and it was filled with a curious pale light, which certainly did not come through any window or other opening. The colour of that pale light was uncertain; it seemed to change softly from one hue to another—now it was red, as if it were the reflection of a very distant fire; now it was green, as if diffused through invisible waters that covered them; now it was darker and half obscured by vapour; now those vapours were dispelled and the clear pallor of early dawn exhibited itself within the room. To this changing phenomenon of light the two men paid no attention; they were gazing at a table which stood in the centre.

It was a table made of some strange kind of wood: so much could be seen from the single central support which opened at the bottom into four foot-pieces, and each of these again into some twelve or fourteen claws, upon the whole fifty-six of which the table rested. But the top was hidden, for it was covered by a plate of what looked like gold, marked very intricately with a pattern, or perhaps with two patterns, one of squares, and one of circles, so that the eyes, as with a chess-board, saw now one and now the other as predominant. Upon that plate of gold were a number of little figures, each about three inches high, also of gold, it seemed, very wonderfully wrought; so that the likeness to the chess-board was even more pronounced, for to any hasty spectator (could such a one ever have penetrated there) the figures might have seemed like those in a game; only there were many of them, and they were all in movement. Gently and continuously they went, immingling, unresting—as if to some complicated measure, and as if of their own volition. There must have been nearly a hundred of them, and from the golden plate upon which they went came a slight sound of music—more like an echo than a sound—sometimes quickening, sometimes slowing, to which the golden figures kept a duteous rhythm, or perhaps the faint sound itself was but their harmonized movement upon their field.

Henry took a few steps forward, slowly and softly, almost

as if he were afraid that those small images would overhear him, and softly and slowly Aaron followed. They paused at a little distance from the table, and stood gazing at the figures, the young man in a careful comparison of them with his memory of the newly found cards. He saw among them those who bore the coins, and those who held swords or staffs or cups; and among those he searched for the shapes of the Greater Trumps, and one by one his eyes found them, but each separately, so that as he fastened his attention on one the rest faded around it to a golden blur. But there they were, in exact presentation—the Juggler who danced continuously round the edge of the circle, tossing little balls up and catching them again; the Emperor and Empress; the masculine and feminine hierophants; the old anchorite treading his measure and the hand-clasped lovers wheeling in theirs; a Sphinx-drawn chariot moving in a dancing guard of the four lesser orders; an image closing the mouth of a lion, and another bearing a cup closed by its hand, and another with scales but with unbandaged eyes—which had been numbered in the paintings under the titles of strength and temperance and justice; the wheel of fortune turning between two blinded shapes who bore it; two other shapes who bore between them a pole or cross on which hung by his foot the image of a man; the swift ubiquitous form of a sickle-armed Death; a horned mystery bestriding two chained victims; a tower that rose and fell into pieces, and then was re-arisen in some new place; and the woman who wore a crown of stars, and the twin beasts who had each of them on their heads a crescent moon, and the twin children on whose brows were two rayed suns in glory—the star, the moon, the sun; the heavenly form of judgement who danced with a skeleton half freed from its grave-clothes, and held a trumpet to its lips; and the single figure who leapt in a rapture and was named the world. One by one Henry recognized them and named them to himself, and all the while the tangled measure went swiftly on. After a few minutes he looked round: "They're certainly the same; in every detail they're the same. Some of the attributed meanings aren't here, of course, but that's all."

"Even to that?" Aaron asked in a low voice, and pointed to the Fool in the middle of the field.

It was still: it alone in the middle of all that curious dance did not move, though it stood as if poised for running; the lynx or other great cat by its side was motionless also. They paused —the man and the beast—as if struck into inactivity in the very midst of activity. And all about them, sliding, stepping, leaping, rolling, the complex dance went on.

"That certainly," Henry said, turning slowly away.

The old man took a step to meet him. "But then," he whispered, so that his faint voice blended with the faint music, "but then we can find out—at any moment—what the dance says? We can tell what the future will be—from what the present is?"

Henry spread out his hands towards the table, as if he were laying something down. "That could be done, I suppose," he answered. "But if the Fool does not move, how will it affect divination? Don't your books tell you anything?"

"There are no writings which tell us anything at all of the Fool," Aaron said.

They stood still for what might have been two or three minutes, watching that unresting movement, hearing that unceasing sound, themselves changed from moment to moment in that altering light; then Aaron said, "Come away now. I don't like to watch too long, unless I am working at the order of the dance."

Henry stood for a moment longer. "I wonder if you can know the dance without being among the dancers," he said.

"But we are," the old man answered hurriedly; "we are—everything is."

"O, as everything is," Henry uttered scornfully, "as stones or winds or ships. But stones and winds and ships don't *know*.

The Hermit

And to know——" He fell silent, and stood meditating till the other pulled at his arm; then, a little reluctantly, he turned to withdraw, and between the curtains and through the doorway they came into the outer room. Aaron locked the door and went back to his seat at the table, whence he looked inquiringly at his grandson.

"What will you do now about the cards?" he asked.

Henry came back from his secret thoughts with an abrupt movement of his body, and smiled, though his eyes remained brilliant and sombre. "I don't know," he admitted. "Remember, I've only just seen them."

"This owner, this father—will he sell them?" Aaron asked.

Henry played a tune on the table. "If he doesn't," he answered slowly, "I don't know quite how . . . He is supposed, at his death—or before, perhaps—to give them to the British Museum. All of them."

"What?" Aaron cried out in something like terror. "But that's imbecile. Surely he'd sell—if we offered him enough?"

Henry shook his head. "I don't know," he said. "He's a man who's got pretty well everything he wants and finds it entirely useless to him. He doesn't need money at all badly. He can think of nothing that will give him pleasure, and because of that he doesn't like other people to have too much pleasure. No, he isn't cruel; he's even kind in his own way. But he holds on to his own as a child does to a broken toy— because one day it might want it or because it doesn't like to see another child playing with what was once its own."

"But money?" Aaron urged.

"I tell you he doesn't want money," Henry said.

"Wouldn't he give it to his daughter?" Aaron asked more hopefully. "Are you going to marry her?"

"He can't easily give her one pack out of the whole collection, and the rest to the Museum," Henry answered. "Yes— I shall marry her. I think perhaps—but that doesn't matter. But if he gives her the whole lot he will be bothered by his

31

friend's wish; and if he gives her one pack he will be bothered
by the explanations; and if he leaves it all to the Museum he
will be bothered by losing it."

"But how will he lose it—if he keeps it while he's alive?"
the old man asked.

"I think he's already unhappy, even while he's alive, at the
idea of losing at his death so much that he could never enjoy,"
Henry said. "He is for ever waiting for satisfaction."

Aaron Lee leaned forward. "But it's necessary that he should
sell it or give it—or lose it somehow," he said anxiously.

"It would be very difficult for him to lose it," the other
answered. "And how do you know what virtue might pass
from the cards?"

"Only violence . . . that's unwise," Aaron answered. "But
to take them . . . to take them for this purpose . . . I don't
see the wrong."

"Mr. Lothair Coningsby would see the wrong," Henry said
drily. "And I doubt if I could persuade Nancy."

"What's she to do with it?" his grandfather asked con-
temptuously.

Henry smiled again, a bright but almost threatening flash
of amusement. "I wonder," he said. "But, whatever I wonder,
be certain, grandfather, that I'm determined not to go against
her till . . ."

He stopped for so long that Aaron said, "Till—till when?"

"Till I've seen whether the image of the Lovers has another
use," Henry finished. "To know—to see from within—to be
aware of the dance. Well, we shall see." His eyes fixed on the
inner door, he added slowly, "Nancy—Nancy—Nancy."

Aaron said: "But you must do something soon. We can't
run any risk. An accident——"

"Or a spasm of gloom," Henry added, "and the cards would
be in the Museum. Yes, you're right; we can't wait. By the
way, do you ever see anything of Joanna?"

"I haven't seen her for months," the old man answered,

with a slight shudder. "She came here in the summer—I told you."

"I know you did," Henry said. "Is she still as mad as ever? Is she still crying out on the names of the old dead gods?"

The other moved uneasily. "Don't let's talk of it. I am afraid of Joanna."

"Afraid of her?" Henry said scornfully. "Why, what can she do to harm us?"

"Joanna's mad, with a terrifying madness," Aaron said. "If she knows that the Tarots might be brought back to their originals and the working of the mystery be complete——"

"What could an old woman and an idiot boy do?" Henry asked.

"Call them an insane prophetess and a young obedient Samson," Aaron answered. "I dream of her sometimes as if she belonged to *them*. If she thought the body of her child was found and formed and vivified . . . and if she knew of the cards, she might . . . A mad hierophant . . . a hieratic hate. . . ."

"Mightn't she be appeased if she thought her child was found?" Henry asked.

"If she thought that we kept it from her?" the old man said. "Ask your own blood, Henry, what your desire would do. Your spirit is more like hers than mine. When she and I were young together, I set myself to discover the prophetic meaning of the dance, but she imagined herself a partner in it, and she studied the old tales and myths of Egypt—thirty years she studied them, and her child was to be a Mighty One born within the measure. It was born, and the same day it died——"

Henry interrupted him sharply. "You've never told me this," he said. "Did Joanna mean knowingly to create life within the dance? Why did the child die? Who was the father?"

"Because its heart was too great, perhaps, or its body too feeble: how should I know?" his grandfather answered. "She married a man who was reckoned knowledgeable, but he led an evil life and he was a plaything compared to Joanna. She longed to adore him, and she could only mock at him and herself. Yet she was fierce for him after the flesh, and she made him her child's father and hated him for his feebleness. She would strike and taunt him while the child was in her womb —for love and anger and hate and scorn and fear. The child was a seven-months' child, and it died. The father ran away from her the day before it was born, and the same night was killed in a street accident when he was drunk. But Joanna, when she heard that the child was dead, screamed once and her face changed, and the Tarot cards that she sought (as we have all done), and the myth of gods that she studied, and the child that should have been a lord of power and was instead a five-hours-old body of death—these tangled themselves in her brain for ever; and for fifty years she has sought the thing that she calls Osiris because it dies and Horus because it lives and at night little sweet names which only Stephen hears. And it has one and twenty faces, which are the faces of them within and of the Tarots, and when she finds the limbs that have been torn apart by her enemy, who is her husband and is Set and is we who seek the cards also, she thinks she will again become the Queen of Heaven, and the twice twenty-one gods shall adore her with incense and chanting. No doubt she is mad, Henry, but I had rather deal with your other mad creature than with her."

Henry meditated for some time, walking about the room in silence; then he said, "Well, there's no reason why she should hear of it, unless she snuffs the news up out of the air."

"She may even do that," Aaron said. "Her life is not as ours, and the air and the lords of the sceptres are one."

"In any case, I don't see what she can do to interfere with us," Henry answered. "She had her chance and lost it. I will see that I don't lose mine. As for Coningsby——" He walked up and down the room for a few minutes in silence; then he said, "I've a good mind to try and get them here for Christmas.

The Hermit

It's a month off—that ought to give me time. You could manage, I suppose?"

"What good would that be?" his grandfather asked.

Henry sat down again. "Why, it's clear", he said, "that we shall have to let them know something—Nancy and her father anyhow. If he's got to give us the cards he's got to have a reason for doing it, and so far as I can see——"

"You're not going to show him *them?*" Aaron exclaimed, glancing over his shoulder at the door of the inner room.

"Why not?" Henry asked lightly. "What does it matter? There're all sorts of explanations. Besides, I want to show Nancy, and she'll be able to work on him better if he's seen them."

"But he'll tell people!" Aaron protested.

"What can he tell them?" Henry asked. "And, if he does, who's to believe him? Besides—after we've got the cards . . . well, we don't know what we can do, do we? I'm sure that's the best. See, I'll ask Nancy—and she'll bring her aunt, I suppose——"

"Her aunt?" Aaron interrupted sharply. "How many are you going to bring? Who is this aunt?"

"Her aunt", Henry said, "is just the opposite to her father. As serene and undisturbed as . . . as *they* are. Nothing puts her out; nothing disturbs her. Yet she isn't a fool. She'll be quite harmless, however: it won't matter whether she sees or not. She'll be interested, but not concerned. Well, Nancy and her aunt and her father. I'll try and dodge the brother; he's simply a bore. There'll be the three of them, and me; say, for— Christmas Day's on a Saturday, isn't it?—say, from Thursday to Tuesday, or a day or two longer. Well?"

"But will he come?" Aaron asked doubtfully.

"I think he may," Henry said. "Oh, of course he won't want to, but, as he won't want to do anything else in particular, it may be possible to work it. Only you'd better keep Joanna out of the way."

"I don't know in the least where she is," the old man said irritably.

"Can't you find out by the cards?" Henry smiled. "Or must you wait for the Tarots?" On the word his face changed, and he came near to the table. "We will certainly have them," he said in a low, firm voice. "Who knows? perhaps we can find out what the Fool means, and why it doesn't dance."

Aaron caught his sleeve. "Henry," he breathed, "if—if there should be an accident—if there should—who would get the cards?"

"Don't be a fool," Henry said roughly. "Haven't you always told me that violence breaks the knowledge of the cards?"

"They told me so," the old man answered reluctantly, "but I don't see . . . anyhow, we needn't both . . ."

"Wait," his grandson answered, and turned to pick up his coat. "I must get back." He stretched himself, and laughed a little. "Nancy told me to have a good night," he said, "and here I am spending it talking to you."

"Don't talk too much to these people of yours," Aaron grumbled, "Nancy or any of them."

His grandson pulled on his coat. "Nancy and I will talk to one another," he said, "and perhaps what we say shall be stranger talk than ever lovers had before. Good night. I will tell you what I can do about it all in London."

Chapter Three

THE SHUFFLING OF THE CARDS

The Coningsbys usually went to Eastbourne for Christmas. The habit had been begun because Mr. Coningsby had discovered that he preferred hotel life for those few days to having his own house treated as an hotel. Groups of young people would arrive at any hour of day or night, and Nancy or Ralph, if in, would leap up and rush to welcome them or, if not in, would arrive soon after, inquiring for friends who had already disappeared. Mr. Coningsby disapproved strongly, but for once found himself helpless, so sudden was the rush; he therefore preferred to be generous and give everyone a thorough change. It was never quite clear whether he regarded this as on his sister's account chiefly or on his children's. She was supposed to need it, but they were supposed to enjoy it, and so after the first year they all went back each Christmas to the same hotel, and Mr. Coningsby put up with playing bridge and occasionally observing the revels and discussing civilization with other gentlemen of similar good nature.

It annoyed him slightly at times that Sybil never seemed quite grateful enough for the mere change—as change. Even the profound content in which she normally seemed to have her being—"sluggish, sluggish," Mr. Coningsby said to himself when he thought of it, and walked a little more briskly— even that repose must surely be all the pleasanter for a change. There were always some nice women about for her to talk to. Of course, she was pleased to go—but not sufficiently pleased to gratify Mr. Coningsby: he was maddened by that continuous equable delight. She enjoyed everything—and he, he enjoyed nothing.

But this year things were different—had got, or anyhow were going, to be different. It had begun with Ralph, who, rather confusedly, had intimated that he was going to have a still more thorough change by going off altogether with some friend of his whose people lived somewhere near Lewes. Mr. Coningsby had not said much, or did not seem to himself to have done so, but he had made it clear that he disliked such secession from the family life. To summer holidays spent with friends he had (he hoped) never objected, but Christmas was different. Christmas was, in fact, the time when Mr. Coningsby most nearly realized the passage of time and the approach of age and death. For Christmas every year had been marked by small but definite changes, through his own childhood, his youth, his marriage, his children's infancy and childhood, and now there were only two possibilities of change—the coming of a third generation or the stopping of Christmas. Each year that Mr. Coningsby succeeded in keeping Nancy and Ralph by him for Christmas postponed either unwelcome change, and enabled him to enter the New Year with the pretence that it was merely the Old Year beginning over again. But this year his friend's death had already shaken him, and if he and Sybil and Nancy—an engaged Nancy—were to be without Ralph, the threat of an inevitable solitude would loom very near. There would be a gap, and he had nothing with which to fill the gap or to meet what might come through it; nothing except the fact that he was a Warden in Lunacy, and had all the privileges of a Warden—such as going in to dinner before the elder sons of younger sons of peers. He did not know where, years before, he had picked up that bit of absurd knowledge, in what odd table of precedence, but he knew it was so, and had even mentioned it once to Sybil. But all the elder sons of younger sons of peers whose spectres he could crowd into that gap did not seem to fill it. There was an emptiness brought to mind, and only brought to mind, for it was always there, though he forgot it. He filled it with his office, his occupation, his family, his house, his friends, his politics, his food, his sleep, but sometimes the emptiness was too big to be filled thus, and sometimes it rolled up on him, along the street when he left the home in the morning, blowing in at evening through the open window or creeping up outside when it was shut, or even sometimes looking ridiculously at him in the unmeaning headlines of his morning paper. "Prime Minister", he would read, "Announces Fresh Oil Legislation"—and the words would be for one second all separate and meaningless—"Prime Minister"—what was a Prime Minister? Blur, blot, nothingness, and then again the breakfast-table and *The Times* and Sybil.

Ralph's announced defection therefore induced him unconsciously to desire to make a change for himself, and induced him again to meet more equably than he otherwise might have done Nancy's tentative hints about the possibility of the rest of them going to Henry's grandfather. It didn't strike him as being a very attractive suggestion for himself, but it offered him every chance of having Nancy and Henry as well as Ralph to blame for his probable discomfort or boredom or gloom, and therefore of lessening a concentration on Ralph, Ralph's desertion, change, age—and the other thing. Sybil, when he consulted her, was happy to find him already half-reconciled to the proposal.

"I'm afraid it'll be very dull for you," he said.

"O, I don't think so," she answered. "It'll have to be very dull indeed if it is."

"And of course we don't know what the grandfather's like," he added.

"He's presumably human," Sybil said, "so he'll be interesting somehow."

"Really, Sybil," Mr. Coningsby answered, almost crossly, "you do say the most ridiculous things. As if everybody was interesting."

"Well, I think everybody is," Sybil protested, "and things apart from their bodies we don't know, do we? And considering what funny, lovely things bodies are, I'm not especially anxious to leave off knowing them."

Her brother kept the conversation straight. "I gather that he's old but quite active still, not bed-ridden or anything."

"Then we shan't be expected to sit with him," Sybil said happily, "and, as Nancy and Henry certainly wouldn't want to, you and I will be much freer."

"If I thought I was expected to sit with a senile old man ——" Mr. Coningsby said in alarm, "but Henry implied that he'd got all his faculties. Have you heard anything?"

"Good heavens, no!" said Sybil, and, being in what her brother called one of her perverse moods, added, "I love that phrase."

"What phrase?" Mr. Coningsby asked, having missed anything particular.

"Good heavens," Sybil repeated, separating the words. "It says everything almost, doesn't it? I don't like to say 'Good God' too often; people so often misunderstand."

"Sometimes you talk exactly in Nancy's irresponsible way, Sybil," her brother complained. "I don't see any sense in it. Why should one want to say 'Good God'?"

"Well, there isn't really much else to say, is there?" Sybil asked, and added hastily, "No, my dear, I'm sorry, I was only . . ." She hesitated for a word.

"I know you were," Mr. Coningsby said, as if she had found it, "but I don't think jokes of that kind are in the best of taste. It's possible to be humorous without being profane."

"I beg your pardon, Lothair," Sybil said meekly. She tried her best not to call her brother "Lothair", because that was one of the things which seemed to him to be profane without being humorous. But it was pain and grief to her; there wasn't all that time to enjoy everything in life as it should be enjoyed, and the two of them could have enjoyed that ridiculous name so much better together. However, since she loved him, she tried not to force the good God's richness of wonder too much on his attention, and so she went on hastily, "Nancy's looking forward to it so much."

"At her age", Mr. Coningsby remarked, "one naturally looks forward."

"And at ours," Sybil said, "when there isn't the time there isn't the necessity: the present's so entirely satisfactory."

Mr. Coningsby just stopped himself saying, "Good God," with quite a different intonation. He waited a minute or two and said, "You know Henry's offered to take us down in his car?"

"Nice of him," Sybil answered, and allowed herself to become involved in a discussion of what her brother would or would not take: at the end of which he suddenly said, "O, and by the way, you might look through those packs of cards and put in a few of the most interesting—and the catalogue— especially the set we were looking at the other evening. Nancy asked me; it seems there are some others down there, and Henry and she want to compare them. A regular gipsy taste! But if it amuses them . . . He's promised to show her some tricks."

"Then I hope", Miss Coningsby said, "that Nancy won't try to show them to us before she's practised them. Not that I mind being surprised in an unintentional way, but it'd show a state of greater sanctity on her part."

"Sanctity!" Mr. Coningsby uttered derisively. "Nancy's not very near sanctity."

"My dear, she's in love," his sister exclaimed.

"And what's that got to do with sanctity?" Mr. Coningsby asked triumphantly, and enjoyed the silence to which Sybil sometimes found herself driven. Anyone who didn't realize the necessary connexion between love and sanctity left her incapable of explanation.

"Tricks" was hardly the word which Nancy would have

used that same evening, though it was one which Henry himself had used to her a week or so before. It wanted still some ten days to Christmas, and in the fortnight that had elapsed since the examination of the late Mr. Duncannon's legacy the subject of the cards had cropped up several times between the two young people. Nancy had the natural, alert interest of youth, as Sybil had the—perhaps supernatural—vivid interest of age, and Henry's occasional rather mysterious remarks had provoked it still more. She had, in fact, examined the cards by herself, and re-read the entry in the catalogue, and looked up "Tarot" in the encyclopædia without being much more advanced. As she sat now coiled in front of the dining-room fire, playing gently with her lover's fingers, at once stirred and soothed by the contact, she suddenly twisted round to face him in the deep chair to her right.

"But, Henry, dearest, what *is* it you mean?" she said. "You keep on talking of these cards as if they were important."

"So they are," Henry answered. "Exactly how important depends on you, perhaps."

Nancy sat up on her heels. "Henry," she said, "are you teasing me or are you not? If you are, you're not human at all;"

"Then you don't know what you'd miss," Henry said.

Nancy threw out her arms. "O wretched me!" she cried dramatically. "Henry, if I pretend I don't want to know, are you sure you'll play up? You won't take a mean advantage, will you?"

"If you really don't want to know," he told her, "I certainly won't tell you. That's the whole point. Do you *really* want to know?"

"Have I bared my heart to have it mistrusted?" she said. "Must I pine away in an hour or so to persuade you? Or will it do if I sob myself to sleep on the spot? As I used *not* to say when we did *Julius Caesar* at school, if you don't tell me, 'Portia is Brutus's harlot, not his wife.' What a nasty little cad and cat Portia was—to squeeze it out of him like that! But I swear I'll give myself a wound 'here in the thigh' unless you *do* tell me, and bleed to death all over your beautiful trousers."

He took her hand in his so strongly that her eyes changed to immediate gravity.

"If you want to know," he said, "I will tell you what I can here; and the rest—there. If you can bear it."

"Do as you will," she answered seriously. "If it's no joke, then try me and let me go if I fail. At that", she added with a sudden smile, "I think I won't fail."

"Then bring the Tarot cards now, if you can," he said. "But quietly. I don't want the others to know."

"They're out—father and Ralph," she answered. "I will go and get them," and on the word was away from the room.

For the few minutes that elapsed before she returned he stood looking absently before him, so that he did not at once hear her entrance, and her eyes took him in, his frown, his concentrated gaze, the hand that made slight unpurposed movements by his side. As she looked, she herself unconsciously disposed herself to meet him, and she came across the room to him with something in her of preparation, as if, clear and splendid, she came to her bridal; nor did they smile as they met, though it was the first time in their mutual acquaintance that so natural a sweetness had been lacking. He took the cards from her, and then, laying his hand on her shoulder, lightly compelled her towards the large table in the middle of the room. Then he drew the cards from their case, which he threw carelessly from him to the floor, and began to separate them into five piles.

"Look," he said, "these are the twenty-two cards—the twenty-one and the one which is nothing—that we looked at the other night. Those are the Greater Trumps, and there's nothing to tell you about them now; they must wait till another time. But these others are the four suits, and you will see what we did not carefully look at then—they're not the usual de-

43

signs, not clubs and spades and hearts and diamonds, but staffs or sceptres, and swords and cups and coins—or deniers: those last are shaped sometimes as pentacles, but this is the better marking. And see—there are fourteen and not thirteen in each suit, for besides the Knave and Queen and King there is in these the Knight: so that here, for instance, are the Knave—or Esquire—of sceptres, and the Knight, Queen, and King of sceptres; and so with the swords, the cups, and the deniers. Look, here they are."

She bent above them, watching, and after a moment he went on.

"Now these cards are the root and origin of all cards, and no one knows from where they came, for the tale is that they were first heard of among the gipsies in Spain in the thirteenth century. Some say they are older, and some even talk of Egypt, but that matters very little. It isn't the time behind them, but the process in them, that's important. There are many packs of Tarot cards, but the one original pack, which is this, has a secret behind it that I will show you on Christmas Eve. Because of that secret this pack, and this only, is a pack of great might."

He paused again, and still she made no movement. He glanced at her hands resting on the edge of the table, and resumed.

"All things are held together by correspondence, image with image, movement with movement: without that there could be no relation and therefore no truth. It is our business—especially yours and mine—to take up the power of relation. Do you know what I mean?"

As she suddenly looked up at him, she almost smiled.

"Darling," she murmured, "how couldn't I know *that*? I didn't need the cards to tell me. Ah, but go on: show me what it means in them."

For another second he paused, arrested: it was as if she had immediately before her something which he sought far off. A little less certainly he again went on, his voice recovering itself almost immediately.

"There is in these suits a great relation to the four compacted elements of the created earth, and you shall find the truth of this now, if you choose, and if the tales told among my people and the things that were written down among them are true. This pack has been hidden from us for more than two centuries, and for all that time no one, I think, can have tried it till to-night. The latest tale we know of is that once, under Elizabeth, a strange ancestor of mine, who had fled to England from the authority of the King of Spain, raised the winds which blew the Armada northward past Scotland."

Nancy wrinkled her forehead as he paused. "Do you mean," she began, "do you mean that he . . . I'm sorry, darling, I don't seem to understand. How could he raise the winds?"

" 'The beating of the cards is the wind'," he answered, "but don't try and believe it now. Think of it as a fable, but think that on some point of the sea-shore one of those wild fugitives stood by night and shook these cards—these"—he laid his hand on the heap of the suit of staffs or sceptres—"and beat the air with them till he drove it into tumult and sent the great blasts over the seas to drive the ships of King Philip to wreck and destruction. See that in your mind; can you?"

"I can," she said. "It's a mad picture, but I can."

He stooped to pick up the case, and restored to it the swords, the staffs, and the cups, and the Greater Trumps, all in silence; then he laid it by, and took up the suit deniers, or coins, or pentacles.

"Now," he said, smiling at her, "shall we see what your hands and mine can do?"

"Tell me," she answered.

He gave the fourteen cards to her, and, standing close by her, he made her hold them in both hands and laid his own over hers. "Now listen," he said in her ear, speaking slowly and commandingly; "you will think of earth, garden-mould, the

45

stuff of the fields, and the dry dust of the roads: the earth your flowers grow in, the earth to which our bodies are given, the earth which in one shape or another makes the land as parted from the waters. Will you do as I say?"

Very serious, she looked up at him. "Yes, Henry," she said, and her voice lingered a little on the second word, as if she gave herself so the more completely to his intention. He said again: "Earth, earth of growing and decaying things—fill your mind with the image of it. And let your hands be ready to shuffle the cards. Hold them securely but lightly, and if they seem to move let them have their way. Help them; help them to slide and shuffle. I put my hands over yours; are you afraid?"

She answered quite simply, "Need I be?"

"Never at all," he said, "neither now nor hereafter. Don't be afraid; these things can be known, and it's good for us to know them. Now—begin."

She bent her mind to its task, a little vaguely at first, but soon more definitely. She filled it with the thought of the garden, the earth that made it up, dry dust sometimes, sometimes rich loam—the worms that crawled in it and the roots of the flowers thrusting down—no, not worms and roots—earth, deep thick earth. Great tree-roots going deep into it —along the roots her mind penetrated into it, along the dividing, narrowing, dwindling roots, all the crannies and corners filled with earth, rushing up into her shoulder-pits, her elbows sticking out, little bumps on those protracted roots. Mould clinging together, falling apart; a spade splitting it, almost as if thrust into her thoughts, a spadeful of mould. Digging—holes, pits, mines, tunnels, graves—no, those things were not *earth*. Graves—the bodies in them being made one with the earth about them, so that at last there was no difference. Earth to earth—she herself earth; body, shoulders, limbs, earth in her arms, in her hands.

There were springs, deep springs, cisterns and wells and rivers of water down in the earth, water floating in rocky channels or oozing through the earth itself; the earth covering, hampering, stifling them, they bursting upwards through it. No, not water—*earth*. Her feet clung to it, were feeling it, were strangely drawing it up into themselves, and more and more and higher and higher that sensation of unity with the stuff of her own foundation crept. There were rocks, but she was not a rock—not yet; something living, like an impatient rush of water, was bubbling up within her, but she felt it as an intrusion into the natural part of her being. Her lips were rough against each other; her face must be stained and black. She almost put up her wrist to brush the earth from her cheek—not her hand, for that also was dirty; her fingers felt the grit. They were, both hands, breaking and rubbing a lump of earth between them; they were full and heaped with earth that was slipping over them and sliding between the fingers, and she was trying to hold it in—not to let it escape.

"Gently, gently," a voice murmured in her ear. The sound brought her back with a start, and dispelled the sensation that held her; she saw again the cards in her hands, and saw now that her hands, with Henry's lying over them, were shuffling the cards, each moment more quickly. She was trying to keep up with the movement, she wasn't initiating it—and that feeling of earth escaping was in fact only this compulsion which the cards were exercising. They were sliding out and sliding back—now she saw the four of deniers on top, and now the ace, and now the Esquire, and now the King, a hatted figure, with a four-forked beard, holding the coin—or whatever it was—in a gloved hand. It shone up at her, and a card from below slipped out, and her fingers thrust it back, and it covered the King—the nine of deniers. A slight sound reached her—a curious continuous sound, yet hardly a sound at all, a faint rustle. The cards *were* gritty, or her hands were; or was it the persistent rubbing of her palms against the edges of the cards? What was that rustling noise? It wasn't her mere fancy, nor was it mere fancy that some substance was slipping between

47

her fingers. Below her hands and the cards she saw the table, and some vague unusualness in it attracted her. It was black—well, of course, but a dull heavy black, and down to it from her hands a kind of cloud was floating. It was from there that the first sound came; it was something falling—it was earth, a curtain, a rain of earth falling, falling, covering the part of the table immediately below, making little sliding sounds—earth, real black earth.

"Steady," said the voice in her ear. She had a violent impulse to throw the cards away from her—if she could, if she could rend her hands from them, but of course she couldn't: they, earthy as they were, belonged to this other earth, the earth that was slipping everywhere over and between her fingers, that was already covering the six of deniers as it slid over the two. But there were other hands; hers weren't alone; she pressed them back into her lover's, and said, keeping her voice as steady as she could: "Couldn't we stop?"

Breath deeply drawn answered her: then Henry's voice. "Yes," it said. "Steady, steady. Think with me, think of the cards—cards—drawings—just drawings—line and colour. Press them back, harder: *use* your hands now—harder."

It was as if a brief struggle took place between her hands and that which they held: as if the thing refused to be governed and dominated. But it yielded; if there had been any struggle, it ceased. Her strong hands pressed back the cards, pushed them level; her thumb flicked them. Henry's hands left hers and took the suit. She let hers drop, took a step away, and looked at the table. There lay on it a little heap of what seemed like garden mould.

Faintness caught her; she swayed. Henry's arm round her took her to a chair. She gasped out, "I'm all right. Stop a minute," and held on to the arm. "It's nothing," she said to herself, "it's quite simple. It's only that I'm not used to it—whatever it is." That it was any kind of trick did not even enter her mind; Henry and that sort of trick could not exist together. Earth on the dining-room table. Aunt Sybil would wonder why it was there. She deliberately opened her eyes again, and her mouth opened in spite of her. It was still there.

"All right?" Henry's voice said.

Nancy made a great effort. "Yes," she said. "Henry, what's happened? I mean——"

"You're frightened!" he said accusingly.

"I'm not frightened," she said.

"If you are, I can't tell you anything," he said. "I can't share with you unless you want me to. This is only the beginning: you'd better understand that at once."

"Yes, darling," she said. "Don't be cross with me. It's a little sudden, isn't it? Is it . . . is it real?"

He picked up some of the earth and scattered it again.

"Quite," he said. "You could grow evergreens in it."

"Then", said Nancy, with a slightly hysterical note in her voice, "I think you'd better ring for Agnes to clear it up."

"Touch it," he said, "feel it, be sure it's real."

"I wouldn't touch it for anything," she exclaimed. "Do ring, Henry. I want to see Agnes taking it away in a dustpan. That'll prove it's real."

Agnes indeed removed it in a dustpan, without any other emotion than a slight surprise and a slight perplexity. It was clear that she couldn't think what Miss Nancy and her young man had been about; but it was also clear that she supposed whatever they had been about had resulted in a small heap of earth on the dining-room table, which she efficiently removed, and then herself disappeared. Nancy lay back in her chair, and there was a complete silence for a long time.

At last she stirred and looked at Henry. "Tell me now," she said.

He leaned against the mantelpiece, looking down on her. "I've told you," he answered. "I told you at first; at least, I hinted at it. There is correspondence everywhere; but some

49

correspondences are clearer than others. Between these cards"
—he pointed to the leather case in which he had replaced the
denier suit—"and the activities of things there is a very close
relation. . . ."

She broke in. "Yes, darling; don't explain it, just tell me,"
she said. "What you said about the wind, and this, and
everything."

"Earth, water, air, and fire," he said. "Deniers, cups,
sceptres, swords. When the hands of a man deal in a certain
way with the cards, the living thing comes to exist."

She looked down at the hands that lay in her lap. "Hands,"
she said. "Can they do it?"

"They can do anything," he said. "They have power."

"But why the cards . . . ?" she asked.

He smiled at her, and suddenly she threw out her arms to
him and he leant and caught her in his own. The movement
gathered her, but it was she who was raised from her chair, not
he who was brought down to that other level, and even while
he murmured to her his voice was charged with an exultant
energy, and when upon her moving he loosed her at last there
was in his action something of one who lays down a precious
instrument till it shall be required. Or, since he kept his eyes
on her, something of one who watches a complex and delicate
piece of machinery to see if everything runs smoothly, and the
experiment for which it is meant may be safely dared.

Nancy patted her hair and sat down again. "Next time",
she said, "I shall be more prepared."

"There is to be a next time?" he asked, testing a screw in
the machinery.

Her eyes were seriously upon him. "If you choose," she said,
"and you will, won't you? If you want me to help, I will. But
next time perhaps you'd better tell me more about it first.
Why *does* it happen?"

"I don't know why," he said, "but how is clear enough.
These cards are in touch with a thing I'll show you at Christ-

mas, and they're in touch with . . . well, there aren't any words for it—with the Dance."

"The Dance?" she asked.

"The Dance that is . . . everything," he answered. "You'll see. Earth, air, fire, water—and the Greater Trumps. There's a way to all knowledge and prophecy, when the cards and they are brought together. But, O Nancy, Nancy, if you'll see what I see and want what I want, there's a way—if it can be found, there's a way." He caught her hands in his. "Hands," he cried, "hands among *them* and all that they mean. Feel it; give it to me; take it."

She burned back to his ardour. "What will you do?" she asked, panting.

He held her hands more tightly. "Who knows?" he answered, rising on the wings of his own terrific dream. "Create."

Chapter Four

THE CHARIOT

On the Wednesday before Christmas, Henry had arranged to take the Coningsbys to his grandfather's house. Mr. Coningsby had decided to give them a week of his Christmas vacation from the preoccupations of a Warden in Lunacy, and Henry was very willing that the chances of those critical days should have so long a period in which to be tested. The strange experiment which he and Nancy had tried had left him in a high state of exaltation; he felt his delight in her as a means to his imagined end. Of its effect upon Nancy herself he found it difficult to judge: she did not refer to it again, and was generally rather more silent with him than was her wont. But his own preoccupations were intense, and it may be it was rather his preoccupation than her own which shrouded and a little constrained her. To the outer world, however, she carried herself much as usual, and only Sybil Coningsby noted that her gaiety was at times rather a concealment than a manifestation. But then among that group only Sybil was aware of how many natural capacities are found to be but concealments, how many phenomena disappear before the fact remains. It was long since in her own life the search had begun; with eyes that necessarily veiled their passion she saw in her niece the opening of some other abyss in that first abyss which was love. Mr. Coningsby had spoken more truly than he thought when he accused Sybil of an irresponsibility not unlike Nancy's; their natures answered each other across the years. But between them lay the experience of responsibility, that burden which is only given in order to be relinquished, that task put into the hands of man in order that his own choice may render it back to its creator, that yoke which, once wholly lifted and put on, is immediately no longer to be worn. Sybil had lifted and relinquished it; from the freedom of a love more single than Nancy's she smiled at the young initiate who from afar in her untrained innocence beheld the conclusion of all initiations.

She stood now on the steps of the house and smiled at Henry, who was beside her. Nancy was in the hall; Mr. Coningsby was telephoning some last-minute instructions in lunacy to the custodians of lunacy who were for a while to occupy the seat of the warden. Ralph had gone off that morning. It was late afternoon; the weather was cold and fine.

Sybil said: "Have I thanked you for taking us down, Henry?"

He answered, his voice vibrating with great expectation, "It's a delight, Aunt Sybil: mayn't I call you that too?"

She inclined her head to the courtesy, and her eyes danced at him as she said, "For Nancy's sake or mine?"

"For all our sakes," he answered. "But you're very difficult to know, aren't you? You never seem to move."

"Simeon Stylites?" she asked. "Do I crouch on a tall pillar in the sky? What an inhuman picture!"

"I think you are a little inhuman," he said. "You're everything that's nice, of course, but you're terrifying as well."

"Alas, poor aunt!" she said. "But nowadays I thought maiden aunts were nothing uncommon?"

"A maiden aunt——" he began and stopped abruptly. Then he went on with a note of wonder in his voice, "That's it, you know; that's exactly it. You're strange, you're maiden, you're a mystery of self-possession."

She broke into a laugh, almost as delightful, even to him, as Nancy's. "Henry, *mon vieux*," she said, "what do you know about old women?"

"Enough to know you're not one," he said. "Aunt Sybil——

53

Sibyl—your very name means you. You're the marvel of virginity that rides in the Zodiac."

"That", she said, "is a most marvellous compliment. If I wasn't in furs I'd curtsey. You'll make me wish myself Nancy's age—for one evening."

"I think it's long", he said, "since you have wished yourself anything but what you are."

She was prevented from answering by Mr. Coningsby, who hurried Nancy out before him on to the steps and shut the door. They all went down to the car, and a policeman on the pavement saluted Mr. Coningsby as he passed.

"Good evening, good evening, constable," he said. "Here." Something passed. "A merry Christmas."

"Gracious," Nancy said in Henry's ear, "father's almost jovial."

"That", Henry answered, "is because he doesn't regard the police as human. He'd never be harsh to a dog or a poor man. It's those of his own kind that trouble and fret him."

"Well, darling," she said, "I've never heard you speak of standing a policeman a drink." She slipped her hand into his. "O, I'm so thrilled," she went on, "what with you and Christmas and . . . and all. Is that policeman part of it, do you think? Is he in the sceptres or the swords? Or is he one of your mysterious Trumps?"

"What about the Emperor?" Henry threw at her, as Mr. Coningsby, who had stopped to speak to the constable, probably about the safety of the house, came to the car. Sybil was already in her seat. Nancy slipped into hers, as Mr. Coningsby got in next to Sybil: Henry closed the door, sprang in, and started the car.

There was silence at first. To each of them the movement of the car meant something different and particular; to the two men it was movement *to* something, to the two women it was much more like movement *in* something. Mr. Coningsby felt it as a rush towards an immediate future to which he had

54

been compelled and in which he gloomily expected defeat. Henry's desire swept on to a future in which he expected trial and victory. But to Nancy and Sybil separately the future could not be imagined except as a blessed variation on what they knew; there was nowhere to go but to that in which they each existed, and the time they took to go was only the measure of delight changing into delight. In that enclosed space a quadruple movement of consciousness existed, and became, through the unnoticeable, infinitesimal movements of their bodies, involved and, to an extent, harmonized. Each set up against each of the others a peculiar strain; each was drawn back and controlled by the rest. Knowledge danced with knowledge, sometimes to trouble, sometimes to appease, the corporeal instruments of the days of their flesh.

A policeman's hand held them up. Henry gestured towards it. "Behold the Emperor," he said to Nancy.

"You're making fun of me, my dear," she half protested.

"Never less," he said seriously. "Look at him."

She looked, and, whether the hours she had given to brooding over the Tarots during the last few days, partly to certify her courage to herself, had imposed their forms on her memory, or whether something in the policeman's shape and cloak under the lights of the dark street suggested it, or whether indeed something common to Emperor and Khalif, cadi and magistrate, prætor and alcalde, lictor and constable, shone before her in those lights—whichever was true, it was certainly true that for a moment she saw in that heavy official barring their way the Emperor of the Trumps, helmed, in a white cloak, stretching out one sceptred arm, as if Charlemagne, or one like him, stretched out his controlling sword over the tribes of Europe pouring from the forests and bade them pause or march as he would. The great roads ran below him, to Rome, to Paris, to Aix, to Byzantium, and the nations established themselves in cities upon them. The noise of all the pausing street came to her as the roar of many peoples; the white cloak held them by a gesture; order and law were there. It moved, it fell aside, the torrent of obedient movement rolled on, and they with it. They flashed past the helmed face, and she found that she had dropped her eyes lest she should see it.

With the avoidance of that face she seemed to have plunged herself deeper into the dream, as if by avoiding it she had assented to it and had acknowledged its being and power. They were not stopped again, but yet, as the car ran smoothly on, she seemed to see that white-clothed arm again and again, now in the darkness beyond the headlights, now pointing forward just outside the window. The streets were busy with Christmas shoppers, but the car shut them out and her in, and, though they were there, it was running steadily away from them—as if down a sloping road while they were all on the high level banks on either hand. They never actually did go down that road, but—as in nightmare—they were always on the very point of plunging. Nancy held desperately to her recollection of a car and a policeman and Henry; she was really beginning to pull herself together when suddenly—somewhere on the outskirts of London—the car slowed for a moment outside the gate of a large building. Over the gate was a light, and under the light was a nurse holding a big key. A gate—a light—a nurse; yet one lobe of her brain showed her again a semblance of one of the Tarot cards—ceremonial robes; imperial headdress, cloak falling like folded wings, proud, austere face lifted towards where in the arch of the gate, so that the light just caught it, was a heraldic carving of some flying creature. Someone, somewhere—perhaps her father behind her—grunted a little, and the grunt seemed to her as if it were wrung from a being in profound pain. And then the car quickened again, and they were flying into the darkness, and away in the roads behind them was that sovereign figure and the sound of a suffering world coming up to it out of the night.

She would have liked to speak to Henry, but she couldn't.

The Chariot

She and he were in the same car, side by side, only she wasn't
at all clear that there was anyone else in the car at all, or that
it was a car, that it was anything but herself mysteriously defined to her own knowledge. She was in a trance; the car,
though moving, was still—poised, rushing and motionless at
once, at the entrance to a huge, deep, and dark defile, from
which on either side the mighty figures rose, themselves at once
swift and still, and fled past her and yet were for ever there.
Indefinable, they defined; they made and held steady the path
that was stretched for her. It was a cloud; it was the moon;
it was vapour and illusion—or it was the white cloak of the
Emperor and the clear cold face of the Empress, as she had
seen them when she pored over the Greater Trumps. But the
darkness of the low defile awaited her; deeper and deeper,
motionless and rushing on, they—she and her companions—
were sinking into it. She dared not speak to Henry; he was
there, but he was guiding the car; if he were distracted for a
moment they might all crash into utter ruin. She let herself
take one side-glance at him, a supplication in her heart, but
never a finger stirring; and, even as she saw his face, she remembered to have seen it elsewhere. There was a painting—
somewhere—of a chariot, driven by some semi-Greek figure
scourging on two sphinxes who drew that car, and the face in
the painting was Henry's. Henry's, and yet there was a difference . . . there was some other likeness: was it (most fantastic
of all dreams!) her aunt? The faces, the figures, all rushed
together suddenly; something that was neither nurse nor
policeman, Empress nor Emperor, Sybil nor Henry, sphinx
nor charioteer, grew out of and possessed them all. It was this
to which they were rushing, some form that was immediately
to be revealed, some face that would grow out of . . .

The car slowed, wheeled as if sweeping round a curve in the
road, and suddenly—despite herself—she screamed. For there,
with light full on it, thrown up in all its terrible detail, gaunt,
bare, and cold, was a man, or the image of a man, hanging by

57

his hands, his body thrust out from the pole that held it, his head dropping to one side, and on it a dreadful tangled head-dress. It hung there right before her, and she only knew that it was the wrong way up—the head should have been below; it was always so in the cards, the Hanged Man upside down. But here the Hanged Man was, livid and outstretched before her, his head decked but above. She screamed and woke. At least, everyone supposed she woke. Henry was solicitous and her father was irritable, and, after all, it was only a village war memorial with a rather badly done crucifix.

They took her away from it and Henry comforted her, and she settled down again, apologizing with the most utter shame. A bad dream, of course.

"Darling, of course it was," Henry murmured.

"Of course it was," her father snapped.

"Of course it is," Sybil Coningsby said. "One wakes, Nancy."

So then they went on again, and, except for one other un-usual incident—but that was certainly not a dream—reached their destination undisturbed. The incident indeed occurred not far away.

The car had slid through a village—the nearest village to his grandfather's, Henry told them, and at that a couple of miles away. It had issued thence past the church and rectory on to an upland road, and climbed steadily across the Downs. Mr. Coningsby looked out at the winter darkness and shud-dered, thinking of London, Eastbourne, and the next five or six days. Henry had just looked over his shoulder to say "Not far now," much as one of Dante's demons might have spoken to a soul he was conducting to its particular circle in Hell. He looked back, swore, and jammed on the brakes. The car pro-tested, slid, and came to a standstill. Six feet in front of it an old woman squatted on the ground, right in the middle of the road. Two feet behind her stood a tall, rough-looking young fellow, as if waiting.

"Good God!" said Mr. Coningsby.

The Chariot

The old woman was apparently speaking, but, shut in the car, they could not hear. Henry opened the door and jumped out. Mr. Coningsby opened his window; Nancy and Sybil instinctively did the same.

"Welcome home, Henry!" the old creature said, in a high shrill voice. Henry took a couple of steps forward—the unknown man moved level with the squatting hag. In the lights of the car she was seen to be very old, shrivelled, and brown. She was wrapped head and body in a stained shawl that had once been red; one foot, which was thrust out from under a ragged skirt, wore a man's heavy boot. She pushed a hand out from beneath the shawl and waggled the skinny fingers at Henry as if in grotesque greeting.

"What are you doing here?" he asked fiercely.

"He, he!" the grotesque being tittered at him. "I've come to see Aaron, Henry. I'm very tired. Won't you take me up in your grand coach? Me and Stephen. Good little Stephen— he takes care of his grandmother—his gran——" She went off into an indescribable fit of chuckling and choking. Henry looked at Stephen. "Get her out of the way," he said.

The man looked stupidly back. "She does what she likes," he said, and turned his eyes again on the old woman.

"Two nice ladies and one nice gentleman," she babbled. "Kind lady"—she peered at Nancy, who was leaning from the window—"kind lady, have your fortune told? He"—she jerked a thumb at Henry—"thinks he knows fortunes, but is he a goddess? Good luck to you, kind lady, to meet a goddess on the roads. Great good luck for you and your children to have a goddess tell you your doom."

Henry said something in a low voice that the others couldn't hear. Sybil opened her door and got out of the car. Mr. Coningsby said sharply, "Sybil, come back," but she only threw him a smile and remained standing in the road. Most reluctantly he also got out. The hag put her head on one side and looked at them.

The Chariot

"Is the young miss afraid of the goddess?" she said. "Or will she help me look? Blessings on whoever finds him."

"Out of my way, Joanna," Henry said, with anger in his voice.

"Henry dear," Sybil said, "is she going our way?"

He made a fierce gesture, but did not reply.

"Do you know her, Henry?" Mr. Coningsby said sharply.

"Father!" Nancy breathed, and touched his arm. "Don't be cross with us; Henry couldn't help it."

"Us," Mr. Coningsby thought. "You . . . us . . . O!"

"Do you want to come to the house?" Henry asked.

"What house?" she shrilled. "Fields, rivers, sea—that's his house. Cover for you, beds for you, warmth for you, but my little one's cold!"

Henry looked over at his friends and made a sign to them that all would be well in a moment. The hag thrust her head on one side and looked up at him.

"If you know——" she cried, more wildly than before. "Curses on you, Henry Lee, if you know and don't tell me. I'm an old fool, aren't I, and you're a clever man and a lawyer, but you've gone to live in houses and forgotten the great ones who live in the gipsy tents. And if you find so much as a shred of skin and don't tell me, so much as the place where a drop of blood has soaked into the ground and don't tell me, you shall be destroyed with the enemy when I and my son take joy in each other again. I'll curse you with my tongue and hands, I'll lay the spell on you, I'll——"

"Be quiet," he said harshly. "Who are *you* to talk, Joanna, the old gipsy-woman?"

"Gipsy I was," she said, "and I'm something more now. Ha, little frightend ones! Ha, Henry Lee the accursed! Stephen! Stephen!"

"Aye, grandmother," the man said.

"Say the answers, say the answers. Who am I?"

The man answered in a voice entirely devoid of meaning, "A goddess are you."

"What's the name of the goddess?" she shrilled.

"Isis the Wanderer," he said mechanically.

"What does Isis the Wanderer seek?"

"The flesh and the bones and the heart of the dead," he answered, and licked his lips.

"Where are the flesh and the bones and the heart of the dead?" she shrilled again.

"Here, there, everywhere," he said.

"Good Stephen, good Stephen," she muttered, appeased; and then suddenly scrambled to her feet. Henry jumped forward to interpose himself between her and the other women, and found himself in turn blocked by Stephen. They were on the point of closing with each other when Sybil's voice checked them.

"And where does the Divine Isis search?" she asked in a perfectly clear voice of urgent inquiry.

The old woman turned her eyes from Nancy to Sybil, and a look of delight came into her face. She took a step or two towards the other.

"Who are you," she said, "to speak as if you knew a goddess? Where have we seen each other?"

Sybil also moved a step forward. "Perhaps in the rice-fields", she said, "or in the towns. I don't remember. Have you found anything that you look for?"

The old creature came nearer yet, and put out her hand as if to feel for Sybil's. In turn Miss Coningsby stretched out her own, and with those curiously linked hands they stood. Behind, on the one side, the two young men waited in an alert and mutually hostile watch; on the other, Mr. Coningsby, in a fever of angry hate, stood by Nancy at the car door; the Downs and the darkness stretched about them all.

"Aren't you a stranger and a Christian rat?" the hag said. "How do you know the goddess when you meet her in Egypt?"

"Out of Egypt have I called my son," Sybil said. "Could you search for the god and not belong to his house?"

"Worship me then, worship me!" the insane thing cried out. "Worship the Divine Isis!"

"Ah, but I've sworn only to worship the god," Sybil answered gently. "Let Isis forgive me, and let us look for the unity together."

"They've parted him and torn him asunder," the creature wailed. "He was so pretty, so pretty, when he played with me once."

"He will be so lovely when he is found," Sybil comforted her. "We'll certainly find him. Won't you come with me and look?"

The other threw up her head and snuffed the air. "It's coming," she said. "I've smelt it for days and days. They're bringing him together—the winds and waters are bringing him. Go your way, stranger, and call me if you find him. I must be alone. Alone I am and alone I go. I'm the goddess." She peered at Sybil. "But I will bless you," she said. "Kneel down and I'll bless you."

Mr. Coningsby made a sound more like a real Warden in Lunacy than ever in his life before as the tall furred figure of his sister obeyed. But Nancy's hand lay urgently on his shoulder, even had he meant to interfere. Sybil kneeled in the road, and the woman threw up her arms in the air over her, breaking into a torrent of incomprehensible, outlandish speech, which at the end changed again to English—"This is the blessing of Isis: go in peace. Stephen! Stephen!" He was by her in a moment. "We'll go, Stephen—not with them, not to-night. Not to-night. I shall smell him, I shall know him, my baby, my Osiris. He was killed and he is coming. Horus, Horus, the coming of God!" She caught the young man by the arm, and hastily they turned and fled into the darkness. Sybil, unaided, rose to her feet. There was a silence, then she said charmingly, "Henry, don't you think we might go on now? . . . It doesn't look as if we could be of any use."

He came to hold the door for her. "You've certainly done it," he said. "How did you know what to say to her?"

"I thought she talked very sensibly," Sybil said, getting into the car. "In her own way, of course. And I wish she'd come with us, that is, if . . . would it be very rude to say I gathered she had something to do with your family?"

"She's my grandfather's sister," he answered. "She's mad, of course; she—but I'll tell you some other time. Stephen was a brat she picked up somewhere; he's nothing to do with us, but she's taught him to call her 'grandmother', because of a child that should have been."

"Conversation of two aunts," said Sybil, settling herself. "I've known many wilder minds."

"What were you at, Sybil?" Mr. Coningsby at last burst out. "Of all the scandalous exhibitions! Really, Henry, I think we'd better go back to London. That my sister should be subjected to this kind of thing! Why didn't you interfere?"

"My dear, it would mean an awful bother—going back to London," Sybil said. "Everything's settled up there. I'm a little cold, Henry, so do you think we could go fairly fast? We can talk about it all when we get in."

"Kneeling in the road!" Mr. Coningsby went on. "O, very well—if you will go. Perhaps *we* shall smell things too. Is your grandfather anything like his sister, Henry? If so, we shall have a most agreeable Christmas. He might like me to kneel to him at intervals, just to make things really comfortable."

Sybil laid a hand on his knee. "Leave it to me to complain," she said. "All right, Henry; we all know you hated it much more than the rest of us." Nancy's hand came over the seat and felt for hers; she took it. "Child, you're frozen," she said. "Let's all get indoors. Even a Christian rat—all right, Henry— likes a little bacon-rind by the fire. Lothair dear, I was going to ask you when we stopped—what star exactly is that one over there?"

"Star!" said Mr. Coningsby, and choked. He was still choking over his troubles when they stopped before the house, hardly visible in the darkness. He was, however, a trifle soothed by the servant who was at the door and efficiently extricated them, and by the courtesies which the elder Mr. Lee, who was waiting just within the hall, immediately offered them. He found it impossible not, within the first two minutes, to allude to the unfortunate encounter; "the sooner", he said to himself, "this—really rather pleasant—old gentleman understands what his sister's doing on the roads the better."

The response was all he could have wished. Aaron, tutored at intervals during the last month by his grandson in Mr. Coningsby's character and habits, was highly shocked and distressed at his guests' inconvenience. Excuses he proffered; explanations he reasonably deferred. They were cold; they were tired; they were, possibly, hungry. Their rooms were ready, and in half an hour, say, supper. . . . "We won't call it dinner," Aaron chatted on to Mr. Coningsby while accompanying him upstairs; Sybil and Nancy had been given into the care of maids. "We won't call it dinner to-night. You'll forgive our deficiencies here—in your own London circle you'll be used to much more adequate surroundings."

"It's a very fine house," said Mr. Coningsby, stopping on what was certainly a very fine staircase.

"Seventeen-seventeen," Aaron told him. "It was built by a Jacobite peer who only just escaped attainder after the Fifteen and was compelled to leave London. It's a curious story; I'll tell it you some time. He was a student and a poet, besides being a Jacobite, and he lived here for the rest of his life in solitude."

"A romantic story," Mr. Coningsby said, feeling some sympathy with the Jacobite peer.

"Here's the room I've ventured to give you," Aaron said. "You can't see much from the windows to-night, but on a clear day you can sometimes just catch a glimpse of the sea. I hope you've everything. In half an hour, then, shall we say?"

He pattered away, a small, old, rather bent, but self-possessed figure, and Mr. Coningsby shut his door. "Very different

from his sister," he thought. "Curious how brothers and sisters
do differ." His mind went to Sybil. "In a way," he went on to
himself, "Sybil's rather irresponsible. She positively encouraged that dreadful old woman. There's a streak of wildness in
her; fortunately it's never had a chance to get out. Perhaps if
that other had had different surroundings . . . but if this is her
brother's house, why's she wandering about the country? And,
anyhow, that settles the question of giving Henry those cards.
I shall tell Nancy so if she hints at it again. Fancy giving poor
dear Duncannon's parting gift—the things he left me on his
very death-bed—to a fellow with a mad gipsy for an aunt!
Isis," he thought, in deep disgust, "the Divine Isis. Good God!"

Chapter Five

THE IMAGE THAT DID NOT MOVE

Much to her own surprise when she found it out in the morning, Nancy slept extremely well: rather to his own disgust, so did her father. No one ever thought of asking Sybil—or, at least, no one ever listened to the answer; it was one of the things which wasn't related to her. She never said anything about it, nor, as a consequence, did anybody else; it being a certain rule in this world that what is not made of vivid personal importance will cease to be of social interest. The shoemaker's conversation therefore rightly returns to leather. Nancy woke and stretched, and, as her sense returned, considered healthily, voluptuously, and beautifully the immediate prospect of a week of Henry, interspersed with as much of other people as would make him more rare if not more precious. It occurred to her suddenly that he might already be downstairs, and that she might as well in that case be downstairs herself. But as she jumped out of bed—with the swinging movement—she swung into a sudden change of consciousness. Here they were—at his grandfather's, and here then all his obscure hints and promises were to be explained. He wanted something; he wanted something of her, and she was not at all clear that she wasn't rather frightened, or anyhow a little nervous, when she tried to think of it. She took a deep breath. Henry had something to show her, and the earth had grown in her hands; however often she washed them she never quite seemed to get away from the feel of it. Being a semi-educated and semi-cultured girl, she dutifully thought of *Macbeth*—"the perfumes of Arabia", "this little hand". For the first time in her life, however, she now felt as if Shakespeare had been talking about something more real than she had supposed; as if the words echoed out of her own deep being, and again echoed back into it—"cannot cleanse this little hand". She rubbed her hands together half-unconsciously, and then more consciously, until suddenly the remembrance of Lady Macbeth as she had once seen her on the stage came to her, and she hurriedly desisted. Lady Macbeth had turned—a tall, ghostly figure caught in a lonely perdition—at the bottom corner of the stage, where the Witches . . . what was it they had sung?

> *The weird sisters, hand in hand,*
> *Posters of the sea and land.*

"Posters of the sea and land"—was that what she had been yesterday in the car—in her sleep, in her dreams? Or that mad old woman? The weird sisters—the old woman and Aunt Sybil—hand in hand, posters of the sea and land? Posters—going about the world—from point to point in a supernatural speed? Another line leapt at her—"Peace! the charm's wound up." Wound up—ready for the unwinding; and Henry ready too. Her expectation terrified her: this day which was coming but not yet quite come was infinite with portents. Her heart filled and laboured with its love; she pressed a hand against it to ease the bursting pain. "O Henry," she murmured aloud, "Henry!" What did one do about it? What was the making of earth beside this? This, whatever it was—this joy, this agony—was not out of key with her dreams, with the weird women; it too posted by the sea and land; the universe fell away below the glory of its passion.

She rose, unable any longer to sit still, drawing deep breaths of love, and walked to the window. The morning as it grew was clear and cold; unseen, miles away, lay the sea. Along the sea-shore, between earth and water, was the woman of the roads now hobbling? Or were the royal shapes of the Emperor and the Empress riding out in the dark heavens above the

67

ocean? Her heart laboured with power still, and as that power flooded her she felt the hands that rested on the window-frame receive it; she leaned her head on the window and seemed to expect mysteries. This was the greatest mystery; this was the sea and land about which she herself was now a fortunate and happy poster.

It was too early; Henry wouldn't be about yet. But she couldn't go back to bed; love and morning and profound intention called to her. Her aunt was in the next room; she decided to go there, and went.

Her aunt, providentially, was awake, contemplating nothing with a remote accuracy. Nancy looked at her.

"I suppose you do sleep?" she said. "Do you know, I've never found you asleep?"

"How fortunate!" Sybil said. "For after all I suppose you've generally wanted something—if only conversation?"

Nancy, wrapping herself in her aunt's dressing-gown as well as her own, sat down, and looked again, this time more attentively.

"Aunt Sybil," she said, "are you by any chance being offensive?"

"Could I and would I?" Sybil asked.

"Your eyes are perpetually dancing," Nancy said. "But is it true—do I only come to you when I want something?"

"Why," said Sybil, "if you're asking seriously, my dear, then by and large the answer is yes." She was about to add that she herself was quite content, but she saw something brooding in Nancy's face, and ceased.

"I don't mean to be a pig," Nancy said. Sybil accepted that as a soliloquy and said nothing. Nancy added, "I'm not all that selfish, am I?"

"I don't think you're particularly selfish," her aunt said, "only you don't love anyone."

Nancy looked up, more bewildered than angry. "Don't

68

love?" she said. "I love you and father and Ralph very much indeed."

"And Henry?" Sybil asked.

"Well—Henry", Nancy said, blushing a little, "is different."

"Alas!" Sybil murmured, but the lament was touched with laughter.

"What do you mean—'alas'?" Nancy asked. "Aunt Sybil, do you *want* me to feel about everybody as I do about Henry?"

"A little adjustment here and there," Sybil said, "a retinting perhaps, but otherwise—why, yes! Don't you think so?"

"Even, I suppose," Nancy said, "to Henry's great-aunt or whatever she was?" But the words died from a soft sarcasm to a softer doubt: the very framing of the question, as so often happens, was itself an answer. "Her body thought"; interrogation purged emotion, and the purified emotion replied to the interrogation. To love. . . .

"But I can't", she exclaimed, "turn all *this*"—she laid her hand on her heart—"towards everybody. It can't be done; it only lives for—him."

"Nor even that," Sybil said. "It lives for and in itself. You can only give it back to itself."

Nancy brooded. After a while, "I still don't see how I can love Joanna with it," she said.

"If you give it back to itself", Sybil said, "wholly and utterly, it will do all that for you. You've no idea what a lot it can do. I think you might find it worth trying."

"Do you?" Nancy said soberly; then she sighed, and said with a change of tone, "Of course I simply adore this kind of talk before breakfast. You ought to have been a missionary, Aunt Sybil, and held early services for cannibals on a South Sea island."

"The breakfast", Sybil said gravely, "would have a jolly time listening to the bell before the service—if I had a bell."

"O, you'd have a bell," Nancy said, "and a collection of cowrie-shells or bananas, and open-air services on the beach in the evening. And Henry and I would lean over the side of our honeymoon liner and hear your voice coming to us over the sea in the evening, and have—what is it they have at those times?—*Heimweh*, and be all googly. And father would say, 'Really, Sybil!' without being googly. Well, thank you for your kind interest in a Daughter of the Poor." She kissed her aunt. "I do, you know," she said, and was gone.

The day passed till dinner without anything particularly striking having taken place. They looked over the house; they lunched; they walked. *The Times* arrived, sent up from the village, about midday, and Mr. Coningsby settled down to it. Henry and Nancy appeared and disappeared; Sybil walked and rested and talked and didn't talk, and contemplated the universe in a serene delight. But after dinner and coffee there came a pause in the conversation, and Aaron Lee spoke.

"My grandson thinks", he said to his visitors, "that you'd be interested to see a curiosity which we have here."

"I'm sure anything——" answered Mr. Coningsby, who was feeling rather inclined to be agreeable.

Nancy said to Henry in a low voice, "Is it whatever you meant?" and he nodded.

The old man rose. "If I may trouble you, then, to come with me," he said, leading the way from the room, and Mr. Coningsby sauntered after his sister without the smallest idea that the attack on his possession of the Tarot cards was about to begin. They came into Aaron's room; they crossed it and stood about the inner locked door. Aaron inserted the key; then, before turning it, he looked round and said, "Henry thinks that your ownership of a particular pack of our gipsy cards may make you peculiarly interested in . . . in what you'll see. The pack's rather rare, I believe, and this"—he unlocked the door—"is, I may say, very much rarer."

Henry, from the back, watched him a little anxiously. Aaron had not been at all eager to disclose the secret dancing images to these strangers; it was only the absolute necessity of showing

The Image that did not move

Mr. Coningsby an overpoweringly good reason for giving away the cards that had at last convinced him. A day's actual acquaintance with Mr. Coningsby had done more towards conviction than all Henry's arguments—that, and the knowledge that the Tarot cards were at last in the house, so close to the images to which, for mortal minds, they were the necessary key. Yet, under the surface of a polite and cultured host which he had presented, there stirred a longing and a hostility; he hated this means, yet it was the only means to what he desired. In the conflict his hand trembled and fumbled with the door-handle, and Henry in his own agitation loosed Nancy's arm. She felt his trouble and misunderstood it. "Darling," she murmured, "you don't mind us seeing, do you? If you do, let's go away."

"You *must* see," he answered, low and rapidly, "you especially. And the others too—it's why they're here."

She took his "here" to mean at that door, and his agitation to be the promise of the mystery he had spoken of, and delighted to share it with him. "You'll tell me everything," she whispered. "I'll do whatever you want." Her eyes glowed at him as he looked at her. He met them, but his preoccupation was heavy upon him. "Your father," he whispered back, "get your father to give me the cards."

The door was open. Aaron said, "You'll excuse me if I go first; there's a curtain." He stepped forward, passed between the hangings, stepped aside, and raised them, so that, one by one, the others also came into the light of the inner chamber— Mr. Coningsby first, then Sybil, then the two young ones. Aaron let the curtain fall, and joined them where they stood, he and Henry closing them in on either side.

The light had been tinged with red when they entered; but it changed, so swiftly that only Aaron noticed it, to a lovely green, and then—more slowly—to an exquisite golden beauty. Aaron's eyes went to Henry's, but the young man was looking at the moving images; then they passed to the visitors—to

71

Nancy, who also was raptly gazing at the spectacle; to Mr. Coningsby, who was surveying it with a benevolent generosity, as if he might have shown his host something similar in his own house, but hadn't thought it worth while; to Sybil, who was half-smiling in pure pleasure at the sight.

"These", Aaron said, "are a very ancient secret among the folk from whom Henry and I come, and they have never been shown to anyone outside our own people till now. But since we are to be so closely joined"—he smiled paternally at Nancy —"the reason against revealing them hardly exists."

He had to pause for a moment, either because of his inner excitement or because (as, for a moment, he half-suspected) some sense stronger than usual of the unresting marvel before them attacked him and almost beat him down. He mastered himself, but his age dragged at him, and his voice trembled as he went carefully on, limiting himself to what Henry and he had agreed should be said.

"You see those little figures? By some trick of the making they seem to hold—what we call—the secret of perpetual motion. You see, how they are dancing—they do it continually. They are—we believe—in some way magnetized—by the movements of the earth—and they—they vibrate to it."

He could say no more. He signed to Henry to go on, but Mr. Coningsby unintentionally interrupted.

"Very curious," he said, "very interesting indeed." He looked all round the room. "I suppose the light comes from behind the curtains somehow?"

"The light comes from the figures," Henry said.

"Does it indeed?" Mr. Coningsby said, as if he was perfectly ready to believe anything reasonable, and even to refrain from blaming his host for offering him something perfectly unreasonable. "From the figures? Well, well." He settled his eyeglasses and leaned forward. "Are they moving in any order?" he asked, "or do they just"—he waggled his hand— "jump?"

The Image that did not move

"They certainly move in order," Henry answered, "all but one: the one in the centre. You may recognize them; the figures are those which are painted on the Tarot cards you showed us."

"O, really?" Mr. Coningsby said, a small suspicion rising in him. "Just the same kind, are they? Well, well. But the cards aren't moving the whole time. At least," he added, half in real amusement, half in superior sarcasm, "I hadn't noticed it."

"No," Henry agreed. "But, if you'll excuse me, sir, the point is rather that the cards explain—or anyhow may be supposed to explain—the movements of these figures. We think probably that that's what all fortune-telling by cards comes from, but the origin's been forgotten, which is why it's the decadent and futile thing it is."

Nothing occurred to Mr. Coningsby in answer to this; he didn't understand it but he didn't want to be bothered with an explanation. He strolled forward till he stood by the table. "May one pick them up?" he asked. "It's difficult to examine the workmanship properly while they're all bustling round."

"I don't think I should touch them, sir," Henry said, checking his grandfather's movement with a fierce glance. "The balance that keeps them dancing must be very delicate."

"O, just as you like," Mr. Coningsby said. "Why doesn't the one in the middle dance?"

"We imagine that its weight and position must make it a kind of counterpoise," Henry answered. "Just as the card of the Fool—which you'll see is the same figure—is numbered nought."

"Has he a tiger by him for any particular reason?" Mr. Coningsby inquired. "Fools and tigers seem a funny conjunction."

"Nobody knows about the Fool," Aaron burst in. "Unless the cards explain it."

The Image that did not move

Mr. Coningsby was about to speak again when Sybil forestalled him.

"I can't see this central figure," she said. "Where is it exactly, Mr. Lee?"

Aaron, Henry, and her brother all pointed to it, and all with very different accents said, "There". Sybil stepped slightly forward, then to one side; she moved her head to different angles, and then said apologetically, "You'll all think me frightfully silly, but I can't see any figure in the middle."

"Really, Sybil!" her brother said. "There!"

"But, my dear, it isn't there," she said. "At least, so far as I can possibly see. I'm sorry to be so stupid, Mr. Lee, because it's all quite the loveliest thing I ever saw in the whole of my life. It's perfectly wonderful and beautiful. And I just want, if I can, to see where you say this particular figure is."

Henry leant forward suddenly. Nancy put her left hand up to where his lay on her shoulder. "Darling," she said, "please! You're hurting me." He took no notice; he did not apparently hear her. He was looking with intense eagerness from Sybil to the golden images and back. "Miss Coningsby," he said, reverting unconsciously to his earlier habit of address, "can you see the Fool and his tiger at all?"

She surveyed the table carefully. "Yes," she said at last, "there—no, there—no—it's moving so quickly I can hardly see it—there—ah, it's gone again. Surely that's it, dancing with the rest; it seems as if it were always arranging itself in some place which was empty for it."

Nancy took hold of Henry's wrist and pulled it; tears of pain were in her eyes, but she smiled at him. "Darling, must you squeeze my shoulder quite so hard?" she said.

Blankly he looked at her; automatically he let go, and though in a moment she put her own hand into the crook of his arm he did not seem to notice it. His whole attention was given to Sybil. "You can see it moving?" he uttered.

On the other side, Aaron was trembling, and putting his

fingers to his mouth as if to control it and them. Sybil, gazing at the table, did not see him. "But it seems so," she said. "Or am I just distracted?"

Henry made a great effort. He turned to Nancy. "Can you see it?" he asked.

"It looks to me to be in the centre," she said, "and it doesn't seem to be moving—not exactly moving."

"What do you mean—not exactly moving?" Henry asked, almost harshly.

"It isn't moving at all," said Mr. Coningsby. "It's capitally made, though; the tiger's quite lifelike. So's the Fool," he added handsomely.

"I suppose I meant not moving," Nancy said. "In a way I feel as if I expected it to. But it isn't."

"Why should you expect it to?" Henry asked.

"I can't think," Nancy admitted. "Perhaps it was Aunt Sybil saying it *was* that made me think it ought to be."

"Well," Sybil said, "there we are! If you all agree that it's not moving, I expect it isn't. Perhaps my eyes have got St. Vitus's dance or something. But it certainly seems to me to be dancing everywhere."

There was a short and profound silence, broken at last by Nancy. "What did you mean about fortune-telling?" she said, addressing ostensibly Mr. Lee, but in fact Henry.

Both of them came jerkily back to consciousness of her. But the old man was past speech; he could only look at his grandson. For a moment Henry didn't seem to know what to say. But Nancy's eager and devoted eyes were full on him, and something natural in him responded. "Why, yes," he said, "it's here that fortunes can be told. If your father will let us use his pack of cards?" He looked inquiringly across.

Mr. Coningsby's earlier suspicion poked up again, but he hesitated to refuse. "O, if you choose," he said. "I'm afraid you'll find nothing in it, but do as you like. Get them, Nancy; they're in my bag."

The Image that did not move

"Right," said Nancy. "No, darling," as Henry made a movement to accompany her. "I won't be a minute: you stay here." There had been a slight effect of separation between them, and she was innocently anxious to let so brief a physical separation abolish the mental; he, reluctant to leave Aaron to deal with Mr. Coningsby's conversation, assented.

"Don't be long," he said, and she, under her breath, "Could I?" and was gone. As she ran she puzzled a little over her aunt's difficulty in seeing the motionless image, and over the curious vibration that it seemed to her to possess. So these were what Henry had meant; he would tell her more about them presently, perhaps, because he certainly hadn't yet told her all he meant to. But what part then in the mystery did the central figure play, and why was its mobility or immobility of such concern to him? Though—of course it wasn't usual for four people to see a thing quite still while another saw it dancing. Supposing anyone saw her now, could they think of her as quite still, running at this speed? Sometimes one had funny feelings about stillness and motion—there had been her own sensation in the car yesterday, but that had only been a feeling, not a looking, so to speak. No one ever saw a motionless car tearing along the roads.

She found the Tarot pack and ran back again, thinking this time how agreeable it was to run and do things for Henry. She wished she found it equally agreeable to run for her father. But then her father—it was her father's fault, wasn't it? Was it? Wasn't it? If she could feel as happy—if she *could* feel. Could she? Could she, not only do, but feel happy to do? Couldn't she? Could she? More breathless within than without, she came again to the room of the golden dance.

She was aware, as through the dark screen of the curtain she entered the soft spheral light and heard, as they had all heard, that faint sound of music, of something changed in three of those who waited for her. Henry and her father were standing near each other, as if they had been talking. But also

76

they were facing each other, and it was not a friendly opposition. Mr. Coningsby was frowning, and Henry was looking at him with a dominating hostility. She guessed immediately what had been happening—Henry had himself raised the possibility of his buying or being given or otherwise procuring the cards. And her father, with that persistent obstinacy which made even his reasonable decisions unreasonable, had refused. He was so often in a right which his immediate personal grievance turned into a wrong; his manners changed what was not even an injury into something worse than an insult. To be so conscious of himself was—Nancy felt though she did not define it—an insult to everyone else; he tried to defy the human race with a plaintive antagonism—even the elder sons of the younger sons of peers might (he seemed to suggest) outrage his decencies by treading too closely on his heels. So offended, so outraged, he glanced at Henry now.

She came to them before either had time to speak. Aaron Lee and Sybil had been listening to the finished colloquy, and both of them willingly accepted her coming.

"Here we are," she said. "Henry, how frightfully exciting!" It wasn't, she thought at the same moment, not in the least. Not exciting; that was wholly the wrong word for this rounded chamber, and the moving figures, and the strange pack in her hand by which the wonder of earth had happened, and the two opposed faces, and Aaron Lee's anxious eyes, and the immortal tenderness of Sybil's. No—not exciting, but it would serve. It would ease the moment. "Who'll try first?" she went on, holding out the Tarots. "Father? Aunt? Or will you, Mr. Lee?"

Aaron waved them on. "No, no," he said hurriedly. "Pray one of you—they're yours. Do try—one of you."

"Not for me, thank you. I've no wish to be amused so——" Her father hesitated for an adverb, and Sybil also with a gesture put them by.

"O, aunt, do!" Nancy said, feeling that if her aunt was in it things would be safer.

"Really, Nancy. I'd rather not—if you don't mind," Sybil said, apologetic, but determined. "It's—it's so much like making someone tell you a secret."

"What someone?" Henry said, anger still in his voice.

"I don't mean someone exactly," Sybil said, "but things . . . the universe, so to speak. If it's gone to all this trouble to keep the next minute quiet, it seems rude to force its confidence. Do forgive me." She did not, Nancy noticed, add, as she sometimes did, that it was probably silly of her.

Nancy frowned at the cards. "Don't you think we ought to?" she asked.

"Of course, if you can," Sybil answered. "It's just—do excuse me—that I can't."

"You sound", Henry said, recovering a more normal voice, "on remarkably intimate terms with the universe. Mayn't it cheat you? Supposing it had something unpleasant waiting for you?"

"But," said Sybil, "as somebody says in Dickens, 'It hasn't, you know, so we won't suppose it.' Traddles, of course. I'm forgetting Dickens; I must read him again. Well, Nancy, it's between you and Henry."

Nancy looked at her lover. He smiled at her at first with that slight pre-occupation behind his eyes which always seemed to be there, she thought a little ruefully, since the coming of the Tarots. But in a moment this passed, and they changed, though whether she or that other thing were now the cause of their full, deep concentration, she could not tell. He laid his hand on hers that held the Tarots.

"And what does it matter which?" he said. "But I'd rather we tried yours, if you don't mind."

"Can't we try them together?" she asked, "and say good night to separation?"

"Let's believe we've said it," he answered, "but you shall try them for us both and let me read the fates. Do you believe that it's true?"

The Image that did not move

"Is it true?" she asked.

"As the earth in your hands," he answered, and Mr. Coningsby's hostility only just conquered his curiosity, so as to prevent him asking what on earth Henry meant. "It's between those"—he pointed to the ever-moving images—"and your hands that the power flows, and on the power the cards move. See."

He turned her, and Aaron Lee, who stood between her and the table, moved hastily back. Then, taking the cards from their case, he made her hold them in her hands, as she had held the suit of deniers on that other evening, and the memory of it came back on her with sudden force. But this time, having settled her hands, he did not enclose them in his own; instead, he stepped away from her and waved away Sybil also, who was close on her left side, so that she stood alone, facing the golden table, her hands extended towards it, holding within them the whole pack of cards, opened a little fanwise so that from left to right the edges made a steeply sloping ascent.

"Move forward, slowly," he said, "till I tell you to stop. Go on."

The earth that had lain in her hands . . . and now she was to go forward a step, or stop. It was not beyond her power to withdraw; she might pause and laugh and apologize to them all—and to Henry privately and beyond all—and lay aside the things she held. It was not beyond her power to refuse to enter the light that seemed now to grow to a golden sheen, a veil and mist of gold between her and the table; she could step back, she could refuse to advance, to know, to be. In the large content of the love that filled her she had no strong desire to find her future—if the cards indeed could tell her of it—though she could not feel, as Sybil did, that the universe itself was love. But, pausing on the verge of the future, she could find no reason noble enough for retreat—retreat would be cowardice or . . . no, nothing but cowardice. She was Henry's will; she

79

was her own will to accomplish that will; having no moral command against her, she must needs go on.

She took a step forward, and her heart beat fast and high as she seemed to move into the clouded golden mist that received her, and fantastically enlarged and changed the appearance of her hands and the cards within them. She took another step, and the Tarots quivered in her hold, and through the mist she saw but dimly the stately movement of the everlasting measure trodden out before her, but the images were themselves enlarged and heightened, and she was not very sure of what nature they were. But nothing could daunt the daring in which she went; she took a third step, and Henry's voice cried to her suddenly, "Stop there and wait for the cards."

She half-turned her head towards him at the words, but he was too far behind for her to see him. Only, still looking through that floating and distorting veil of light, she did see a figure, and knew it for Aaron's: yet it was more like one of the Tarots—it was the Knight of Sceptres. The old man's walking-stick was the raised sceptre; the old face was young again, and yet the same. The skull-cap was a heavy medieval head-dress—but as the figure loomed it moved also, and the mist swirled and hid it. The cards shook in her hands; she looked back at them, and suddenly one of them floated right out into the air and slowly sank towards the floor; another issued, and then another, and so they followed in a gentle persistent rain. She did not try to retain them; could she have tried she knew she could not succeed. The figures before her appeared and disappeared, and as each one showed, so in spiral convolution some card of those she still held slipped out and wheeled round and round and fell from her sight into the ever-swirling mist.

They were huge things now, as if the great leaves of some aboriginal tree, the sacred bodhi-tree under which our Lord Gautama achieved Nirvana or that Northern dream of Igdrasil or the olives of Gethsemane, were drifting downward from the cluster round which her hands were clasped. The likenesses were not in her mind, but the sense of destiny was, and the vision of leaves falling slowly, slowly, carried gently upon a circling wind that touched her also in its passage, and blew the golden cloud before it. She grew faint in gazing; the grotesque hands that stretched out were surely not those of Nancy Coningsby, but of a giant form she did not know. With an effort she wrested her eyes from the sight, and looked before her, only more certainly to see the dancers. And these now were magnified to twenty times their first height; they were manikins, dwarfs, grotesques, yet living. More definitely visible than any before, a sudden mingled group grew out of the mist before her. Three forms were there—with their left arms high-arched, and finger-tips touching, wheeling round a common centre; she knew them as she gazed—the Queen of Chalices, holding her cup against her heart; and the naked figure of the peasant Death, his sickle in his right hand; and a more ominous form still, Set of the Egyptians, with the donkey head, and the captives chained to him, the power of infinite malice. Round and round, ever more swiftly, they whirled, and each as it passed seemed to stretch out towards her the symbol of itself that it carried; and the music that had been all this while in her ears rose to the shrieking of a great wind, and the wind about her grew strong and cold. Higher still went the shrieking; more bitterly against her the fierce wind beat. The cold struck and nipped her; she was alone and her hands were empty, and the bleak wind died; only she saw the last fragments of the golden mist blown and driven upon it. But as it passed, and as she graspingly realized that her lover and friends were near her, she seemed yet for a moment to be the centre of that last measure: the three dancers whirled round her, their left hands touching over her head, separating and enclosing her. Some knowledge struck to her heart; and her heart ached in answer, a dull pain unlike her glorious agony when it almost broke with the burden of love. It existed and it ceased.

The Image that did not move

Henry's voice said from behind her: "Happy fortune, darling. Let's look at the cards."

She felt for the moment that she would rather he looked at her. There she was, feeling rather pitiable, and there were all the cards lying at her feet in a long twining line, and there was her father looking a trifle annoyed, and there was Henry kneeling by the cards, and there was Aaron Lee bending over him, and then between her and the table at which she didn't want to look came the form of her aunt. So she looked at her instead, which seemed much more satisfactory, and went so far as to slip an arm into Sybil's, though she said nothing. They both waited for Henry, and both with a certain lack of immediate interest. But this Henry, immersed in the cards, did not notice.

"You're likely to travel a long distance," he said, "apparently in the near future, and you'll come under a great influence of control, and you'll find your worst enemy in your own heart. You may run serious risks of illness or accident, but it looks as if you might be successful in whatever you undertake. And a man shall owe you everything, and a woman shall govern you, and you shall die very rich."

"I'm so glad," Nancy said in a small voice. She was feeling very tired, but she felt she ought to show a little interest.

"Henry," she went on, "why is the card marked nought lying right away from the others?"

"I don't know," he said, "but I told you that no one can reckon the Fool. Unless you can?" he added quickly, to Sybil.

"No," said Sybil. "I can see it right away from the others too." She waited a minute, but, as Henry showed no signs of moving, she added in a deliberately amiable voice: "Aren't you rather tired, Nancy? Henry dear, it's been the most thrilling evening, and the way you read fortunes is superb. I'm so glad Nancy's to be successful. But would you think it very rude if she and I went to bed now? I know it's early, but the air of your Downs . . ."

The Image that did not move

"I beg your pardon?" Henry said. "I'm afraid I wasn't listening."

Sybil, even more politely, said it all again. Henry sprang to his feet and came over to them. "My darling, how careless of me," he said to Nancy, while his eyes searched and sought in hers, "of course you must be fagged out. We'll all go back now—unless", he added politely to Mr. Coningsby, "you'd like to try anything further with"—there was the slightest pause—"your cards."

"No, thank you," Mr. Coningsby said frigidly. "I may as well take them down myself"; and he looked at them where they lay on the floor.

"I'll come back and collect them as soon as I've seen Nancy along," Henry answered. "They'll be safe enough till then."

"I think I would as soon take them now," Mr. Coningsby said. "Things have a way of getting mislaid sometimes."

"Nothing was ever mislaid in this room," Henry answered scornfully.

"But the passages and other rooms might be less fortunate," Mr. Coningsby sneered. "Nancy can wait a minute, I'm sure."

"Nancy", he said, "will pick them up while you're talking about it," and moved to do it. But Henry forestalled him, though his dark skin flushed slightly, as he rose with the pack, restored it to its case, and ostentatiously presented it to Mr. Coningsby, who clasped it firmly, threw a negligent look at the dancing figures, and walked to the opening in the curtains. Henry drew Nancy from her aunt into his own care, and followed him; as they passed through she said idly: "Why do you have curtains?"

He leaned to her ear. "I will show you now, if you like," he said; "the sooner the better. Are you really too tired? or will you see what larger futures the cards show us?"

She looked back at the room. "Darling, will to-morrow do?" she said. "I do feel rather done."

"Rest, then," he answered; "there's always sound sleep in

this house. To-morrow, I'll show you something else—if," he added, speaking still more softly, "if you can borrow the cards. Nancy, what good can they possibly be to your father?"

She smiled faintly. "Did you quarrel with him about them?" she said, but as she saw him frown added swiftly, "None."

"Yet he *will* hold on to them," Henry said. "Don't you think they belong to—those behind us?"

"I suppose so," Nancy said uncertainly. "I feel as if we all belonged to them, whatever they are. Your golden images have got into my bones, darling, and my heart's dancing to them instead of to you. Aren't you sorry?"

"We'll dance to them together," he said. "The images and the cards, and the hands and the feet—we'll bring them all together yet."

"That's what your aunt said," she answered, "something coming together. What did she mean by Horus?"

"My aunt's as mad as your father," he answered, "and Horus has been a dream for more than two thousand years."

Chapter Six

THE KNOWLEDGE OF THE FOOL

It was some time later, their visitors having all retired, after more or less affectionate partings, that Henry came to his grandfather in the outer room. The old man was waiting eagerly; as the door shut behind his grandson he broke out, "Did you hear? Did she mean it?"

Henry came across and sat down. "She must have meant it," he said; "there's no conceivable way by which she could have known what we need. Besides, unless she was playing with us—but she wouldn't, she's not that kind. So if she saw ——" He got up again and walked in extreme excitement about the room. "It can't be—but why not? If we've found the last secret of the images! If time's at last brought sight along with the cards!"

Aaron put his hand to his heart. "But why should she be able to see? Here have all our families studied this for centuries, and none of them—and not you nor I—has ever seen the Fool move. There's only a tale to tell us that it does move. Why should this woman be able to see it?"

"Why should she pretend if she doesn't?" Henry retorted. "Besides, I tell you she's a woman of great power. She possesses herself entirely; I've never seen anything dismay or distract her. She's like the Woman on the cards, but she doesn't know it—hierophantic, maid and matron at once."

"But what do you mean?" Aaron urged. "She knew nothing of the cards or the images. She didn't know why they danced or how. She's merely commonplace—a fool, and the sister of a fool."

The Knowledge of the Fool

"None of us has ever known what the Fool of the Tarots is," the other said. "You say yourself that no one has ever seen it move. But this woman couldn't see it in the place where we all look for it. She saw it completing the measures, fulfilling the dance."

"She doesn't know the dance," Aaron said.

"She doesn't know what she does or doesn't know," Henry answered. "Either she was lying, I tell you, or by some impossible chance she can see what we can't see: and if she can, then the most ancient tale of the whole human race is true, and the Fool does move."

"But then she'll know the thing that's always been missing," Aaron almost sobbed. "And she's going away next week!"

"It's why she could manage Joanna as she did," Henry went on unheeding. "She's got some sort of a calm, some equanimity in her heart. She—the only eyes that can read the future exactly, and she doesn't want to know the future. Everything's complete for her in the moment. It's beautiful, it's terrific—and what do we do about it?" He stopped dead in his walk and stared at Aaron.

"She's going away next week," the old man repeated.

Henry flung himself back into a chair. "Let us see," he said. "The Tarots are brought back to the images; there is a woman who can read the movements rightly; and let us add one more thing, for what it's worth—that I and Nancy are at the beginning of great experiments. On the other hand, the Tarots may be snatched from us by the idiot who pretends to own them; and the woman may leave us and go God knows where; and Nancy may fail. But, fail or not, that's a separate thing, and my own business. The other is a general concern, and yours. When the Tarots have been brought back to the dancers, and we can read the meaning of the dance, are you willing to let them go?"

"But let us see then", Aaron said, "what we can do to keep them."

The Knowledge of the Fool

Henry looked over at him and brooded. "If we once let them out of this house we may not see them again—they will be hidden in the Museum while we and our children die and rot: locked in a glass case, with a ticket under them, for hogs' faces of ignorance to stare at or namby-pamby professors to preach about." He leapt to his feet. "When I think of it," he said, "I grow as mad as Joanna, with her wails about a dismembered god. Shall we let the paintings and the images be torn apart once more?"

Aaron, crouching over the table, looked up sneeringly. "Go and pray to Horus, as Joanna does," he said, "or run about the fields and think yourself Isis the Divine Mother. Bah! why do you jump and tramp? I'm an old man now, desire is going out of me, but if I'd your heat I'd do more with it than waste it cursing and shouting. Sit down; let us talk. There are four days before they go."

Henry stamped. "You can't be sure of four hours," he said. "Any moment that fool may take offence and be off. Get over to-morrow safely, and he can't go on Christmas Day, but after that how can we keep him against his will?"

"By leaving him to use his will," Aaron said.

Henry came slowly back to the table. "What do you mean?" he asked. "You won't run the risk of violence, will you? How can we? We don't know what the result on the Tarots may be; there are warnings against it. Besides—it would be hard to see how to do it without—— O no, it's impossible."

Aaron said, "He has the Tarots—can't he be given to the Tarots? Is wind nothing? Is water nothing? Let us give him wind and water, and let us see if the obstinacy that can keep the cards will bring him safely through the elements of the cards. Don't shed blood, don't be violent; let's loose the Tarots upon him."

Henry leaned forward and looked at the ground for a long time. "I've thought of something of the sort," he said at last. "But there's Nancy."

Aaron sneered again. "Spare the father for the child's sake, hey?" he said. "You fool, what other way is there? If you steal the cards from him, if you could, can you show them to her or use them with her? D'you think she won't be bothered and troubled, and will that be good for your experiment? She'll always be worried over her honesty."

"I might show her that our use and knowledge is a high matter," Henry said uncertainly, "and teach her. . . ."

"All in time, all in time," the old man exclaimed, "and any day he may give the Tarots to the Museum. Besides, there's the woman."

"The woman!" Henry said, "That's as great a difficulty. Can you persuade her to come and live with you and be the hierophant of the images of the cabalistic dance?"

"If," said Aaron slowly, stretching out a hand and laying it on the young man's arm, "if her brother was—gone, and if her niece was married to you, would it be so unlikely that she should live with her niece? If her niece studied the images, and loved to talk of them, and asked this woman for help, would it be so unlikely that she would say what she can see?" He ceased, and there was a pause.

At last—"I know," Henry said. "I saw it—vaguely—even to-night I saw it. But it may be dangerous."

"Death is one of the Greater Trumps," Aaron said. "If I had the strength, I would do it alone; as it is, I can't. I haven't the energy or will to control the cards. I can only study and read them. You must do the working, and however I can help you I will."

"The Greater Trumps——" Henry said doubtfully. "I can't yet use—that's the point with Nancy—I want to see whether she and I can live—and she mustn't know——"

"There are wind and water, as I told you before," the old man answered. "I don't think your Mr. Coningsby will manage to save himself even from the twos and threes and fours of the sceptres and cups. He has no will. I am more afraid of Joanna."

The Knowledge of the Fool

"Joanna!" Henry said. "I never heard that she saw the movement of the Fool."

Aaron shrugged. "She looked to find that out when she had succeeded in carrying out her desire," he said.

"She was right," Henry said.

"And has Sybil Coningsby carried out her desire?" Aaron asked. "What was it, then?"

"I can't tell you," Henry said, "but she found it and she stands within it, possessing it perfectly. Only she doesn't know what she's done. But she doesn't matter at the moment, nor Joanna. Only Nancy and . . . and that man."

"Shall there then be only Nancy?" Aaron asked softly.

Henry looked back at him steadily. "Yes," he answered, "unless he can overcome the beating of the cards."

"Be clear upon one thing," Aaron said. "I will have no part in this which you are wanting to achieve with *them*. I do not want even to know it. If all things go well, it will be enough for me to have restored the knowledge of the dance, and perhaps to have traced something of the law of its movement. But supposing Nancy—later—discovers somehow, in the growth of her wisdom, what you've done? Have you considered that?"

"I will believe", Henry said, "that if indeed it's the growth of her wisdom that discovers it, her wisdom will justify me. She'll know that one man must not keep in being the division of unity; she'll acknowledge that his spirit denied something greater than itself and perished inevitably. His spirit? His mere habitual peevish greed."

"You will take that risk?" Aaron said.

"It is no risk," Henry answered; "if it were, then the whole intention is already doomed."

Aaron nodded, and got to his feet. "Yet ten minutes ago you weren't so certain," he said.

"I hadn't then determined," Henry answered. "It's only when one has quite determined that one understands."

"When will you do it?" Aaron asked. "Do you want me to help you? You should consider that if what you do succeeds, then the girl may be too distressed to go your way for a while."

"If it may be," Henry said slowly, "I will wait over to-morrow, for to-morrow I mean to show her the fortunes of nations. But we must not wait too long—and you're right in what you say: she will need time, so that I won't try to carry her with me till later. And if after Christmas her father should determine to go . . . it would be done more conveniently here. Let's see how things fall out, but if possible let it be done on Christmas Day. He always walks in the afternoon—he told me weeks ago that he hasn't missed a sharp walk on Christmas afternoon for thirty-four years."

"Let it be so, then," his grandfather answered. "I will talk to the women, and do you rouse the winds. If by any chance it fails, it can be tried again. At a pinch you could do it with the fire in the car when you return."

Henry made a face. "And what about Nancy and her aunt?" he asked.

Aaron nodded. "I forgot," he said. "Well, there will be always means."

Chapter Seven

THE DANCE IN THE WORLD

The sense of strain that had come into being on the Thursday night existed still on the morning of Christmas Eve. Henry and Mr. Coningsby were markedly the centres of conflicting emotions, and Mr. Coningsby was disposed to make his daughter into the battle-field since she seemed to hesitate to support him with a complete alliance. He alluded, as the two of them talked after a slightly uncomfortable breakfast, to the unusual sight which had been exposed to them the night before.

"I must say", he remarked, "that I thought it showed poorer taste than I had hoped for in Henry, to try that trick of the moving dolls on us."

"But why do you call it a trick, father?" Nancy objected. "They *were* moving: and that was all Henry said."

"It was not by any means all," Mr. Coningsby answered. "To be quite candid, Nancy, he disappointed me very much; he practically tried to swindle me out of that pack of cards by making an excuse that the dolls were very much like them. Am I to give up everything that belongs to me because anyone has got something like it?"

Nancy thought over this sentence without at once replying.

Put like that, it did sound unreasonable. But how else could it be put, to convince her father? Could she say, "Father, I've created earth, and seen policemen and nurses become emperors and empresses, and moved in a golden cloud where I had glimpses of a dance that went all through my blood?" Could she? Could she tell him that her mind still occasionally remembered, as if it were a supernatural riddle, the shock of seeing the crucifix with its head above its feet, and the contrast with the Hanged Man of the cards? She said at last, "I don't think Henry meant it quite like that. I'd like you to be fair to him."

"I hope I'm always fair," said Mr. Coningsby, meaning that he couldn't imagine Eternal Justice disagreeing with him, "but I must say I'm disappointed in Henry."

Nancy looked at the fire. Dolls? She would have been annoyed, only she was too bothered. Her father must be there, if she could only get at him. But, so far as that went, he might as well be shut away from her in the gleaming golden mist. He might as well be a grey automaton—he was much more like a moving doll than the images of the hidden room, than Henry, than Sybil and Joanna hand in hand, than the white-cloaked governor of the roads, than Henry, than the witches of Macbeth's encounter, than the staring crucifix, than the earth between her hands, than Henry . . . She looked at him dubiously. She had meant to ask him if she and Henry might have the Tarot pack again that evening, because Henry wanted to tell her something more, and she wanted to know. But he wouldn't, he certainly wouldn't. Might she borrow them for an hour without asking him? It wouldn't hurt them or him. They were on his dressing-table; she had seen them there, and wondered why he hadn't locked them away. But she knew—it was because he hadn't really expected them to be taken; he had only wanted to be nasty to Henry. Suppose she asked him and he refused—it would be too silly! But was she to lose all this wonder, which so terrified and exalted her, because he wanted to annoy Henry? O, in heaven's name what would a girl who was trying to love *do*?

Love (presumably) at that moment encouraged Mr. Coningsby, meditating on his own fair-mindedness and his generous goodwill, to say, "I'd always be willing for him to borrow them, if I could be sure of getting them back. But——"

Nancy lifted eyes more affectionate than she knew. "If I promised I'd give them back, father, whenever you liked?"

Mr. Coningsby, a little taken aback, said evasively, "It isn't you I'm doubtful about. You're my daughter, and you know there's such a thing as decency."

It would be only decent, Nancy thought, for her not to take the cards for use without his consent; but it would also be only decent for him to lend them. She said, "You'd trust me with them?"

"Of course, of course, if the necessity arose," Mr. Coningsby said, a trifle embarrassed, and feeling glad that the necessity couldn't arise. Nancy, relieved from her chief embarrassment, decided that the necessity *had* arisen. She felt that it would be silly to compel her father to a clearer statement. She said, as clearly as possible, "I'll take care of them," but Sybil came into the room at that moment and the remark was lost. Nancy, a little bewildered by the sudden appearance in her life of a real moral problem, and hoping sincerely that she had tried to solve it sincerely, slid away and went to look for Henry.

It was with Henry, and holding the Tarots, that she entered the room that evening and passed the curtains; together they stood before the golden images. Nancy felt the difference; what had on the previous night been a visit of curiosity, of interest, was now a more important thing. It was a deliberate repetition, an act of intention, however small; but it was also something more. By her return, and her return with Henry, she was inviting a union between the mystery of her love and the mystery of the dance. As she stood, again gazing at it, she felt suddenly a premonition of that union, or of the heart of it. It must be in herself that the union must be, in a discovery of some new state perhaps as unlike her love and her vision as they were unlike the ignorant Nancy of the previous year—there was no other place nor other means, whatever outward change took place. All that she did could but more deeply reveal her to herself; if only the revelation could be as good and lovely as . . . as Henry found her. Could she believe in herself so? Dared she trust that such a beauty was indeed the final answer, or could be made so?

But before she could search out her own thoughts he spoke to her.

"You saw last night how fortunes can be told," he said. "The cards that you held are the visible channel between the dance and you. You hold them in your hands and——"

"Tell me first," she said, "now we're here alone, tell me more of this dance. It's more than fortune-telling, isn't it? Why do the cards make earth? Why do you call of them the Greater Trumps? Is it only a name? Tell me; you must tell me now."

He drew a deep breath, began to speak, and then, checking, made a despairing movement with his hands. "O, how shall I explain", he cried out, "what we can only be taught to imagine? what only a few among my own people can imagine? I've brought you here, I've wanted you here, and now it's too much for me. There aren't any words—you'll think me as mad as that wretched woman on the roads."

"How do you know I think her mad?" Nancy said. "Did Aunt Sybil seem to? You must try and tell me, Henry—if you think it's important. If you don't," she added gravely, lifting serious eyes to his, "I should be sorry, because it would all be only a conjurer's trick."

He stood away from her a step or two, and then, looking not at her but at the table, he began again to speak. "Imagine, then, if you can," he said, "imagine that everything which exists takes part in the movement of a great dance—everything, the electrons, all growing and decaying things, all that seems alive and all that doesn't seem alive, men and beasts, trees and stones, everything that changes, and there is nothing anywhere that does not change. That change—that's what we know of the immortal dance; the law in the nature of things— that's the measure of the dance, why one thing changes swiftly and another slowly, why there is seeming accident and incalculable alteration, why men hate and love and grow hungry, and cities that have stood for centuries fall in a week, why the smallest wheel and the mightiest world revolve, why blood flows and the heart beats and the brain moves, why your body is poised on your ankles and the Himalaya are rooted in the earth—quick or slow, measurable or immeasurable, there is nothing at all anywhere but the dance. Imagine it—imagine it, see it all at once and in one!"

She did not speak, and after a minute's silence he broke out again.

"This is all that there is to learn; our happiest science guesses at the steps of a little of it. It's always perfect because it can't be anything else. It knows nothing of joy or grief; it's movement, quick as light, slow as the crumbling of a stone tomb in the jungle. If you cry, it's because the measure will have it so; if you laugh, it's because some gayer step demands it, not because you will. If you ache, the dance strains you; if you are healthy, the dance carries you. Medicine is the dance: law, religion, music, and poetry—all these are ways of telling ourselves the smallest motion that we've known for an instant before it utterly disappears in the unrepeatable process of *that*. O Nancy, see it, see it—that's the most we can do, to see something of it for the poor second before we die!"

The very dance itself seemed to have paused in her, so motionless her light form held itself, so rapt in its breathless suspension as the words sounded through her, and before her eyes the small shapes of glory turned and intertwined.

"But once," he went on, "—some say in Egypt long before the Pharaoh heard of Yussuf Ben-Yakoob, and some in Europe while the dreaming rabbis whispered in the walled ghetto over fables of unspeakable words, and some in the hidden covens of doctrine which the Church called witchcraft—once a dancer talked of the dance, not with words, but with images; once a mind knew it to the seventy-eighth degree of discovery, and

95

not only knew it, but knew how it knew it, so beautifully in one secret corner the dance doubled and redoubled on itself. And then the measure, turning here and there, perpetually harmonious, wrought out these forms of gold in correspondence with something at least of itself, becoming its own record, change answering to change. We can't guess who, we can't tell how, but they were carried in the vans of the gipsies about Europe till they were brought here, and here they still are."

She moved a hand and he paused; as if willing to speak from herself, she said—the voice and the words desiring a superfluous but compensating confirmation, as of step answering to step: "To look at these then is to have the movement made visible? this is what is going on . . . now, immediately now? Isn't there anything anywhere that isn't happening there?"

He pointed to the table. "This is the present," he said, "and this is the only present, and even that is changed before it can be known."

"Yet you said", she answered, "that this unknown man knew how it was to be known. How was that? and why, dearest, are the figures—the images, I mean—made as they are?"

"It would need another seer to explain," he said, "and that seer would have to pass behind the symbols and see them from within. Do you understand, Nancy? Do you understand that sometimes where one can hardly go, two may? Think of that, and think what might be seen and done within the dance if so much can be seen without. All we know is that the images are the twenty-one and the nought, and the four fours and the four tens. Doubtless these numbers themselves are of high necessity for proper knowledge, but their secret too is so far hidden within the dance."

"Yet you must have considered the shapes, darling?" she asked.

"The shapes, perhaps, are for two things," he answered more slowly, "for resemblance and for communication. On the one hand they must mean some step, some conjunction, some—what we call a fact—that is often repeated in the infinite combinations; on the other, it must be something that we know and can read. This, I think, is what was meant, but even the secondary meaning has been lost—or was lost while the cards were separated from the golden images, as if a child were taken from its mother into some other land and never learned her language, that language which should have been the proper inheritance of its tongue."

He stopped short, as if the thought troubled him, and the girl, with the same memory in her mind, said, "Did the woman on the road mean that when she talked to us?"

"I don't care what she meant," he said almost harshly. "Neither she nor anyone but ourselves concerns us now. No one but ourselves has a proper right to talk of the cards or the images."

He glanced at her as he spoke, but, smiling very slightly, she let the utterance die, and said only: "Tell me more of the cards."

"The cards were made with the images," he answered; "the mark in the corner of each of them is the seal of the bottom of each golden shape; seventy-eight figures and as many seals on as many cards. The papyrus paintings are exactly the same as the figures; they are the paintings of the figures. This, as I told you a month ago, when we first saw them, is the only perfect set, correspondence to correspondence, and therefore the only set by which the sublime dance can be read. The movement changes incessantly, but in every fractional second it is *so*, and when these cards are brought to it they dispose themselves in that order, modified only by the nature of the hands between which they are held, and by the order into which they fall we read the fortune of whoever holds them."

"But the suits, you said, are the elements?" she asked.

He nodded. "But that is in the exterior world; they are the increasing strength of the four elements, and in the body of a man there are corresponding natures. This is the old doctrine of humours which your schoolmistress taught you, no doubt, that you might understand Ben Jonson or what not."

"And the others?" she said; "the Greater Trumps?"

He came near to her and spoke more low, almost as if he did not want the golden dancers to know that he was talking of them. "They", he said, "are the truths—the facts—call them what you will—principles of thought, actualities of corporate existence, Death and Love and certain Virtues and Meditation and the Benign Sun of Wisdom, and so on. You must see them—there aren't any words to tell you."

"The Devil—if it is a devil?" she said.

"It is the unreasonable hate and malice which moves in us," he answered.

"The Juggler—if it is a juggler?" she asked.

"It is the beginning of all things—a show, a dexterity of balance, a flight, and a falling. It's the only way he—whoever he was—could form the beginning and the continuation of the dance itself."

"Is it God then?" Nancy asked, herself yet more hushed.

Henry moved impatiently. "What do we know?" he answered. "This isn't a question of words. God or gods or no gods, these things are, and they're meant and manifested thus. Call it God if you like, but it's better to call it the Juggler and mean neither God nor no God."

"And the Fool who doesn't move?" she said after a pause.

"All I can tell you of that", he said grimly, "is that it is the Fool who doesn't move. There are tales and writings of everything but the Fool; he comes into none of the doctrines or the fortunes. I've never yet seen what he can be."

"Yet Aunt Sybil saw him move," she said.

"You shall ask her about it some time," he answered, "but not yet. Now I have told you as much as I can tell of these things; the sense of them is for your imagination to grasp. And when you have come to understand it so, then we may see whether by the help of the Tarots we may find our way into the place beyond the mists. But meanwhile I will show you something more. Wait for me a minute."

He paused, considering; then he went to a different part of the curtains and disappeared through what she supposed was another opening in them. She heard a sound, as if he were opening a window, then he came back to her.

"If you look up at this room from without," he said, "you will see it has four windows in it. I have opened the eastern one. Now see."

He went to the part of the table nearest to the window he had opened, and, feeling beneath it, drew out a curved ledge, running some third of the way round the table. It was some three feet wide, and it reached, when it was fully extended, almost to the curtains; it also was of gold, and there were faint markings on it, though Nancy could not see very well what they were—some sort of map of the world, she thought. Henry turned a support of wood to hold it rigid and began to lay the Tarot cards upon it. He spread the Greater Trumps along the table edge in the order of their numbering. But he began, not with the first, but with the second card, which was that of the Empress, and so on till he came to the pictures which were called xx The Last Judgement—where a Hand thrust out of cloud touched a great sarcophagus and broke it, so that the skeleton within could arise, and xxi The World—where a single singing form, as of a woman, rose in a ray of light towards a clear heaven of blue, leaving moon and sun and stars beneath her feet. The first, however, which showed a Juggler casting little balls into the air, he laid almost in the middle, resting it upon the twelfth card, which was the Wheel of Fortune, and supporting it against the edge of the table itself behind, over which it projected; under the Wheel of Fortune he hid the Fool. Having done this carefully, he went on very quickly with the rest of his task. He took the four suits and laid them also on the ledge from left to right, the deniers, the cups, the sceptres, the swords. Of each suit he laid first, against and slightly overlapping the Greater Trumps, the four Court cards —the King, the Queen, the Knight, the Esquire; in front of, and again overlapping these, the ten, the nine, the eight, and the seven; then, similarly arranged, the six, the five, and the four; then the three and the two; and in front of all, pointing outwards, the ace of each suit, so that the whole company of the Tarots lay with their base curved against the table of the dance, and pointing with a quadruple apex towards the curtains behind which was the open window.

As soon as this was done he stepped back to Nancy, thrust an arm round her, and said: "Look at the curtains." She obeyed, but not continuously; her eyes turned back often to the cards on the ledge, and it was while she gazed at them that she became aware how, in the movement of the dance, the Juggler among the images had approached the corresponding card. He seemed to her to run swiftly, while still he kept the score or so balls spinning over him in the air, and as he went he struck against the card and it slid from its place. Its fall disturbed the Wheel of Fortune on which it stood, and immediately the whole of the cards were in movement, sliding over and under each other—she gazed, enchanted, till Henry whispered in her ear, "The curtain!"

She looked, and at first instead of a curtain she saw only the golden mist in which she had found herself on the previous night. But it was already gathering itself up, dissipated, lost in an increasing depth of night. At first she thought the curtains had disappeared and she was looking out through the open window, but it was hardly that, for there was no frame or shape. The dark hangings of the room here lost themselves in darkness. She had not passed through the mist, but she was looking beyond it, and as within it her own fortune had been revealed so now some greater thing came into conjunction with the images, and the cards moved under the union of the double influence. For within the darkness a far vision was forming. She saw a gleam of green close before her; she heard for an instant what seemed the noise of waves on the shore. Then against that line of greenish-blue a shore actually grew; she saw the waves against it. As she gazed, it dwindled, growing less as what was beyond it was shaped in the darkness. Small and far, as if modelled with incredible minute exactitude, there emerged the image of a land with cities and rivers, railways and roads, The shape defined itself and was familiar; she was looking at a presentation of Holland and Belgium and Northern France, and—for, even as she understood, the limits expanded and what she saw seemed to grow smaller yet, as wider stretches came into view—there were the Alps, there was Italy; that dome of infinitesimal accuracy, above like infinitesimal detail, was St. Peter's—and beyond were more seas and islands and the sweep of great plains. Before her breath had thrice sighed itself out she saw India and Asia, with its central lakes, and Everest, its small peak dazzling white against the dark, and, as she breathed again, Tibet expanded into China, and the horizon of that mysterious night fled farther away and closed at length upon the extreme harbours of Japan. The whole distance lay before her, and she knew certainly within her that she was seeing no reproduction or evoked memory, but the vast continents themselves, with all that they held. She looked on the actual thing; earth was stretched before her, and the myriad inhabitants of that great part of earth.

Fast in Henry's arm, as if leaning forward from a height, she strained to see; and something of man's activities she did indeed discern. There were moving specks on certain roads— especially away in Northern China; and, since there chiefly she could trace movement, without deliberate intention concentrated on it. It grew larger before her, and the rest of the vision faded and diminished. She unconsciously desired to see, and she saw men—companies of men—armies—all in movement—details she could not hold her gaze steadily enough to observe, but there was no doubt that they were armies, and moving. There was a town—they were about it—it was burning. Her concentration could not but relax, and again all this receded, and again before her the whole of Europe and of Asia lay. But now the seas and continents were no longer still; they were shaken as if with earthquake; they were dissolving, taking fresh shapes, rising into, changing into, the golden images that danced upon their golden ground. Only here they danced in night upon no ground. They started from the vanishing empires and nations; cities leapt together, and Death came running instead; from among the Alps the Imperial cloak swept snow into itself; rivers poured into the seas and the seas into nothing, and cups received them and bearers of cups, and a swift procession of lifted chalices wound among the gathering shapes. From Tibet, from Rome, some consummation came together, and the hierophant, the Pope of the Tarots, took ritual steps towards that other joined beauty of the two lovers for which her grateful heart always searched. All earth had been gathered up: this was the truth of earth. The dance went on in the void; only even there she saw in the centre the motionless Fool, and about him in a circle the Juggler ran, for ever tossing his balls.

She felt, being strangely, and yet not strangely, conscious of his close neighbourhood, Henry draw himself together as if to move. She felt him move—and between those two sensations she saw, or she thought she saw, a complete movement in the dance. Right up to the hitherward edge of the darkness the two lovers came; they wheeled back; her eyes followed them, and saw suddenly all the rest of the dancers gathering in on either side, so that the two went on between those lines towards where the Fool stood still as though he waited them. After them other opposing forms wheeled inward also, the Emperor with the Empress, the mitred hierophant with the woman who equalled him; and the first twain trod on the top of the Wheel of Fortune and passed over; before them rose the figure of the Hanged Man, and they disjoined to pass on either side and went each under his cross, and Death and the Devil ran at them, and they running also came to a tower that continually fell into ruin and was continually re-edified; they passed into it, and when they issued again they were running far from each other, but then the golden light broke from each and met and mingled, and over them stars and the moon and the sun were shining; yet a tomb lay in their path, and the Fool—surely the motionless Fool!—stretched out his hand and touched it, and from within rose a skeleton; and it joined the lovers in their flying speed, and was with each, and the Fool was moving, was coming; but then she lost sight of lovers and skeleton, and of all the figures there were none left but the Juggler who appeared suddenly right under her eyes and went speedily up a single path which had late been multitudinous, and ran to meet the Fool. They came together; they embraced; the tossing balls fell over them in a shower of gold—and the golden mist covered everything, and swirled before her eyes; and then it also faded, and the hangings of the room were before her, and she felt Henry move.

Chapter Eight

CHRISTMAS DAY IN THE COUNTRY

It had been settled at dinner on Christmas Eve that the three Coningsbys would go to the village church on Christmas Day. Mr. Coningsby theoretically went to church every Sunday, which was why he always filled up census forms with the statement "Church of England". Of the particular religious idea which the Church of England maintains he had never made any special investigation, but he had retained the double habit of going to church on Christmas morning and for a walk on Christmas afternoon. In his present state of irritation with the Lees he would rather have walked to church than not have gone, especially as Aaron pleaded his age and Henry professional papers as reasons for not going. But Aaron had put the car and chauffeur at his disposal for the purpose, so that he was not reduced to any such unseemly effort. Mr. Coningsby held strongly that going to church, if and when he did go, ought to be as much a part of normal life as possible, and ought not to demand any peculiar demonstration of energy on the part of the church-goer.

Sybil, he understood, had the same view; she agreed that religion and love should be a part of normal life. With a woman's natural exaggeration, she had once said that they were normal life, that they were indeed life. He wasn't very clear whether she usually went to church or not; if she did, she said nothing much about it, and was always back in time for meals. He put her down as "Church of England" too; she never raised any objection. Nancy went under the same heading, though she certainly didn't go to church. But her father felt that she would when she got older; or that, anyhow, if she didn't she would feel it was right to do so. Circumstances very often prevented one doing what one wished: if one was tired or bothered, it was no good going to church in an improper state of mind.

Nancy's actual state of mind on the Christmas morning was too confused for her to know much about it. She was going with her father partly because she always had done, but even more because she badly needed a short refuge of time and place from these shattering new experiences. She felt that an hour or so somewhere where—just for once—even Henry couldn't get at her was a highly desirable thing. Her mind hadn't functioned very clearly during the rest of the time they had spent in the inner room; or else her memory of it wasn't functioning clearly now. Henry had explained something about the possibility of reading the fortunes of the world in the same manner as those of individuals could be read, but she had been incapable of listening; indeed, she had beaten a rather scandalous retreat, and (for all his earlier promises of sound sleep) had lain awake for a long time, seeing only that last wild rush together of the Fool and the Juggler, that falling torrent of balls breaking into a curtain of golden spray, which thickened into cloud before her. One last glance at the table had shown her upon it the figure of the Fool still poised motionless, so she hadn't seen what Aunt Sybil had seen. But she had seen the Fool move in that other vision. She wanted to talk to her aunt about it, but her morning sleep had only just brought her down for breakfast, and there had been no opportunity afterwards before church. She managed to keep Sybil between herself and her father as they filed into a pew, and sat down between her and a pillar with a sense of protection. Nothing unusual was likely to happen for the next hour or two, unless it was the vicar's new setting of the Athanasian Creed. Aaron Lee had remarked that the man was a musical enthusiast, doing the best he could with the voices at his disposal, assisted by a few friends whom he had down at Christmas. This Christmas, it seemed, he was attempting a little music which he himself had composed. Nancy was quite willing that he should—nothing seemed more remote from excitement or mystery than the chant of the Athanasian Creed. During the drive down her father had commented disapprovingly on the Church's use of that creed. Sybil had asked why he disliked it. Mr. Coningsby had asked if she thought it Christian; and Sybil said she didn't see anything very un-Christian about it—not if you remembered the hypothesis of Christianity.

"And what," Mr. Coningsby said, as if this riddle were entirely unanswerable, "what do you call the hypothesis of Christianity?"

"The Deity of Love and the Incarnation of Love?" Sybil suggested, adding, "Of course, whether you agree with it is another thing."

"Certainly I agree with Christianity," Mr. Coningsby said. "Perhaps I shouldn't put it quite like that. It's a difficult thing to define. But I don't see how the damnatory clauses——"

However, there they reached the church. Nancy thought, as she looked at the old small stone building, that if Henry was right about the dance, then this member of it must be sitting out some part of the time on some starry stair. Nothing less mobile had ever been imagined. But her intelligence reminded her, even as she entered, that the apparent quiescence, the solidity, the attributed peace of the arched doorway was one aspect of what, in another aspect, was a violent and riotous conflict of . . . whatever the latest scientific word was. Strain and stress were everywhere; the very arch held itself together by extreme force; the latest name for matter was Force, wasn't it? Electrical nuclei or something of that sort. If this antique beauty was all made of electrical nuclei, there might be—there must be—a dance going on somewhere in which even that running figure with the balls flying over it in curves would be

Christmas Day in the Country

outpaced. She herself outpaced Sybil by a step and entered the pew first.

And she then, as she knelt decorously down, was part of the dance; she was the flying feet passing and repassing; she was the conjunction of the images whose movement the cards symbolized and from which they formed the prophecy of her future. "A man shall owe you everything"—everything? Did she really want Henry to owe her *everything*, or did she—against her own quick personal desire—desire rather that there should be something in him to which she owed everything? "And a woman shall govern you"—that was the most distasteful of all; she had no use at all for women governing her; anyhow, she would like to see the woman who would do it. "And you shall die very rich"—by this time she had got up from her knees, and had sat down again—well, that was very fortunate. If it meant what it said—"You shall die very rich" —but the forms of Death and the Devil and the Queen of Chalices had danced round her, and the words shook with threat, with promise, with obscure terror. But what could even that do to harm her while Henry and she together dared it? While that went on, it was true in its highest and most perfect meaning; if that went on, she would die very rich.

A door opened; the congregation stirred; a voice from the vestry said: "Hymn 61. 'Christians, awake,' Hymn 61." Everyone awoke, found the place, and stood up. The choir started at once on the hymn and the procession. Nancy docilely sent her voice along with them.

> *Christians, awake, salute the happy morn,*
> *Whereon the Saviour of the world was born:*
> *Rise to a——*

Her voice ceased; the words stared up at her. The choir and the congregation finished the line—

> *adore the mystery of love.*

107

"The mystery of love." But what else was in her heart? The Christmas associations of the verse had fallen away; there was the direct detached cry, bidding her do precisely and only what she was burning to do. "Rise to adore the mystery of love." What on earth were they doing, singing about the mystery of love in church? They couldn't possibly be meaning it. Or were they meaning it and had she misunderstood the whole thing?

The church was no longer a defence; it was itself an attack. From another side the waves of some impetuous and greater life swept in upon her. She turned her head abruptly towards Sybil, who felt the movement and looked back, her own voice pausing on "the praises of redeeming love". Nancy, her finger pointing to the first of those great verses, whispered a question, "Is it true?" Sybil looked at the line, looked back at Nancy, and answered in a voice both aspirant and triumphant, "Try it, darling." The tall figure, the wise mature face, the dark ineffable eyes, challenged, exhorted, and encouraged. Nancy throbbed to the voice that broke into the next couplet—"God's highest glory was their anthem still."

She looked back at the hymn and hastily read it—it was really a very commonplace hymn, a very poor copy of verses. Only that one commanding rhythm still surged through her surrendered soul—"Rise to adore the mystery of love." But now everyone else was shutting up hymn-books and turning to prayer-books; she took one more glance at the words, and did the same.

The two lovers had run straight on—not straight on; they had been divided. Separately they had run up the second part of the way, separately each had danced with the skeleton. She could see them now, but more clearly even than them she remembered the Juggler—"neither God nor not God," Henry had said—running to meet the unknown Fool. "Amen," they were singing all round her; this wasn't getting very far from the dance. It hadn't occurred to her that there was so much

singing, so much exchanging of voices, so much summoning
and crying out in an ordinary church service. Sybil's voice
rose again—"As it was in the beginning, is now——" What
was in the beginning and was now? Glory, glory.

Nancy sat down for the Proper Psalms, though she was aware
her father had looked at her disapprovingly behind Sybil's
back. It couldn't be helped; her legs wouldn't hold her up in
the midst of these dim floods of power and adoration that
answered so greatly to the power and adoration which abode
in her heart, among these songs and flights of dancing words
which wheeled in her mind and seemed themselves to become
part of the light of the glorious originals of the Tarots.

She was still rather overwhelmed when they came to the
Athanasian Creed, and it may have been because of her own
general chaos that even that despised formulary took part in
the general break-up which seemed to be proceeding within
her. All the first part went on in its usual way; she knew
nothing about musical setting of creeds, so she couldn't tell
what to think of this one. The men and the boys of the choir
exchanged metaphysical confidences; they dared each other,
in a kind of rapture—which, she supposed, was the setting—
to deny the Trinity or the Unity; they pointed out, almost
mischievously, that though they were compelled to say one
thing, yet they were forbidden to say something else exactly
like it; they went into particulars about an entirely impossible
relationship, and concluded with an explanation that something wasn't true which the wildest dream of any man but the
compiler of the creed could hardly have begun to imagine.
All this Nancy half-ignored.

But the second part—and it was of course the setting—for
one verse held her. It was of course the setting, the chance that
sent one boy's voice sounding exquisitely through the church.
But the words which conveyed that beauty sounded to her full
of sudden significance. The mingled voices of men and boys
were proclaiming the nature of Christ—"God and man is one

in Christ"; then the boys fell silent, and the men went on, "One, not by conversion of the Godhead into flesh, but by taking of the manhood into God." On the assertion they ceased, and the boys rushed joyously in, "One altogether, not"—they looked at the idea and tossed it airily away—"*not* by confusion of substance, but by unity"—they rose, they danced, they triumphed—"by unity, by unity"—they were silent, all but one, and that one fresh perfection proclaimed the full consummation, each syllable rounded, prolonged, exact—"by unity of person".

It caught the young listening creature; the enigmatic phrase quivered with beautiful significance. Sybil at her side somehow answered to it; she herself perhaps—she herself in love. Something beyond understanding but not beyond achievement showed itself, and then the choir were plunging through the swift record of the Christhood on earth, and once more the attribution of eternal glory rose and fell—"is now," "is now—and ever shall be". Then they were all kneeling down and the vicar was praying in ritual utterance of imperial titles for "our sovereign lord King George".

For the rest of the service Nancy moved and rose and sat and knelt according to the ritual, without being very conscious of what was going on. She felt two modes of being alternating within her—now the swift rush of her journey in the car, of her own passion, of the images seen in the night, of the voices roaring upward in the ceremonies of Christmas; now again the pause, the silence and full restraint of the Emperor, of Sybil, of her own expectation, of that single voice declaring unity, of the Fool amid the dance of the night. She flew with the one; she was suspended with the other; and, with downcast eyes and parted lips, she sought to control her youth till one should disappear or till both should come together. Everything was different from what it had so lately seemed; even the two who sat beside her. Her respect for her aunt had become something much more like awe; "Try it, darling," was a summons to her from one who was a sibyl indeed. Her father was different too. He seemed no more the absurd, slightly despicable, affected and pompous and irritating elderly man whom she had known; all that was unimportant. He walked alone, a genie from some other world, demanding of her something which she had not troubled to give. If she would not find out what that was, it was no good blaming him for the failure of their proper relation. She, she only, was to blame; the sin lay in her heart whenever that heart set itself against any other. He might be funny sometimes, but she herself was very funny sometimes. Aunt Sybil had told her she didn't love anyone; and she had been slightly shocked at the suggestion. The colour swept into her cheeks as she thought of it, sitting still during the sermon. But everything would be different now. She would purify herself before she dared offer herself to Henry for the great work he contemplated.

At lunch it appeared that his ordinary work, however, was going to occupy him for the afternoon as well as the morning. He apologized to her for this in a rather troubled way, and she mocked him gently.

"Father's going," she said, "and you'll be shut up. It'll be perfect heaven to look at the furniture or read a murder story —only your grandfather doesn't seem to have many murder stories, does he, darling? All his literature seems so very serious, and quite a lot of it's in foreign languages. But there's yesterday's paper, if I'm driven to it."

"I must do it," Henry said, rather incoherently. "There's no other way."

"Where there's a will there's a way," she said. "You haven't got the will, Henry. You don't think the world's well lost for me."

"I've a will for what's useful," he said, so seriously that she was startled.

"I know you have, dearest," she said. "I'm not annoying you, am I? You sounded as if you were going to do something frightfully important, that I hadn't a notion of."

Christmas Day in the Country

He found no answer to that, but wandered off and stood looking out of the window into the frosty clearness of the day. He dared not embrace her lest she should feel his heart beating more intensely than ever it had beaten for his love; nor speak lest his voice should alarm her sensitive attention to wonder what he purposed. It was one thing to see what had to be done, and if it had not been for Nancy he could have done it easily enough, he thought. But to sit at lunch with her and "the murdered man". If she ever knew, would she understand? She must, she must! If she didn't, then he had told his grandfather rightly that all his intention was already doomed. But if she did, if she could see clearly that her father's life was little compared to the restoration of the Tarots, so that in future there might be a way into the mystical dance, and from within their eyes might see it, from within they—more successful than Joanna—might govern the lesser elements, and perhaps send an heir to all their knowledge out into the world. If they perished, they perished in an immense effort, and no lesser creature, though it were Nancy's father or his own—though it were Nancy herself, should she shrink—must be allowed to stand in the way. She would understand when she knew; but till she had learned more he dared not tell her. It would be, he told himself, cruel to her; the decision for both of them must be his.

The sombre determination brooded over the meal. As if a grey cloud had overcast the day and the room, those sitting at the table were dimmed and oppressed by the purpose which two of them cherished. Aaron's eyes fixed themselves, spasmodically and anxiously, on the women whom his business was to amuse; Henry once or twice, in a sudden sharp decision, looked up at Mr. Coningsby, who went on conversing about Christmas lunches he had known, about lunches in general, the ideal lunch, the discovery of cooking, fire, gas-fires, air, space, modern science, science in the Press, the present state of newspapers, and other things. Sybil assisted him, more talkative than usual, because the other three were more silent. Nancy felt unexpectedly tired and chilly, though the room was warm enough. A natural reaction of discouragement took her, a natural—yet to her unnatural—disappointment with Henry. Her eyes went to him at intervals, ready to be placated and delighted, but no answering eyes met hers. She saw him, once, staring at his own hands, and she looked at them too, without joy, as if they were two strange instruments working at a little-understood experiment. The dark skin, the long fingers, the narrow wrists—the hands that had struck and caressed hers, to which she had given her free kisses, which she had pressed and stroked and teased—they were so strange that they made her union with them strange; they were inhuman, and their inhumanity crept deeper into the chill of her being. Her glance swept the table; five pairs of hands were moving there, all alien and incomprehensible. Prehensile . . . monkeys swaying in the trees: not monkeys . . . something more than monkeys. She felt Sybil looking at her, and refused to look back. Her father's voice maddened her; he was still talking—stupid, insane talk. He a Warden in Lunacy! He was a lunatic himself, the worse for being uncertifiable. O, why didn't he die?'

A fork and spoon tinkled. Mr. Coningsby was saying that forks came in with Queen Elizabeth. She said, quite unexpectedly, "In Swift's time people used to say 'Queen Elizabeth's dead' instead of 'Queen Anne's dead'."

Henry's hand jerked on the cloth, like some reptile just crawled up from below the table. She went on perversely, "Did you know that, Henry?"

He answered abruptly, "No," and so sharp was the syllable that it left all five of them in silence, a silence in which either Elizabeth or Anne might have passed from a world she knew to a world she could not imagine. Sybil broke it by saying, "It was the change of dynasty that made their ends so important, I suppose? No one ever said 'George II is dead', did they?"

"Aren't we being rather morbid?" Aaron asked, in a kind of high croak, almost as if the reptile Nancy had imagined had begun to speak. Cold . . . cold . . . and cold things making discordant noises. O, this wouldn't do: she was being silly. She made an effort and reminded herself that this was Mr. Lee speaking—and it was a gloomy conversation: not so much gloomy as horrid. Everyone was unnatural—at least, Henry was unnatural, and her father was overwhelmingly natural, and Mr. Lee . . . He was saying something else. She bent her attention to it.

"There are some manuscripts", he was saying, "you might like to look at this afternoon. Some poems, part of a diary, a few letters."

"I should like to very much," Sybil said. "What sort of a man does he seem to have been?"

"I'm afraid I've not read them carefully enough to know," Aaron replied. "He was, of course, disappointed; the cause had been ruined, and his career with it."

Sybil smiled. "He believed that?" she asked. "But how foolish of him!"

Henry said, "Is it foolish to give oneself to a purpose and die if it perishes?"

"Disproportioned, don't you think?" Sybil suggested. "One might die rather than forsake a cause, but if the cause forsakes you——? They're pathetic creatures, your lonely romantics. They can't bear to be mistaken."

Nancy shivered again. Even Sybil's lovely voice couldn't help giving the word "mistaken" rather a heavy and fatal sound. "Mistaken"—utterly mistaken. To mistake everything life had concentrated in, to be *wrong*, just *wrong*. . . . O, at last the meal was ending. She got up and followed her aunt and Aaron to the drawing-room, loathing herself and everybody else, and especially the manuscript relics of the unfortunate peer.

Henry saw Mr. Coningsby off. "Which way shall you go?" he asked.

Christmas Day in the Country

"I shall walk as far as the village and back," his guest said. "If I see the vicar I shall congratulate him on the service this morning—bright, short, and appropriate. A very neat little sermon too. Quiet and convincing."

"What was it about?" Henry said, against his will trying to delay the other. He looked at him curiously: "bright, short, and appropriate" were hardly the words for the thing that was gathering round him who had spoken. The reared tower of his life was already shaking; and it was Henry whose hand pushed it.

"O, behaving kindly—and justly," Mr. Coningsby said. "Very suitable to the villagers who go. Well, I mustn't delay. I'll be off."

"Take care you take the left path at the division as you come back," Henry said.

"Quite, quite; the left," Mr. Coningsby said, and disappeared. Henry went his own way—not to the drawing-room, where Nancy, with all her heart but much against her temper, expected him to look in for a few minutes. He didn't. She cursed herself, and went on staring at the peer's extremely eighteenth-century diary, taking no part in the chat of the other two. Sybil began reading a poem aloud.

TO CLARINDA: ON RECEIVING A LETTER

Ah, cruel Clarinda, must this Paper show
All of thy Fortune that I now may know?
Though still the Town retain thee, perjured Maid,
May not some Thought of me the Town invade?
Was I forgotten when I did depart,
And thou oblivious of a Faithful Heart?
Despair to thee is but a grateful Pain,
Coolly pretended by the Amorous Swain;
But O, in me Despair is all my Sense
As hateful as impoverished Joy's Pretence——

Christmas Day in the Country

"Impoverished Joy's pretence"—Nancy knew that was what she was feeling, and knew how hateful it was. At the same time she realized that she was feeling tired—O, so absolutely tired. She must get away and lie down and rest: she'd be better then by tea-time. And perhaps Henry would be free, and impoverished Joy need no longer pretend. When the poem was finished, she said, rather ungrateful to the wretched peer, "He wasn't a very good poet, was he? I suppose Clarinda had thrown him over. Mr. Lee, would you think me a perfect pig if I went and lay down and went to sleep? I'm only just keeping my eyes a little way open."

"My dear girl, of course," Aaron said. "Anything you like. I'm so sorry. You're not overtired, are you?"

"No, O no," Nancy protested. "It's just . . . it's just . . . that I'm unutterably sleepy. I can't think what's come over me."

As he went to open the door, she smiled at her aunt. Sybil said in a low voice, "Being in love is a tiring business—I mean getting into love. Sleep well, darling."

She slept at least without dreams, unless that sudden vision of her father falling from a high precipice from which she woke and sprang up was a dream. It was his scream that had wakened her; was it—or was it that howling wind? There was something driving against the windows; for a moment she thought it was a great white face staring in, then she knew it for snow—heavy, terrific snow. Bewildered, she blinked at it. The day had changed completely: it was dark, and yet, from the unlit room, white with snow. The wind or the scream sounded again, as, still half-asleep, she clung to the bed and gazed. Her father—he must be in by now. It was close on five. Her father—faces looking for him—her father crying out. She ran uncertainly to the door, and, driven by an unknown fear, went hurrying to the hall. There was Sybil and Aaron—Sybil with her coat on, Aaron protesting, offering. . . . Nancy came up to them.

"Hallo," she said. "I say, aunt, you're not going out, are you?"

Sybil said something that was lost in the noise of the blizzard; Nancy looked round. "Where's father?" she asked.

"Out," Sybil said. "I was just going to meet him."

"Hasn't he come back?" Nancy said. "But, I say, he'll never find his way. . . ." If only she hadn't dreamed of his being thrown over a precipice. There was no precipice here. But he'd screamed.

"But it's absurd," Aaron said. "Henry'll go. I'll call him. I've let the chauffeur go home. But Henry'll go."

Sleep was leaving Nancy, but dream and fear and cold took her. Her father ought to have been back long ago—and where *was* Henry? He couldn't be working all this time, in this tumult. He and her father were missing—and her aunt was going out—and she?

"I'll go," she said. "You can't go, aunt. I'll go."

"You", Sybil said, "can go and look for Henry. We can't leave Mr. Lee to do everything. I've no doubt your father's all right, but he may be glad of an arm. Even mine. Help Mr. Lee to shut the door."

If her father had taken the wrong road—if hands were guiding him the wrong way—if he were being thrust——

Sybil opened the door: the wind struck at their throats and half-stifled them; the snow drove at their faces. Over her shoulder Sybil said, "It is rather thick."

"O, don't go," Nancy said. "You'll be flung over the edge too. I'll go—I hated him—I'll go. What can you *do*?"

"You go and find Henry," Sybil said, leaning forward against the wind. "I can adore the mystery of love." The tall figure was poised for a moment against the raging turmoil beyond and around, then it took a couple of steps forward and was lost to sight. Aaron struggled to close the door, desperately alarmed; it had been no part of his intention that Sybil also should be exposed to the powers that were abroad. But he hadn't been able to stop her. Nancy, in a torment of anger at herself, flung forward to help him; that done, she turned and fled to find Henry. Where was Henry? Some terror beat in her: Henry and her father—a scream in the storm. She ran into Henry's room; he wasn't there. She rushed out again—to other rooms; she raced through the house, and couldn't find him. Was he in the room of the images? If so, the old man must open it for her. But Aaron had vanished too, and the wind was howling even louder round the house. She burst in on the maids in the kitchen thrilling at the storm—"Mr. Lee; where's Mr. Lee?" Before they could answer with more than the beginning of stammered ignorance she was off again. Well, if he wasn't here she would go without him. She *must* go. She rushed into her own room, and as she pulled on her coat she gazed out of the window on the wild chance of seeing her father's returning figure, though (could she have thought) she would have remembered that her room looked out over the terrace at the side of the house. But it was then that she saw Henry.

He was standing at one end of the terrace facing slantingly out so as to command from a distance the road that led to the village, and to be himself unseen except from one or two higher windows. He was standing there; she could only just see his figure through the dark snow-swept day, but it was he— certainly it was he. What he was doing there she couldn't think; he couldn't be watching for her father—that would be silly. He must have a reason, but, whatever the reason, it must wait; his business now was to come with her. She flew out of the room, downstairs, along a corridor that led to a small door giving on to the other end of the terrace, just beside the drawing-room which occupied the bottom corner of the house; not more than thirty yards from Henry she'd be then. She opened it and desperately fought her way out.

The next thing she knew was that the wind had flung her back against the wall of the house and was holding and stifling her there. Bludgeons of it struck her; snow and wind together

118

choked her. She turned her head to face the wall, drew a sob-
bing breath or two, and cried out "Henry" once. Once, for
she could hardly hear herself, and with her remaining intelligence she kept her breath for other things. Surely Henry
couldn't be out in this; the wind beat and bruised her again,
thrusting her against the wall. For a moment she forgot everything, and reached out to find the doorway and drag herself
into shelter, but even as her hand touched the edge she tore
it away. No, Henry wasn't indoors and he was out here; and
her business was to get to him. She began to edge along the
wall. He had been standing at the extreme end of the terrace;
so if she worked along the wall, and then (if necessary) crawled
out on her hands and knees, she ought to find him. Unless he
had gone. . . .

She ventured to look over her shoulder. The wind, even in
its violence, was rhythmical; it rose to its screaming height
and ceased a little, and then began to rise again. In a pause
she looked and could see only the falling snow. She looked
back just in time to avoid a blast that seemed almost to smash
at her as if it were a great club, and went on struggling along
the wall. Aunt Sybil was out in this, and her father, and Henry.
In God's name, why Henry? Her father by accident, and Sybil
by—by love. Love—O, to get away from this, and anyone who
liked could have love! "No, no," she gasped. "No, darling;
I'm sorry." She looked round once more and saw—not Henry,
but another shape. In the snow, leaping through the air, pre-
luding the new blast of wind that blinded and strangled her,
there swept a wild figure waving in each hand a staff of some
kind, and another like it followed. She saw the swinging clubs,
she heard shrieking—the wind shrieking—and almost lost her
footing as the renewed strength of it came against her. For
some minutes she clung to the wall; mad memories that the
crisis of the last half-hour had driven from her mind returned.
Death with the sickle—earth from the deniers—the gipsy who
drove the Armada—and the powers of the wind screamed

again as if once more they saw the dismasted and broken ships swept before them through the raging seas. Henry—where was Henry? What was Henry doing out at the end of the terrace? Before the thought had formed in her mind she herself screamed—one protesting shriek: "Henry, my darling, don't, don't!" And as she did so she began to struggle on again towards an end which she did not dare imagine. Whatever it was, she must be there; Sybil had told her to find Henry—but Sybil must be dead by now; nothing could live in this storm, any more than the Spanish vessels flung on the Scottish rocks. Sybil must be dead—well, then, it all lay on her; she was left to do the bidding of a greater than herself. And if Sybil wasn't dead—Sybil who had seen the Fool moving, who had said "Try it, darling." "Try it"—and she was crawling along the house-wall! Though Death ran at her, though the Hanged Man faced her, though the Tower fell upon her, though a skeleton rose in her path—"Rise to adore the mystery of love." She pulled herself upright and passionately flung round to face the wind and snow.

Something, away, among them was moving: something was sweeping up and down. She forced herself a step out from the wall: there was the end, there was where Love meant her to be, there then was where she was except for the slight inconvenience of getting there. Another step; another—she was, by the mere overwhelming force of the storm, driven down, she stumbled and fell on to one knee; there she looked up to those moving shapes and knew them for hands. Regularly, monotonously, they swept down and out, holding something; they were huge, gigantic—as her own had seemed in the golden mist. As her own in the golden mist, so these in the white surges of the snow, and the snow swept out from them. On one knee she fought to get nearer—to face another terror, she dimly felt, but of a different kind. This, if that other were true, this could be stopped. The great hands swept down again, and colossal snowflakes drove towards her on a renewed blast that drove her down literally to hands and knees. But she crawled and dragged herself on; she was almost there; she was under them—those awful moving origins of storm. She kneeled upright, she struck up at them and missed, they had swept right outward and as they more lightly turned she flung at them with her own hands outstretched. She caught and held them, but as they struggled with hers in that first surprise, and dragged themselves away and up, bringing her to her feet with them, something that they held slipped and was gone. She clutched and clung to them, holding them in, pressing them back, and as she did so and was drawn inward with them she fell forward and knew suddenly that she lay on Henry's breast.

Lost in the concentration and movement of the spell, he did not know she was near him till his hands were seized and, pulling them frantically away, he dragged her grey-coated form up with them out of the storm. It was against his heart before he knew it; he had one spasm of terror lest something unknown had turned on him, lest an elemental being, a bearer of staffs, had crept near to embrace its master. He cried out, then, recovering, checked, and then again broke into a shout of rage. "You fool," he cried, "you fool! You've knocked the cards away!" In his hand he held but a few; peering at them in the dusk, he discerned but the four princely chiefs; the rest, as she clutched them, had slipped or blown off, and were now tossing in the wind which rose from them, seething with power, vagabond and uncontrolled. Even with her weight against him he took a step or two forward, but her arms clung round his shoulders and he could not shake himself free. The catastrophe —the double catastrophe, for the magical instruments were lost, and the wild whirlwind was free—struck at his heart; he stood still, stricken. She half-raised her head. "Henry, please don't," she murmured.

"You've stopped it," he said. There could be no secrets now; by another way than either had intended they had been brought into knowledge of each other, and might speak clearly.

"Stop it now," she urged. "Darling, don't do it. Not this way."

"I can't stop it," he said. "I haven't got them. You've—— Get in, get in; we mustn't be here. Anything may happen."

In that great ending of both their spirits they could not clamour. The Tower that each had raised—the Babel of their desired heavens—had fallen in the tumult of their conflicting wills and languages, and a terrible quiet was within their hearts. They were joined in an unformulated union of despair. He accepted the arm about his shoulder; he put his own arm round her. "Back," he said, "to the wall; to the door. Come."

The storm was still soaring upward and outward from around them, so that their way was at first easier. But before they reached their refuge it had spread more wildly; battle raged in the air, and the heavens, once disturbed only at a distance where the invoked disturbance struck them, were now themselves in full action. Natural and supernatural riot ruled everywhere. Once Nancy was torn from him, and only as if by chance their clutching hands re-gripped, frenzied with the single desire and power of preservation. Twice they were beaten down amid the already heaping snow, and had to drag themselves along till an accidental and local lull in their enemy let them scramble to their feet. They were dashed against the wall; they were held motionless by the madness of the elements. At last they came, almost broken, to the harbour of the open doorway. They stumbled through the drift that was forming in it, and the need for new labour presented itself. But other human aid was near. Henry, half-blind, staggered towards the kitchen, called the maids, and ordered one of them to help him to clear the doorway and fasten the door, while the other took charge of Nancy. With his last effort he saw the lock turned, the bolt driven home; then he dropped to the floor of the passage, unconscious at once of his purpose, his thwarting, and his accomplishment.

Chapter Nine

SYBIL

S ybil Coningsby stepped out into the storm and tried to
see before her. It was becoming very difficult, and the
force of the wind for the moment staggered and even
distressed her. She yielded to it a little both in body and mind;
she knew well that to the oppositions of the world she could in
herself offer no certain opposition. As her body swayed and
let itself move aside under the blast, she surrendered herself
to the only certain thing that her life had discovered: she
adored in this movement also the extreme benevolence of Love.
She sank before the wind, but not in impotence; rather as the
devotee sinks before the outer manifestations of the God that
he may be made more wholly one with that which manifests.
Delaying as if both she and it might enjoy the exquisite
promise of its arrival, it nevertheless promised, and, as always,
came. She recovered her balance, swaying easily to each
moment's need, and the serene content which it bestowed filled
again and satisfied her.

It satisfied, but for no more than the briefest second did she
allow herself to remain aware of that. Time to be aware, and
to be grateful for that awareness, she enjoyed; literally enjoyed,
for both knowledge and thankfulness grew one, and joy was
their union, but that union darted out towards a new subject
and centre. Darted out and turned in; its occupation was
Lothair Coningsby, and Lothair was already within it. It did
not choose a new resting-place, but rather ordered its own
content, by no greater a movement than the shifting of the
accent from one syllable back to the other. So slight a variation

as gives the word to any speaker a new meaning gave to this pure satisfaction a new concern. She was intensely aware of her brother; she drew up the knowledge of him from within her, and gave it back within her. In wave after wave the ocean of peace changed its "multitudinous laughter" from one myriad grouping to another. And all, being so, was so.

Such a state, in which the objects of her concern no longer struck upon her thoughts from without, recalled by an accident, a likeness, or a dutiful attention, but existed rather as they did in their own world—a state in which they were brought into being as by the same energy which had produced their actual natures—had not easily been reached. That sovereign estate, the inalienable heritage of man, had been in her, as in all, falsely mortgaged to the intruding control of her own greedy desires. Even when the true law was discovered, when she knew that she had the right and the power to possess all things, on the one condition that she was herself possessed, even then her freedom to yield herself had been won by many conflicts. Days of pain and nights of prayer had passed while her lonely soul escaped; innocent joys as well as guilty hopes had been starved. There had been a time when the natural laughter that attended on her natural intelligence had been hushed, when her brother had remarked that "Sybil seemed very mopy". She had been shocked when she heard this by a sense of her disloyalty, since she believed enjoyment to be a debt which every man owes to his fellows, partly for its own sake, partly lest he at all diminish their own precarious hold on it. She attempted dutifully to enjoy and failed, but while she attempted it the true gift was delivered into her hands.

When the word Love had come to mean for her the supreme greatness of man she could hardly remember: one incident and another had forced it on her mind—the moment when her mother, not long before death, had said to her, "Love, Sybil, if you dare; if you daren't, admit it"; the solemn use of the name in the great poets, especially her youthful reading of

Dante; a fanatic in a train who had given her a tract: *Love God or go to Hell*. It was only after a number of years that she had come to the conclusion that the title was right, except perhaps for *go to*—since the truth would have been more accurately rendered by *be in Hell*. She was doubtful also about *God*; *Love* would have been sufficient by itself but it was necessary at first to concentrate on something which could be distinguished from all its mortal vessels, and the more one lived with that the more one found that it possessed in fact all the attributes of Deity. She had tried to enjoy, and she remembered vividly the moment when, walking down Kingsway, it had struck her that there was no need for her to try or to enjoy: she had only to be still, and let that recognized Deity itself enjoy, as its omnipotent nature was. She still forgot occasionally; her mortality still leapt rarely into action, and confused her and clouded the sublime operation of—of It. But rarely and more rarely those moments came; more and more securely the working of that Fate which was Love possessed her. For it was fatal in its nature; rich and austere at once, giving death and life in the same moment, restoring beyond belief all the things it took away—except the individual will.

Its power rose in her now and filled her with the thought of her brother. As she came from the drive into the road she looked as alertly as she could before her in case he staggered into sight. Whether she was going to find him or not she couldn't tell, but it was apparently her business to look for him, or she wouldn't have felt so strongly the conviction that, of all those in the house, she alone was to go out and search. That she should be walking so lightly through the storm didn't strike her as odd, because it wasn't really she who was walking, it was Love, and naturally Love would be safe in his own storm. It was, certainly, a magnificent storm; she adored the power that was displayed in it. Lothair, she thought, wouldn't be adoring it much at the moment: something in her longed passionately to open his eyes, so that the two of them could walk in it happily together. And Nancy, and Henry—O, and Aaron Lee, and Ralph, and everyone they all knew, until the vision of humanity rejoicing in this tumultuous beauty seemed to show itself to her, and the delight of creation answered the delight of the Creator, joy triumphing in joy.

It was the division in the road where Lothair might go wrong: to take the right-hand path would lead him away over the Downs. If she got there without meeting him, should she go on or herself turn up the other road? She had long ago discovered that Love expected you to do the best you could to solve such questions before leaving It to decide. The intellect had to be finely ready before It deigned to use it. So she tried to think, and kicked something in the road.

It wasn't her brother at any rate, she thought, yet it had felt as if it were soft and alive. She bent down, put her hand out, and, grasping something just at her feet, gathered it up—to discover that it was a rather large kitten. Where it came from she couldn't think—probably from the Lees' house. She warmed and caressed and petted it, till the half-frozen brute began to pay some attention, then she undid a button of her coat and thrust in her hand and wrist, extended upon which the kitten lay contentedly purring. Sybil went on, smiling to think that perhaps Lothair had passed her and was already safe; the Power that governed her would be quite capable of dragging her out of the house to save a kitten from cold. She adored It again: perhaps the kitten belonged to some child in the village, and she was taking a four-mile walk in a snowstorm to make a child and a kitten happy. Lothair, she thought, would be honestly puzzled by that, and (she thought more regretfully) while he was honestly puzzled he probably wouldn't be encouraged to take the four-mile walk. So everyone would be satisfied.

The storm lifted, and she found herself at the parting of the roads, and there, by the hedge, on the extreme wrong side, was a crouching figure. The snow was beginning to pile round it; the wind and flakes seemed to be rushing at it and centring on it. Sybil, holding the kitten firmly, went quickly across the road. For a moment, as she ran, she thought she saw another form, growing out of the driving snow—a tall figure that ran down on the white stairs of the flakes, and as it touched earth circled round the overwhelmed man. Before it a gleam of pale gold, as of its own reflection, since no break in the storm allowed the sinking sun to lighten the world, danced in the air, on the ground, on hands that were stretched out towards the victim. They seemed to touch him, as in the Sistine Chapel the Hand of God for ever touches the waking Adam, and vanished as she reached it. Only, for a moment again, she saw that gleam of flying gold pass away into the air, lost within the whiteness and the gloom. Then she was by him; she leaned down; she touched a shoulder, and held and shook it gently. She herself knelt in the snow to see the better—it was Lothair. His hat was gone; his glasses were gone; his coat was half-off him, flying loose; the buttons, she found, as she tried, with one hand, to pull it round him, were all off. He was blue and dangling.

"What a thing it is to be a Warden in Lunacy," Sybil thought, "and how much like a baby the dear looks! and how he'd hate to think so! Lothair! Lothair, darling! Lothair!"

He took no notice, save that he seemed to relax and sink even lower. "O dear," Sybil sighed, "and I can't put the kitten down!" She pulled at the coat till she got it more or less properly over him; then she stood up, put her left arm round him beneath the shoulders, and made an enormous effort to pull him up also. It was impossible; he was too heavily irresponsible. She stilled herself—either Love would lift him or Love would in some other way sufficiently and entirely resolve the crisis that held them. The practised reference possessed her, and then, kneeling by him, she went on shaking him and calling to him: "Lothair! Lothair! Lothair!"

He opened dull eyes on her. "'S that you, Sybil?" he said. "Are you go'?"

"Are who gone?" she said. "Do take me home, Lothair. It's such a terrific storm."

"'ur quite all righ'," he muttered. "Jus' res' a min' an' I'll get alon'. Are they go'?"

She shook him again. "I've never been out in such weather. Lothair, you always look after me. Do, please, please, take me back!"

She put a poignant wail into her voice that disturbed him. He made his first movement. "I'll look a'ter you," he said. "I'll take . . . back in min'. Didn' know you were here."

"I came to you to meet you," she said, distraught and appealing. "And I'm out in it too."

He gently shook his head, as he had often done over her folly. "Silly o' you," he said. "Ver' silly. Stop indoors. Did they hit you?"

She clutched his shoulder with a strength that brought him back to clear consciousness. "Ow!" he said, "Sybil, be careful. We must get on. You shouldn't have come out." But even as he began to struggle slowly to his feet he looked round, still only half-restored. "Funny," he went on. "Sure I saw them. Running by me, beating me. Each side. Great men with clubs."

She thought of the figure she had seemed to see, but she answered, "I've not seen them, my dear. O, Lothair, help me up." Her arm was in his as she spoke, and, so twined, they both struggled awkwardly to their feet. The kitten, alarmed at the earthquake, stuck its claws into Sybil's wrist. She rubbed it with her little finger to pacify it, and it slowly removed them. Once on his feet, Mr. Coningsby began to take charge. "Keep your arm in mine, and don't be frightened. It was a good thing you saw me—you'd have been quite lost. I'd stopped for a minute—get my breath. Had you better hold on—both hands?"

"One's enough, I think," Sybil said. "We'd both better keep our coats round us, and we shall have to hold them."

Sybil

She didn't feel like producing the kitten, and also she was engaged in secretly getting him on to the right road: she didn't think Love meant them to stand in the snow arguing which was the way to go. And if Lothair thought it was the left. . . .

He vacillated, but not between the roads. The screaming and howling of the blizzard grew louder, and as they moved away from the hedge, both huddled against the wind, for his crouching dragged her upright body down, he paused. "I wonder", he gasped, "if . . . hadn't better . . . shelter there . . . a bit."

"O, take me back," said Sybil. "I've got you." The ambiguity of those words pleased her immensely, and she said them over again, more slowly, separating them, enjoying the exquisite irony of the universe, which made them even more subtle than at first she had seen. For certainly *she* hadn't got him; something other than she was, as she had known it would, carrying and encouraging them both.

"Yes," Mr. Coningsby panted. "You're quite all right."

"Good God," said Sybil—she thought she might allow herself that, in the circumstances—"yes. Only don't leave me."

"I won't——" he began, but had to abandon it, and merely gasp, "No."

They went on, struggling back along the way she had come so easily. Most of the time he hung on her arm, leaned on her, or even stumbled and fell against her. But he murmured protective assurances at intervals, and Sybil, her arm pulled and wrenched, her breath knocked from her at every stumble, couldn't help thinking how really charming and affectionate he was. Because he certainly thought he was helping her on, and he never grew irritable through all that task of salvation, or not beyond panting once or twice, "Can't think . . . why you . . . came out. Horrible day"; and once, "Good thing you . . . found me."

"It was," she answered. "I'm very grateful." He was really moved, even in his present state, by the thought of her danger;

129

he was very good. "My dear," she said, pressing his arm.

Slowly, under that imperious command of death, they drove their way onward; each, with more or less strength and intensity, devoted to the other's preservation. Away on the terrace, Nancy clung to the terrible moving hands, and the magical invocation of wind and snow broke from the hands of the practitioner and rode free: storm to the tenth degree of power was loosed without control.

Fortunately, when, unknown to them, that mischief chanced, they were already near the drive; fortunately for them also, the wider dissemination of the origins of storm weakened it a little directly round them. But as they turned in for the last effort to reach the house, Mr. Coningsby almost halted; only Sybil's determination kept him moving; as a mere human being, she felt that if the kitten stuck its claws in her once more she should forget that she loved it. It had done so whenever he dragged her over to him. "Need you hold on *quite* so firmly, darling?" she silently asked it. "You're quite safe, you know. Sparrows falling to the ground, and so on. I suppose you're like us; you've made your mind up *not* to fall to the ground, whether your heavenly Father knows it or not. O, Lothair dear, you nearly had me over. Kitten, don't please. That is, if either of you could possibly manage without."

Mr. Coningsby almost halted. Right in front of them—in the blind tumult they had almost collided—were other figures; three of them, it seemed. Sybil peered forward.

"I . . . told . . . you so . . ." her brother managed to articulate; "men . . . with clubs."

One figure seemed to have a kind of club; indeed, as it struggled on, Sybil saw that it had, but it was rather a staff on which it leant than a club. But the other two hadn't. They were all going more slowly than the two behind them, who had, indeed, everything considered, come along with remarkable speed. Or, *everything* considered, perhaps not so remarkable.

"They're making for the house, I expect," Sybil said.

Sybil

"Though how they can see their way . . ." Unobtrusively she guided her brother to one side. "We'd better catch them up," she added.

Mr. Coningsby nodded. He was drifting again towards unconsciousness. "Then all of us have good res'," he said; Sybil could only just hear him. "Nice quiet time."

There was, even Sybil admitted, something attractive in the idea of a nice quiet time. She peered again at the other travellers as they drew level, and saw that the middle one of the three was a woman, a small woman hanging on the arms of the others, but talking. Sybil could just catch the sound of a voice: then the man nearest her turned his face towards her, and she recognized it.

"Ralph!" she cried.

"Hallo, aunt!" Ralph gasped. "Hell of a day . . . what . . . you doing . . . out in it?"

"Walking," Sybil said vaguely, but he couldn't hear her, and the conversation ended. He made some inquiring gesture in front of him; she nodded. All five of them beat on together. But the sound from the woman went on, and even pierced the storm and reached Sybil's ears; it was a kind of chanting. The shrill voice mingled with the wind and was the only thing that was not silenced by it. Its scream answered the wind's scream; though it was blown away, it was not lost, but carried as if on the music of a mad unison. The storm sang with its companion, reinforced her, made way for her. A word or two came to Sybil.

". . . coming . . . coming . . . the whole one shall awake . . ."

Ralph turned his head with difficulty and made a face at her. Discreetly turned from her brother, she grimaced back. She wondered—could it be the old gipsy Henry had called Joanna? That might explain why these others held so straight a course for the house. But with what wild song was she challenging or hailing the blizzard? and what energy of insane vision so filled her as to give her voice and spirit this strength, though her body hung on the arms of her supporters? Certainly it was not for Sybil Coningsby to deny the dismemberment through earth of the ever-triumphant Osiris, nor the victory that the immortal freshness of Love continually won over his enemies. If it was Love that the old woman was praising now, the shrill voice didn't quite sound like it. But it might be; with the sweet irony of Perfection, one could never tell. It was never what you expected, but always and always incredibly more.

Something dim loomed in front of them; they were there—they were right up against the front door, Lothair and the kitten and Ralph and these others and she herself: not for salvation from death, but for the mere manifestation of its power, she adored the Mystery of Love. She pressed the bell steadily; Ralph hammered on the door; the other man—Stephen, if it was Stephen—beat on it with his stick. Her brother fell against the door-post. The old woman turned her head—Sybil and she gazed at one another, their eyes recognizing mysteries of remote initiations.

"Perfect hellish weather!" Ralph said.

They heard someone within. The door was opened by Aaron himself, and the blizzard and they entered together. Sybil helped her brother in; then she gave Ralph a quick hand with the door. It closed gradually and was made fast. Her back against it, Sybil turned gently, removing the kitten from her numb arm, and saw Lothair sinking on to a seat; Stephen leaning against the opposite wall; and Joanna, all dripping with melting snow, facing a snarling Aaron.

"I've come," she cried, "I've come. Don't hide him, Aaron. I've come to see him wake."

Chapter Ten

NANCY

It was still hardly six o'clock. Mr. Coningsby had been put to bed, after Nancy had flown to welcome him and her aunt—to rather more than welcome her aunt, perhaps, for Sybil felt in the clinging embrace something she could have believed to be a clutching despair. She looked at the girl intently as they drew apart. Nancy's face was colourless, her eyes very tired: the new light which had for weeks shone from her was eclipsed, and her movements were heavy and troubled. "Where's Henry?" Sybil casually asked. "O, shut away somewhere," Nancy said, and shut herself away even more secretly.

Ralph was introduced and taken to have hot drinks and a hot bath. It appeared that he had determined to rush across in his car from the house where he was staying, to hurl Christmas greetings at his people on Christmas Day, and then to tear back. He was slightly ashamed of the intention, more especially as in the first excited feeling of safety he had told Sybil that he had thought it would please his father.

"That was very nice of you, Ralph," she said warmly.

"O, I don't know," he answered vaguely. "I mean—he was looking a bit aged the other day, I thought, and if a man's getting on . . . well, I mean he *likes* people to think about him a bit, I suppose. I mean, it wouldn't matter two grey Grimalkins to me whether anyone came to see me on Christmas Day or not; there's always plenty of people about anyhow. But he doesn't seem to get up to more than about forty per h. at at the best, does he?"

"And what's yours normally?" Sybil said gravely.

"O, I don't know; say, a lusty sixty," Ralph meditated. "But I'm rather a quiet one really, Aunt Sybil. I mean——"

Here he was interrupted, and only given time hastily to explain how the storm had caught and held the car; how he had at last got out and gone a little way to see if there was another road or anything; how he had lost his way back, and then encountered the other two wanderers, with whom he had gone along—partly because they had seemed to be aiming somewhere, partly to give Joanna an arm. "And I must say", he added quietly and hastily to Sybil, "the set of carols that she sung all the time curdled anything in me that the snow didn't. O, she was a lively little Robin Redbreast."

Sybil thought, as she herself was carried off—quite unnecessarily, she assured them—that there was something not wholly inapplicable in the phrase. The two women were apparently the least exhausted of all the five. Joanna was sitting on one of the hall chairs, her old red cloak pulled round her, and snow melting and pouring from her on every side. Aaron obviously wasn't a bit pleased, but nothing could be done. He couldn't push Joanna and Stephen out into the blizzard, and no one naturally would help him, and they wouldn't go. "But I wonder", Sybil thought, "why they dislike each other so. Is it just family, or is it something special?"

She would not go to bed, certainly not, but hot drinks—yes; and a hot bath—yes; and a complete change—yes. Drinks and baths and changes were exquisite delights in themselves; part of an existence in which one beauty was always providing a reason and a place for an entirely opposite beauty. As society for solitude, and walking for sitting down, and one dress for another, and emotions for intellect, and snowstorms for hot drinks, and in general movement for repose, repose for movement, and even one movement for another, so highly complex was the admirable order of the created universe. It was all rather like Henry's charming little figures in their perpetual dance; perhaps they were a symbol of it; perhaps that was what was meant by Aaron's uncertain phrase about being magnetized by the earth. They were the most beautiful things, with that varying light irradiating and striking outward from each, and a kind of gold aureole hanging in the air, which had expanded and heightened while Nancy's fortune was being tried. As she saw them again in her mind she saw at the same time the faint golden gleam that had possessed the air around her brother. She knew where the golden light came from among the images; it came from the figure of the Fool who moved so much the most swiftly, who seemed to be everywhere at once, whose irradiation shone therefore so universally upward that it maintained the circle of gold high over all, under which the many other rays of colour mingled and were dominated now by one, now by another. It had been, this afternoon, as if some figure—say, the Fool himself—had come speeding down from his own splendid abode of colour to her brother's side. She contemplated the idea; so, one might imagine, only no imagination could compass it, so did the beautiful perfection which was in and beyond all things make haste to sustain its creatures in their mood; immediacy to immediacy. She moved her foot lazily through the water of the bath, and half-pretended, half-believed, that little sparkles of gold rose and floated off as she did so: then she abandoned the fancy hastily. "I'm getting mythical," she said aloud; "this is the way superstitions and the *tantum mali* arise. Only", she added, in a charming apology, "I knew I was doing it, and I *have* left off. People", she went on thinking, "have killed one another on questions like that—did you or did you not see a golden sparkle? Well, the answer is, no, I didn't, but I saw the ripples in the water, and the top of my toe, and even though it may annoy Lothair, it is a very well-shaped toe. How sweet of Love to have a toe like that!"

She wondered as she dressed where Henry was; she'd rather expected to find him also in the hall. Nancy's "shut away somewhere" had been obscure—not merely in the meaning but in the tone. It hadn't been bitter; it hadn't been plaintive; it had been much more like an echo of despair. Despair? Had Henry refused to come out or something? had he a complex about snow? did it make him go what Ralph—if she had the phrase right—called "ga-ga"? If so, Nancy's winters—except for the luck of the English climate, to which Lothair (judging from his continual protests about it) had a profound objection —Nancy's winters might be rather trying. Henry might have to hibernate. She imagined Nancy teaching her children: "Mother, what animals hibernate?" "Bears, tortoises, hedge-hogs, and your father." Squirrels, snakes? did snakes and squirrels hibernate? It couldn't be that; he wouldn't have become a barrister if the Long Vacation was merely a prelude to a sound sleep. So awkward if he could only have summer clients. "Nobody could have much affiance in a barrister who could only take summer clients."

She re-ordered her thoughts; this was mere dithering. But dithering was rather nice; occasionally she and Nancy had dithered together. Nancy. What was wrong with the child? She had sat down to put on her shoes, and—one off and one on—she turned to her habitual resource. She emptied her mind of all thoughts and pictures: she held it empty till the sudden change in it gave her the consciousness of the spreading out of the stronger will within; then she allowed that now unimportant daily mind to bear the image and memory of Nancy into its presence. She did not, in the ordinary sense, "pray for" Nancy; she did not presume to suggest to Omniscience that it would be a thoroughly good thing if It did; she merely held her own thought of Nancy stable in the midst of Omniscience. She hoped Nancy wouldn't mind, if she knew. If, she thought, as, the prayer over, she put on her other shoe—if she had believed in a Devil, it would have been awkward to know whether or not it would be permissible to offer the Devil to Love in that way. Because the Devil might dislike it very much, and then. . . . However, she didn't believe in the Devil, and

Nancy

Nancy, up to lunch anyhow, had believed in a—if not the—mystery of Love. She determined to go and see if Nancy by any chance would like her to listen. Besides, there was Lothair —who in a strange home would certainly want her to be somewhere about. Also there was Joanna—Sybil rather looked forward to a conversation with Joanna, who seemed to her to have, on the whole, a just view of the world, if rather prejudiced against the enemies of Horus.

On the point of going downstairs, she checked herself. It was possible that Nancy, relieved from anxiety about her father, was not downstairs, but in her own room next door. Sybil considered this, and decided, if she were, that there would be no harm in venturing a visit; it could easily be ended. She went and knocked. A high, shaking voice said, "Come in."

Nancy was lying on the bed; she barely looked round as her aunt entered, and, on the point of speaking, gave up the effort.

She looked worse than she had done downstairs; a more complete collapse showed in her. Sybil, from the door, beheld a dying creature, one in whom the power of Life was on the point of evacuating its last defences. But she looked also a creature betrayed, one in whom the power of Life had changed to Death while she was still aware. The storm that had attacked the bodies of others might have crushed her soul; a wan recognition of the earth lingered in her eyes before she fell into entire ruin. Sybil came swiftly across the room.

"What's the matter, darling?" she said.

Nancy made a small movement with one hand, but didn't answer. Sybil sat down on the bed, and very lightly took the hand in her own. They remained so for some minutes in silence; then, in a voice hardly breathing it, Sybil said:

"All beauty returns. Wait a little."

Nancy trembled, as if the storm shook her from within; she said "No" in a moan and was silent. But the moan was at least life; the denial was at least consciousness; and Sybil ventured then so far as to put an arm round the girl's shoulders. There she rested silent again, bending all the power that she had to find what remote relic of power still existed somewhere in that strange overthrow. Time went past, but after a long while Nancy's fingers had closed ever so little more tightly on Sybil's hand; her shoulder pressed ever so little more willingly against the encircling arm. The blizzard without struck again and again at the window, and suddenly for the first time Nancy shuddered when she heard it. In a horrible stifled voice she said, "You don't know what that is."

Sybil tightened her grasp and gathered Nancy more closely into eternity. As if the remorseless will of that peace broke her into utterance, Nancy said, still in the same horrible voice, "It's Henry killing father."

The executive part of Sybil's mind had been so disciplined that it was not allowed to be startled. She said, and though her voice was low it was full of profounder wisdom than the words seemed to carry: "He came back with me."

"If he didn't," Nancy answered, "if he'd died out there, if I'd died, the storm would have stopped. It won't stop, now. It'll go on for ever. It's Henry killing father, and he can't leave off. I've stopped him."

Her brother's fancy of "great men with clubs" came into Sybil's mind for a perplexing moment. She dismissed it gently, not to break the deeper labour on which she was engaged. She answered with all the tenderness of her certainty: "You couldn't do anything at all unless you were let, could you? And if you were let stop it, then stopping it was the most perfect thing that could happen. Only *you* mustn't stop now."

The storm shook and rattled at the windows. Nancy jerked violently and cried out: "Nothing can stop it. He's lost them; he can't."

"What is it that's lost?" Sybil asked commandingly, and the girl answered in almost a shriek, "The Tarots, the magical leaves." She went on in a high torment: "He had them; he beat them up and down; he made the storm to kill father, and

I knocked them away, and they're gone, and nothing can stop
the wind and the snow for ever. It'll find father and it'll drown
the whole world. Hear it dancing! hear it singing! that's the
dance Henry keeps in his little room."

"I know the dance," Sybil said instantly. "Nancy, do you
hear? I know the dance, and the figures that make the dance.
The crown's gold over them, and there's a movement that
Henry's not known yet. Do you suppose that storm can ever
touch the Fool?"

Why she used the words she didn't know, but something
in them answered the girl in the same terms in which she had
cried out. Her face changed; there came into it a dim memory
of life. She said, arrested in the midst of terror and death, "The
Fool——"

"I saw the gold in the snow," Sybil said, "and your father
was in it and safe. Do you think the Tarots can ever escape
while the Fool is here to hold them?"

"They say he doesn't move," Nancy breathed.

"But I saw him move," Sybil answered, eternal peace in
her voice, "and there's no figure anywhere in heaven or earth
that can slip from that partner. They are all his for ever."

"The snow?" Nancy said.

"And you and I and Henry and your father," Sybil answered. "It is only the right steps we have to mind." She was
not very clear what language she was using; as from the
apostles on Pentecost, the single gospel flowed from her in
accents she had not practised and syllables she had never
learned. She added, deeply significant: "Your father came
back with me; mayn't Henry be waiting for you?"

As a proselyte in the streets of Jerusalem, drawn from the
parts of Libya about Cyrene, hearing a new message in a
familiar tongue, Nancy looked up for the first time.

"Why?" she said.

"Do you think the mystery of Love is only between those
who like one another?" Sybil said. "Darling, you're part of

the mystery, and you'll be sent to do mysterious things. Tell me—no, never mind the storm; it's nothing; it's under the feet of the Fool—tell me what's happened."

Uncertainly at first, and in no sort of order, Nancy began to pour out her story of all that she had known of the Tarots. She broke off, she went back to the beginning and leapt to the end, she confused her own experiences with what Henry had told her, and that again with what she believed Henry to desire, and all of it with her outraged will to love. It was confusion, but in the confusion, as if in a distant unity of person, went the motionless and yet moving figure of the Fool, and about his feet as he went flowed the innocent and ardent desire of the girl who told it to do all that she could—for Henry perhaps, but, even more than for Henry, for the unfathomable mystery of which she had known something and had half-hoped, half-despaired to know more.

Sybil herself, being prepared for anything at any moment, as those who have surrendered themselves must naturally be, all amazement being concentrated in a single adoring amazement at the mere fact of Love, and leaving no startled surprise for the changes and new beauties that attend It—Sybil herself listened gravely and intelligently to the tale. She saw, not in her own mind so much as in Nancy's, the whole earth, under the stress of what had been heard and seen, taking on a strange aspect. She saw—but this more in her own mind—the remote figure of the Juggler, standing in the void before creation was, and flinging up the glowing balls which came into being as they left his hands, and became planets and stars, and they remained some of them poised in the air, but others fell almost at once and dropped down below and soared again, until the creating form was lost behind the flight and the maze of the worlds. She saw, as the girl's excited voice rushed on, the four great figures between whom the earth itself hovered—the double manifestation of a single fact, the body and soul of human existence, the Emperor and the Empress, and diagonally opposite them, the hierophants male and *fe*male, the quadruple security of knowledge and process upon earth. The rushing chariot of the world came from among them, and it again parted, and on one side went the Hermit, the soul in its delighted solitude of contemplation, and on the other the Lovers, the soul in its delighted society of terrestrial love.

"And earth came out of them," Nancy said breathlessly. Earth and air and fire and water—the lesser elements pouring down from below the Greater Trumps, but these also in the dance, and in each of those four cataracts she saw the figure of the Fool, leaping and dancing in joy. "So I thought it was the Hanged Man, and I screamed." Nancy had dashed to another part of the tale, and Sybil remembered the crucifixions of her past, and by each of them, where she herself hung and screamed and writhed, she saw the golden halo and the hands of the Fool holding and easing her, and heard his voice murmuring peace. "And what shall we do? what shall we do?" the young creature babbled at last, and, half-risen, clutched hard at Sybil and broke into a storm of tears. But as she wept and agonized Sybil's hands held and eased her and Sybil's voice murmured peace.

How far her vivid intelligence at the moment believed the tale was another matter. Whether the pieces of painted papyrus and the ever-moving images, the story of newly created earth and the swift storm, Henry's desire and her brother's firmness, the sight of her own eyes and the vision of the rest, Nancy's tragic despair and Joanna's wild expectation—whether all these corresponded to some revelation of ultimate things she could not then tell, nor did she much mind. The thing that immediately concerned her was Nancy's own heart. There was the division; there, justified or not, were bewilderment and fear. If it were delusion that possessed her, still it was clear that that delusion was too deep and far-reaching to be torn up by a few words of bright encouragement. If it were not delusion, if the strange and half-mystical signs and names of

the Greater Trumps had meaning and life, then no doubt in
due time of beneficence her own concern with them would be
revealed. She held Nancy more closely.

"Dearest," she said, "your father's safe. Do you understand
that?"

"Yes," Nancy sobbed.

"Tell me then—there, darling, quietly; all is well, as is most
well—tell me, where's Henry?"

"In his own room, I suppose," Nancy said brokenly. "I—I
ran away from him—when I knew."

"Did he want you to—run away?" Sybil asked slowly.

"I don't know—no," Nancy said. "But I couldn't stop. He'd
been doing that awful thing—and I was terrified and ran away
—and I love him. I can't live if I don't find him—and now
I never shall."

"But, darling, that's not loving *him*," Sybil gently protested.
"That's only preferring to live, isn't it?"

"I don't care what it is," Nancy sobbed again. "If I could
do anything, I would, but I can't. Don't you understand—he
tried to *kill* father? There's just Death between them, and I'm
in the middle of it."

"Then", Sybil said, "there's something that isn't death, at
least. And you might be more important than Death, mightn't
you? In fact, you might be life perhaps."

"I don't know what you mean," Nancy said, wresting herself free suddenly. "O, go away, Aunt Sybil. I'm going mad.
Do go away."

Sybil sat back on the bed. "Stand still and listen," she said.
"Nancy, you said it yourself, there's death and there's you.
Are you going to be part of death against Henry and against
your father? or are you going to be the life between them?
You'll be power one way or another, don't doubt that; you've
got to be. You've got to live in them or let them die in you.
Make up your mind quickly, for the time's almost gone."

"I can't do anything," Nancy cried out.

Nancy

Sybil stood up and went over to her. "Your father came back with me," she said. "Go and see if Henry still has any idea of going anywhere with you. Go and see what he wants, and if you can give it to him, do. I'll see to your father and you see to Henry. Do let's get on to important things."

"*Give* it to him!" Nancy exclaimed. "But . . ."

"Dearest," Sybil said, "he may not want *now* what he wanted two hours ago. People change their minds, you know. Yes, honestly. Go and live, go and love. Get farther, get farther— now, with Henry if you can. If not—listen, Nancy—if *not*, and if you loved him, then go and agonize to adore the truth of Love. Now." She gave the girl a little gentle shake, and moved away to the door, where she stopped, looked over her shoulder, said, "I should be as quick as I could, darling," and went.

Nancy stared after her. "Go to Henry"? "go and live"? "go and love"? To be life or death between her lover and her father? Her hands to her cheeks, she stood, brooding over the dark riddle, seeing dimly some sort of meaning in it. Something had kept her father alive; something held her father and herself—if that something were waiting for her to move? to go to Henry? She couldn't think what she could do there, or of what, divided and united at once by a terrible truth, they could possibly even speak. Life wasn't all speaking. Love was being something, in some way. Was she now to be driven to be *that*, in the way that—who knows what?—chose? Slowly she began to move. Henry probably wouldn't want her, but . . . She went gradually and uncertainly towards his room.

He was sitting, as she had been lying, in darkness. When she had knocked and got no answer, she had taken the risk of annoying him and had gone in, switching on the light. She saw him sitting by his table and switched it off again. Then she went delicately across the room, kneeled by him, touched him lightly, and said, "Henry!"

He did not answer. In a little she said again, "Darling," and as still he made no sound she said no more, only went on kneeling by his chair. After many minutes he said, "Go. Go away."

"I will", she answered sincerely, "if you want me to, if I can't help. Can I help?"

"How can you help?" he said. "There's nothing for any of us but to wait for death. We shall all be with your father soon."

"He's back, quite safe," she said. "Aunt Sybil met him and brought him back."

"It was a pity; the storm will have to find him out again," he answered. "Go and be with him till that happens."

"Must it happen?" she asked, and he laughed.

"Unless you have a trick to lure back the chalices and the staffs," he said. "If you can, you can put them in their order and seal up the storm. But since they are rushing and dancing about the sky I can't tell how you'll do it. Perhaps if you talked to those that are left——"

"Mightn't we?" she asked, but he did not understand her.

"Try it," he mocked her again. "Here are the four princes; take them and talk to them. Perhaps, since you struck all the rest loose, these will tell you where they are. O, to be so near, so near——!"

"I should have done it all the same if I'd known," she said, "but I didn't know—not that I should do that. I only wanted to hold your hands still."

"They'll be still enough soon," he mocked, "and so will yours;" and suddenly his hand felt for and caught hers. "They're beautiful hands," he said; "though they've ruined the world, they're beautiful hands. Do you know, Nancy, that you've done what thousands of priests and scientists have talked about? This is the end of the world. You've killed it—you and your beautiful hands. They've sent the snow and the wind over the whole world, and it'll die. The dance is ending: the Juggler's finished with one ball."

"Love them a little then," she said, "if you're sure. If you're quite sure."

144

"Can you bring back the staffs?" he asked, "from the one to the ten? Shall I open the window for you to call or catch them? Maybe one's on the window-sill now."

"Can't the images help?" she asked. "I don't know, but you should. Isn't there any way in which they could command the Tarots?"

She felt him stiffen in the darkness. "Who told you that?" he said. "I can't tell. I don't know anything of what can be done from within. If . . ."

"If——" she answered, and paused. "I will do anything with you that I can. What would you like me to do?"

His figure turned and leaned towards her. "You?" he said. "But you hated what I was doing, you wanted to save your father—of course you did; I'm not blaming you—but how can you help me now?"

She broke unexpectedly into a laugh, the sound of which surprised some solemn part of her nature, but seemed to bring freedom at once into herself and into the dark room, so that she felt relieved of her lingering fear. "O, Henry darling," she said, "must those dancers of yours concentrate on my father? Haven't they any way of doing things without bothering the poor dear? Don't you think they might manage to save the world and yet leave him alone? Henry sweetest, how serious you are about it all!"

"You can laugh," he said uncertainly, not as a question nor yet in anger, but as if he were feeling after some strange fact. "You can laugh . . . but I tell you it *is* the end of the world."

She scrambled to her feet. "I begin to agree with Aunt Sybil," she said; "it isn't quite decent to break into the poor thing's secrets when it's gone to such trouble to keep them quiet. But since you and I together drove things wrong, shall you and I together see—only see, darling—if we can put them straight?"

"You're afraid of the Tarots," he said; "you always have been."

"Never again," she said, "or yes—perhaps again. I'll be afraid again, I'll fall again, I'll hate and be angry again. But just for a moment there's something that runs and laughs and all your Tarots are flying along with it, and why shouldn't it catch them for us if we ask it very nicely? Only we won't hurt anyone, will we, if we can help it? Nothing's important enough for that."

He got to his feet heavily. "There's no way anywhere without hurting someone," he said.

"Darling, how gloomy you are," she said. "Is this what comes of making blizzards and trying to kill your own Nancy's own father? Perhaps there's a way everywhere without hurting anyone—unless," she added, with a touch of sadness clouding the full gaiety that had seized her, "unless they insist on being hurt. But let's suppose they won't, and let's pretend they don't, and let's be glad that my father's safe, and let's see if the golden dancers can call back the staffs and the cups. I think perhaps we owe the world that." She kissed him lightly. "It was sweet of you to pick out a nice soothing way of doing what you wanted," she said. "Some magicians would have put him in a barn and set it on fire, or forced him into a river and let him drown. You've a nice nature, Henry, only a little perverted here and there. All great geniuses are like it, they say. I think you must be a genius, darling; you take your job so solemnly. Like Milton and Michael Angelo and Moses. Do you know, I don't believe there's a joke in all the Five Books of Moses. I can't see very well, Henry, but I think you're frowning. And I'm talking. And talking and frowning won't do anything, will they? O, hark at it! Come along, my genius, or we shan't save the world before your own pet blizzard has spoilt it."

"There's no other way," he said, "but I warn you that you don't know what may happen. Perhaps even this isn't a way."

"Well, perhaps it isn't," she answered. "But they are dancing, aren't they, dearest? And perhaps, if we mean to love——"

"Do you love me still then?" he asked.

"I never loved you more and yet I never loved you less," she told him. "O, don't let's stop to ask riddles. And, anyhow, I wasn't thinking of you, so there! Come, darling, or your aunt will be doing something curious. Yours is a remarkable family, Henry; you get all het up over your hobbies. And so you shall if you like, bless you! only not just now."

"Joanna——" he exclaimed, unconsciously following her as she drew him towards the door. "Is she here?"

"She is," Nancy said, "but we won't worry about her now. Take me to them, darling, for the dance is in my ears and the light's in my eyes, and this is why I was born, and three was glory in the beginning and is now and ever shall be, and let's run, let's run, for the world's going quickly and we must be in front of it to-night."

Chapter Eleven

JOANNA

In the hall below, the kitten stretched itself and yawned. Sybil had put it down when she was once well inside and asked one of the maids to look after it. But there had been not time yet; Mr. Coningsby, Ralph, Sybil herself, had to be seen to. And now there were still Joanna and Stephen. Aaron Lee, looking at his sister with something very much like watchful hatred, said: "Now you're here, Joanna, you'd better get into bed. And so", he added, jerking his head at Stephen, "had he."

"Yes, Aaron," said Joanna docilely, with a little giggle. "It's a bad night to be out in, isn't it?"

Aaron glanced round him; the three, except for the kitten, were alone in the hall.

"Why have you come?" he asked.

"To see you, dear," the old woman said. "So's Stephen. He's very fond of you, Stephen is. Aren't you, Stephen?"

"Yes, grandmother," Stephen answered obediently.

"He's very big, isn't he?" Joanna ran on. "Much bigger than you, dear Aaron." She hopped off her chair and began to prowl round the hall, sniffing. Presently she came to the kitten and stood staring at it. The kitten rubbed itself against her leg, felt the wet, and sprang aside. The old woman, bending, scratched its head, and began muttering to it in words which the others couldn't hear.

The kitten jumped up, fell down, twisted over itself, dashed off, and dashed back. Joanna gesticulated at it, and it crouched watching her.

"You'd better get to bed, Joanna," Aaron exclaimed to her. "Get those things off and get between the blankets. You'll be ill if you don't."

"You fool, Aaron," Joanna said. "Illness can't touch me any more than death. I shall never be ill. I shall be transformed when the body that's lost is made whole." She turned her face towards him. "And where'll you be then, Aaron? Screeching among the tormentors."

"You're mad," Aaron answered. "You're a mad old woman hobbling about in a dream."

She left the kitten and almost ran back to him. "Dream, hey?" she snarled. "Little dream, Aaron Lee, for you that help to hide my baby."

"Your baby's dead," Aaron snarled back, as the two small old creatures faced each other fiercely and despitefully. "Don't you know that by now?"

She caught at his coat, and at the movement of her arm the water that still ran from her was flung wide-spattering around. "My baby never dies," she cried, "and you know it. That's why you hate me." Her whole manner changed. "But you're right, dear Aaron," she mumbled, "yes, you're right. Give me your bed to sleep in and your plate to eat from and I'll give you a plate and a bed one day in a finer house than this. Give me a kiss first, Aaron, and I'll never set Stephen on to you to twist the news of the grave where you've hidden him out of your throat. Kiss me, Aaron."

She was up against him, and he stepped sharply back to face her. His foot came down on the tail of the kitten, which was smelling at his shoes. It yelped; Aaron tottered and lost his footing, staggering a pace or two away. He turned fiercely on the kitten, which had dashed wildly across the hall.

"Put it out," he cried, "put it back in the snow. Who brought it in? Stephen, catch it and put it out."

The young man, who all this while had been leaning dully against the wall, the snow melting from him, his eyes following

Joanna wherever she went, moved uncertainly. Joanna made no sign, and he, with movements that seemed clumsy but were exact, first attracted the kitten and then caught it up in his great hands.

"What shall I do with it, grandmother?" he said.

"Put it out," Aaron called to him.

"Ah, no, don't put it back in the snow," Joanna said. "Ah, it's a cunning little cat; it's very small, but everything's small at first. It'll grow; it'll grow. Let it sleep in my blankets, Aaron; the cats know where the blood fell, and they sit in a circle round the hidden place watching for God. Have you ever found their eyes looking at you, Aaron, when you were shuffling the cards? little green eyes looking up at you? little claws that scratched? Give it to me, and it'll sleep till the right time comes."

"No cat'll come to you in those drenched clothes," Aaron said, with a curious flat effort at common sense. But, unhearing, she beckoned to Stephen, and, when he came, took the kitten from him. It wriggled a little in her hands and mewed once, but it did not make any serious effort to escape. She held it near her face, peering and muttering at it, and it stared back at her. The colloquy of their eyes lasted some dozen seconds; then Joanna said: "Show me where I'm to rest, Aaron." A maid returned at the moment. Aaron conferred with her and then said abruptly to Joanna, "Go along with Amabel; she'll show you." Then to Stephen, "And you—come with me. You can rub yourself down and have some food."

"Ah, let Stephen sleep in the same room with me," Joanna cried, "for we're used to it and we're uneasy apart. Haystack or lych-gate or king's house or quarry, it's all one to us so long as there's Stephen to watch while I'm dreaming and me to wake while Stephen sleeps. Only he can't see my dreams, and though I see his they're only water and wind and fire, and it's in earth that the other's hidden till Horus comes."

With the word a quietness fell on her; she brought the kitten

against her cheek and crooned to it, ·as she followed the
bothered and dubious Amabel away.

Stephen presumably "had some food", but he was not at
the late and bewildered dinner to which, soon after, Aaron
sat down with Sybil and Ralph. Aaron muttered something
about Henry's probably being busy, and seemed to take it for
granted that Nancy, after her experience of the storm, was
also in bed. Sybil, when she grasped this, thought that Nancy
might have been annoyed to have it thought so, but then even
Sybil had not quite grasped the true history of the afternoon.
She knew that Nancy believed that Henry had loosed the
storm on Mr. Coningsby, by means of the magical operation
of the power-infused Tarots. But she was not aware of the
short meeting of Henry and Aaron, when the younger man had
recovered consciousness to find his grandfather, summoned by
an agitated mind, bending over him. In a few sentences, as he
came to himself, he told Aaron what had happened. Aaron
stepped back, appalled.

"But then", he faltered, "we can't stop the winds," and his
face paled. "We shall all be killed."

"Yes," Henry said. "That's the end of all our dreams."

As he spoke he had gone away to his own room, to sit in
darkness brooding over his hope and his defeat, waiting for
the crash that must come when the force of the released elements broke in on the house, and had sat so till Nancy came
to him. But Aaron had refused, in his own mind, to believe it;
it couldn't be so. Something might happen, some wild chance
might save them. He had never cared much for Henry's intrusion into the place of the powers, and Henry might easily
be wrong. The manuscripts told them this and that, but the
manuscripts might be wrong. In the belief that they were true,
Henry and he had plotted to destroy his guest—but the storm
might be a coincidence; Coningsby might be safe; in an ordinary storm he would be; it wasn't as if, all put together, it was
a long distance or a great danger, *unless*—unless the snow and

wind had been aimed at him. If they were not, if it was chance, if indeed the Tarots and the images had no power in themselves and were but passive reflections of more universal things, if the mystery of both was but a mystery of knowledge and prophecy and not of creation and direction—why then—the stranger would come back safely, and, if he did, why then they would all be safe. That some of the paintings should be lost was indeed a catastrophe; no one now could justly divine the movement of the images and their meaning. The telling of fortunes would be for ever but a childish game, and never the science of wisdom. But he would be alive. The long study in which he had spent his years might partly fail. But he would be alive. On the very verge of destruction, he cried out against destruction; he demanded a sign, and the sign was given him. Lothair Coningsby came stumbling into the hall, and when Aaron saw him he drew great breaths of relief. The storm was but natural; it would cease.

In this recovered quiet of mind he was able to deal with immediate practical questions; he was even able to confront Joanna with his old jealousy and hatred. Since, many years before, the images had come into his possession, since his father and he had—O, away in his boyhood—taken them (with what awful and breathless care! what almost eye-shutting reverence!) from the great round old silver case—only some six inches high, but marvellously huge in diameter—in which for centuries, so his father had told him, his hidden secret of the gipsies had been borne about the world, covered by wrappings and disguises, carried in waggons and carts, unknown even to most of their own wandering bands, who went straying on and did not know that one band of all those restless companies possessed the mystery which long since some wise adept of philosophical truths had made in the lands of the east or the secret houses of Europe: Egyptian or Jew or Christian heretic—Paulician, Bogophil, or Nestorian—or perhaps still farther off in the desert-circled empire of Abyssinia, for there were hints of all in the strange medley of the sign-bearing images, and the symbols wore no accepted or traditional aspect; their familiarity was foreign, they had been before the building of churches and sects, aboriginal, infinite: but, from wherever they came, he who had made them, and the papyrus paintings with them, up to seventy-eight degrees of knowledge, had cased and hidden them, and sent them out on everlasting wanderings without as they kept among themselves the everlasting dance within. But at that making and hiding the Tarot cards had lain in due mysterious order on and about the golden base of the Tarot images, each subtly vibrating to the movements of its mightier golden original, as that in turn moved in correspondence to the movement of that full and separate centre of the created dance which it microcosmically symbolized. There was to be a time, the legends said, when one should arise who should understand the mystery of the cards and the images, and by due subjection in victory and victory in subjection should come to a secret beyond all, which secret—it had always been supposed by those few who had looked on the shapes, and few they had been even over the centuries—had itself to do with the rigid figure of the Fool. But the dark fate that falls on all mystical presentations, perhaps because they are not presentations only, had fallen on this; the doom which struck Osiris in the secular memory of Egypt, and hushed the holy, sweet, and terrible Tetragrammaton in the ritual of Judah, and wounded the Keeper of the Grail in the Castle of the Grail, and by the hand of the blind Hoder pierced the loveliest of all the Northern gods, and after all those still everywhere smote and divided and wounded and overthrew and destroyed; by the sin of man and yet by more and other than the sin of man, for the myth of gods and rebellious angels had been invoked—by reason, no doubt, to explain, but by something deeper than reason to frame the sense of a dreadful necessity in things: the need that was and yet must not be allowed to be, the inevitability that must be denied, the fate that must be rejected, so only and only by such contradictions of mortal thought did the nature of the universe make itself felt by man. Prophesied itself within itself by the Tower that fell continually or by the fearful shape of Set who was the worker of iniquity ruling over his blinded victims, prophesied thus within itself, the doom came to pass on the mystery of the images, none knew when, for some said as long since as the son of the first maker, who fell from his father's wisdom, and others but in the very generation that preceded the speaker's. But, whenever the sin was done, it chanced upon a night that one opened the silver case, sealed with zodiacal signs, and, daring the illustrious beauty that shone forth, thrust in his hands and tore out the translucent painted leaves, thinking that by them alone he might tell the fortunes of men and grow rich by his fellows' yearning to know what was to be, or wantonly please an idle woman in the low chambers of Kieff or Paris. The images he dared not touch, and the golden base that carried them he could not. So he fled, completing the sacrilege, and died wretchedly, the tale said, but rather because it was thought proper that the sinner should suffer than because anything certain was known. Thus the leaves of the presentation were carried one way, and the golden shapes another, and the people of the secret waited in hope and despair, as Israel languishes till the Return, and the Keeper till the coming of the Haut Prince, and Osiris the slain till Horus overcome his foes, and Balder in the place of shades till after Ragnarok, and all mankind till the confusions of substance be abolished and the unity of person be proclaimed. But, even when the paintings had been found by chance and fate and high direction in the house of Lothair Coningsby, yet the wills of the finders had been set on their own purposes, on experiment of human creation or knowledge of human futurity, and again the mystical severance had manifested in action the exile of the will from its end.

To that last conclusion, as his thoughts recalled the myth,

Aaron, sitting at the dinner-table, did not permit himself to reach. In his father's time it had been determined, by a few among the wanderers, that the far-borne images would be carried no farther, since it was yearly becoming more difficult to evade the curiosity and power of the magistrates; enough money, from some rich and many poor, had been gathered, a solitary house had been found, and the treasure had been given into the charge of the oldest of the Lees. The room had been prepared and the silver chest carried in, and, that the influence of the dance might more quickly draw to itself its lesser instruments, the images had been set upon the new-shaped table. But upon their father's death the knowledge of the charge had been, as it were, separated between Aaron and Joanna, and both again misunderstood the requirements of devotion, Joanna in hot dreams of her child, Aaron in cold study of the continuous maze. Her madness drove her wide, his folly kept him still; and when she came to him he forbade her even a sight of the sacred thing. So through years their anger grew between them, and now she lay in his home.

He hated and feared her, yet he did not well know what in her he feared and hated. He did not much think she would dare to touch the images, and, anyhow, without Henry's aid or his own she could not find them through the outer and inner chambers. It was perhaps no more than the intensity of her desire, and the mad energy which for her turned the names of Egypt to living and invocable deities, and within that her own identification of herself with the Divine Mother and Seeker. It was strange and absurd, but it was also rather terrifying—she was so much one with her dream that at times her dream invaded like the mists of the Nile his own knowledge of her as Joanna. But she was here, and nothing could be done. Perhaps Miss Coningsby, who seemed from Henry's account to have been remarkably successful with her on the road, would be able to quieten her if she fell into one of her fits.

Sybil, while she ate and drank, and maintained the conversation as well as could be, considering the spoiled dinner, their preoccupied minds, and the increasing hurricane without, contemplated at the same time the house and its occupants. She saw it, against the background of a dark sky filled with tumultuous snow, part of it yet its opposite, its radiance of enclosed beauty against a devastation of wilder beauty, and in the house she saw the lovely forms of humanity each alive with some high virtue, each to its degree manifesting the glory of universal salvation. Her brother, industrious, as generous as he knew how to be, hungry for peace, assured, therefore, of finding peace; Henry and Nancy—Henry, she thought, had been a little mistaken if he imagined that violence of that kind would bring him to the kingdom; stillness rather, attention, discipline—but Henry and Nancy—she ardently hoped they were together and moving into peace; Ralph with his young freshness and innocence; Aaron with his patient study and courtesy—even if the courtesy had hidden some other intention, as, if Nancy were right, it probably had, still courtesy in itself was good and to be enjoyed: yes, certainly good was not to be denied in itself because motives were a little mixed. Her own motives were frequently mixed; the difference between delighting in . . . well, in the outrageous folly of mankind (including her own) and provoking it grew sometimes a little blurred. She was uneasily conscious that she sometimes lured her brother in London into showing off his pomposity, his masterful attitude towards his employees, because it seemed to her so wonderful that he should be able to behave so. "My fault," Sybil sighed to herself, and offered herself once more as a means whereby Love could more completely love the butcher. Not, of course, that Love didn't completely love the butcher already, but through her perhaps . . . however, that argument was for the theologians. Anyhow, with that sin in her mind it was not for her to rebuke Aaron or Nancy. Before perfect Love there wasn't much to choose between them. At the same time, without excusing herself, it was up to the butcher to see that he wasn't drawn, if he didn't want to be, even as subtly as she knew she did it; and in the same way it was up to her to see that the charm of Aaron's manners didn't any further involve her brother in disagreeable experiences. The courtesy was one thing; the purpose of the courtesy was another thing; there need be no confusion of substance. She smiled back at Aaron. "And where", she asked, "is my kitten?"

"In my sister's room, as a matter of fact," Aaron answered. "If you want it——"

She sighed a negative. "Why, no," she said, "of course not. Did I tell you that I found it in the snow? I thought it must belong to the house."

Aaron shook his head. "Not here," he answered. "We never have any animals here, especially not cats."

"Really?" Sybil said. "Don't you like them, Mr. Lee? Or doesn't the air suit them? Or do they all refuse to live in the country and want to get to London, to the theatres and the tubes? Are the animals also forsaking the countryside?"

He smiled, saying, "It isn't a social law, Miss Coningsby, but it's a rather curious fact. They—the cats we've had from time to time, for one reason or another—they spend all their time round my study door, miaowing to get into the room of the images."

Ralph looked up; this was the first he had heard of a room with images.

"Dogs too," Aaron went on, "they do the same thing. In fact, we've had a mighty business sometimes, getting them away—when we've had one. It'd snarl and bite and go almost mad with rage before it'd be taken back to its kennel. And there was a parrot Henry had when he was a boy—a cousin of mine gave it to him, a magnificent bird—Henry left the door of its cage unfastened by accident one night, and we found it the next morning dead. It had gone on dashing itself againt the door of the room till it killed itself."

There was a moment's silence; then Ralph said: "Parrots

are jolly useful things. I know a man—he's at Scotland Yard, as a matter of fact, and he has to see all sorts of cranks and people who think other people are conspiring or fancy they're on the track of dope-gangs . . . of course not the very silliest kind, but those that there just might be something in—well, he got so fed up that he had a parrot in his room, put it away in the window opposite his table so that it was at the back of anyone else, and he taught it, whenever he stroked his nose several times, to say 'And what about—last—Tuesday—week?' It had an awfully sinister kind of croak in its voice, if you know what I mean, and he swore that about half his people just cleared out of the room without stopping to ask what it meant, and even most of those that didn't were a bit nervy most of the rest of the time. He got a shock once though, because there was a fellow who'd lost a lot of money racing on the Tuesday week, and when he was reminded of it suddenly like that, he just leapt up and cursed for about twenty minutes straight off before getting down to his business again."

"That", said Sybil with conviction, "was an admirable idea. Simple, harmless, and apparently effective. What happened to the parrot, Ralph?"

"O, well, it got all out of hand and a bit above itself," Ralph answered. "It kept on all the time asking 'What about last Tuesday week?' till my friend got sick of it. Especially after some fellow tried to do him in one Tuesday with a hammer. So he had to get rid of it. But he always thought it'd be a brainy notion for solicitors and business men and vicars and anybody who had a lot of callers."

"Beautiful!" Sybil said. "The means perfectly adapted to the end—and no fuss. Would you jump, Mr. Lee, if someone asked you what you were doing last Tuesday week?"

"Alas, I am always leading the same life," Aaron said. "There hasn't been a day for years—until this Christmas—that I've had cause to remember more than any other. No, I shouldn't jump."

"And you, Ralph?" Sybil asked.

"Well—no," Ralph said, "I should have just to think for a minute. . . . I mean, in Scotland Yard and all. But—no, not after a second."

"How innocent the old are," Sybil said, smiling to Aaron. "I shouldn't jump either."

"No, but then you never *do* jump, do you, Aunt Sybil?" Ralph protested. "When that girl we had smashed a whole trayful of china in the hall, you just said, 'O poor dear, how worried she'll be,' and dipped out there like a homing-pigeon."

"Well, so she was worried," Sybil answered. "Frightfully worried. But about your animals, Mr. Lee. What's the explanation, do you think?"

Aaron shrugged delicately and moved his hands. "Who knows?" he answered. "It sounds fantastic to say the images draw them, but what other cause can there be? Some mesmeric power . . . in the balance, in the magnetic sympathies."

"Magnetic sympathy over cats?" Sybil said, a little dubiously. "Cats never struck me like that. But you won't let my kitten bang itself against the door, will you? Or not till we've tried to amuse it in other ways first."

"I'll see to its safety myself," Aaron said. "I shall be looking in on Joanna, and I'll either bring it away or warn her to keep it safe. She'll treat it carefully enough, with her unfortunate delusions about Egypt. Isn't Ra the Sun God shown in a cat's form?"

"I haven't an idea," Sybil answered, smiling. "Perhaps the kitten is Ra, and I carried the Sun God home this afternoon. It doesn't, if one might say so, seem exactly the Sun God's best day."

They listened to the blizzard for a minute or two; then Sybil looked at her watch. "I think, if you'll pardon me, Mr. Lee," she said, "I'll just run and look in on my brother. He might be glad of a word." The three of them rose together.

159

"Present my regrets again," Aaron bowed. "It was an entirely unexpected accident and a most regrettable result."

Sybil curtsied back. "Thank you so much," she murmured. "Lothair will—or will not—think so. But I can't altogether think so myself, if (you don't mind me being frank?), if Henry *did* arrange for the storm."

He stepped back, startled. "The storm," he cried more loudly, "the storm's only winter snow."

"But is all winter snow the same storm?" she asked. "That is, if I've got it right. But isn't it divinely lovely? Do excuse me; I must just see Lothair." She turned and went.

"Aunt Sybil", Ralph said in the pause after her departure, "would find a torture-chamber divinely lovely, so long as she was the one on the rack. Or a broken-down Ford. Or draughts. Or an anaconda."

Chapter Twelve

THE FALLING TOWER

In Aaron's workroom the noise of the blizzard was very high. The two who crossed the room heard it, and heard it roaring still higher as Henry unlocked the inner door. But when they had entered that other room, just as they passed through the curtains, there was a change. The high screech of the wind altered by an infinitely small but complete variation. Nancy heard it no longer screaming, but singing. Her hand in Henry's, she paused between the hangings.

"Do you hear? My dear, do you hear?" she exclaimed. Holding the hangings for her, and listening, he looked back. "I hear," he said. "It's catching us up, Nancy."

"No, but that's gone," she protested. "It sounds different here. Hark!"

As he dropped the curtain, the habitual faint music of the room greeted them. It seemed to the girl that the roar of the wind was removed to an infinite distance, where it mingled with other sounds, and was received into the feet of the dancers, and by them beaten into fresh sound. She stood; she looked; she said to Henry: "Have you the Tarots, darling?"

He held them out, the suit of sceptres, the suit of deniers, the princely cards of cups and staves.

"I wonder", she said, "if we shall be able to find our way in by them alone."

He looked at her fully for the first time since on the terrace their eyes had beheld each other in the snow.

"I can't tell; this has never happened before," he said. "What I tried to do has failed; perhaps it was better that it failed. I did what seemed wise——"

The Falling Tower

"I know you did," she said. "Dearest Henry, I know you did. I do understand that, though I understand so little. There's nothing between us at all. You did—and I did—and now here we are. But you've always talked as if there was a way to—what do you call them?—the Greater Trumps, and as if the Greater ruled the Lesser."

"Certainly they do," he answered, "and therefore the suits are less than the Trumps. But it may be a very dangerous thing to thrust among them as we are, so—half-prepared."

"Still, we can't wait, can we?" she said. "And if time would let us, my heart won't—it's beating too hard. Kiss me, Henry, and, in case we are divided, remember that I always wanted to love. And now for the cards. Look, will you hold them or shall I? and what's the best thing to do?"

"Do as you did the other night", he said, "and I will put my hands round yours, and hold the eight high cards that are left to us; and then let's move towards the table as you did, but this time we will not stop till we are compelled. And God help us now—if there be a God—for I do not know what we can do or say if we come knowingly into the measure of the dance."

"All is well; all is most well," she murmured, and they put themselves in the order he had proposed, but he more fearfully than she. Then, the Tarots pointed towards the dancers, they took the first slow step forward together.

As they did so, the golden mist flowed out again to meet them, and flowed round them as it had compassed her but two nights before. This time, so intent was her will upon its work, she did not look up to him at all, and it was he who was startled by the apparent distortion of her face below his, by the huge enlargement of their hands, by the gigantic leaves that shook and quivered in their clasp, trembling till the very colours upon them seemed to live and move, and the painted figures floated as if of their own volition from the mortal grasp that held them. He did not dare pause, nor could he feel a

162

trace of faltering in the girl who stepped forward, foot by foot, so close to him; only there passed through his mind a despairing ironic consciousness that not thus, certainly not thus, had he purposed to attempt the entrance into the secret dance. He had meant to go victoriously, governing the four elemental powers, governing the twin but obedient heart and mind that should beat and work in time with his, lover and friend but servant also and instrument. By her devotion to his will he had hoped to discover the secret of domination, and of more—of the house of life where conquerors, heroes, and messiahs were sent out to bear among men the signs of their great parentage. And now he was drawn after her. It had been she who had pointed the way, the thought of which had been driven from his mind by the catastrophe that had overwhelmed it. It was she who went first, not by his will but by her own—nor could he then guess how much, to Nancy's own heart, her purpose and courage seemed to derive from him. His power was useless till she drew it forth; it worked through her, but it was from him that it still obscurely rose. Though she ruled instead of him in the place of the mist, it was he who had given her that sovereignty, and it seemed to her then that, though all dominions of heaven and earth denied it, she would acknowledge that profound suzerainty while her being had any knowledge of itself at all.

She pressed on. The great leaves shook and parted and drifted upon the wind, which, as before, seemed to stir in the golden cloud. As one by one they were carried off they took on the appearance of living forms; the transparency which was illumined with the crimson and azure tints of the Queen of Chalices floated before her, farther and farther away, and was indeed a crowned and robed woman bearing the crimson cup; the black and purple of the Esquire of Deniers showed for a moment before it was swallowed up in the cloud as a negro youth in an outlandish garment holding aloft a shining bronze coin, and all surrounded by a halo of light which had once been the papyrus where had been figured the now-living shape. Her hands below her were lucent and fiery in the mist; the golden cloud above those pale shapes, infused with crimson fire of blood, dazzled and dazed her; they were more splendid and terrific even than the visions that rose from them and fled upon the wind. Around them, closing them in, supporting them, were other mighty hands—his. Of his presence otherwise she was by now unaware; she might, but for those other hands, have been alone. But those four hands that by mischance had loosed the winds and the waters on earth were stretched out to recover the power they had inadvertently cast away. The power within her, the offspring of her transmuted love, longed in itself, beating down her own consciousness, for some discovery beyond where mightier power should answer it. She pressed on.

It was at the fourth step that Henry lost her. Still aware of the irony of their movement, still aware of himself as against her, and of both of them as against the mystery of paintings and images, he lost himself for less than a moment in a regret that things should have turned to this result. This was not what he had meant to be; his mind added that this was not what should have been, and almost before his reproach had grown from his pulse into his thought she was gone. His hands were empty; the cloud swirled about him, but he had now no companion. He took a single solitary step; then he ceased to move. He hesitated in the mist; the wind struck him as if it had swept the girl away and was minded to fling him into ruin. He pressed back and fought against it, but not for his own sake then so much as for hers. It pressed him, not in sudden blasts, but with a steady force, so that he could, by leaning against it, just maintain himself. As if he were still on the terrace fighting the storm, he set himself against this oppression, as if indeed all that had chanced since had never been, but for one unrealized change. On the terrace his danger and hers had been known to him with equal urgency. But in fact, since then much had happened. His own schemes had been scattered; her love for him, her love for something greater than him, had shone in his darkness; her laughter had stirred it, her voice had called him from it. Following her, he had come so far; he filled his mind now with desire for her salvation. Let himself go, let the world perish, so only that she walked safely among the perils of this supernatural world. He had mocked at her fear, and now fear for her was in his heart. The mist was in his throat and nostrils; he was choking in it. His eyes were blind, his head swam, in that terrible golden cloud. But, more than that, he knew chiefly that her hands were gone, and that she also was alone.

It was then that the hands took him. At first he did not realize, he did not even notice, what was happening. Filled with a sense of Nancy's possible danger, himself choking and groping in that intolerable shining cloud, and fighting all the time to keep securely upright in the persistent wind, he hardly felt the light clasp that took hold of one ankle. But as he began to move his foot he found it fixed, and fixed by what felt like a hand. He looked hastily down; nothing could be seen through the floating gold. He tried to pull his foot up from the ground; he could not do it. On the point of bending to free his ankle, he hesitated; the mist was so thick down there. He jerked it sharply; the grasp of whatever held it grew tighter, and something slid round the other ankle and held fast. Certainly they were hands; he felt the fingers and thumbs. On the realization he stood still; against these adversaries it was no use battling like a frightened child. Perhaps if something hostile indeed lived in this world he could overcome it—so long as his will held. But what was his will to do?

His feet were being drawn together. He set his will against it, but compulsion moved them. He swept an arm round him, and as it came to his rear his wrist also was seized, and the arm was drawn against his back and held there. The grasp was not harsh, it was even gentle, but it was absolute. It, or another like it, caught his other wrist and drew that also back. The wind ceased; it might have been blowing merely to delay him until the imprisonment was complete.

For what seemed hours nothing more happened, only he was held. His strong and angry imagination strove in vain to find some method of release, and miserably failed. There came to him out of the mist, which had receded a little from him, the sound of music, now increasing, now diminishing, as if something went past him and again returned. He could, once or twice, have believed that he heard voices calling, but they also died away. A faint light shone at intervals; the mist shook as if trembling with a quick passage. But more than these hints of existences he could not catch. He stood there, seeing nothing else. His heart began to faint; this perhaps was the end. Motionless in the place of the Tarots, as motionless as the Fool that stood in the centre—he himself, indeed, a fool of the Tarots. And Nancy—was she also held—her young delight, her immortal courage, her desire for love, in this unchanging golden mist? "If we are divided, remember that I always wanted to love." There was nothing here to love but himself—if indeed he wanted to love.

The hours grew into days, into years. Imperceptibly the grasp had tightened; that round his ankles had drawn them together, and that also round his wrists. He was still incapable of movement, but his incapacity was more closely constrained; he was forced more tightly into the mere straight shape of his enclosed body, for the mist closed again round him and moulded itself to his form. He was defined as himself, a bas-relief of him was shaped on that cloud, now almost plastic in its consistence; he could breathe and that was all. His thoughts began to fail within him; he was aware only of his senses, and they were now limited to the sight and feel of the mist. If it had not been for the slight tingling everywhere which the golden vagueness seemed to cause as it pressed on him, and the strong grasp upon his limbs, he would not have been conscious

166

of anything at all—there would have been nothing of which to be conscious. He could no longer even strive to free himself, for the very idea of freedom was passing from him. There was no freedom for there was no knowledge; he was separated from all that he had been, except that dimly, within or without, in that aeonian solitude, there occasionally loomed something of a memory of one or other of the Greater Trumps of the Tarots. Somewhere, very vaguely, he would think that he saw in front of him, fashioned of the mist, yet thrown up against the mist, the hierophantic Woman or the Lovers, or the great Tower which reached almost out of sight, so loftily it grew up and then always—just as his dimmed eyes strained to see the rising walls—tottered and swayed and began in a horrible silence to fall apart, but never quite apart. It was raised by hands which, from within the rising walls, came climbing over, building themselves into a tower, thrusting those below them into place, fists hammering them down, so that the whole Tower was made up of layers of hands. But as it grew upward they changed; masonry below, thinner levels of masonry above, and, still above, masonry changing into hands, a few levels of moving hands, and (topmost of all) the busy working fists and fingers. And then a sudden spark of sunlight would fall on it from above and the fists would fall back out of sight, and the hands would disjoin, swiftly but reluctantly, holding on to each other till the ruin tore them apart, and the apparent masonry, as it was rent by some invisible force, would again change back into clutching and separating hands. They clung together fantastically; they shivered and writhed to avoid some principle of destruction that lurked within them, and as he felt that ugly living twist and evasion they would altogether fade back into the mist from which they grew. The years went by, and every now and then, once in every four or five, the Tower was again shown, and each time it was a little closer than before.

The years grew into centuries. He was no longer looking at

anything; sight also had departed. Very slowly the Tower had moved right up against him; he could see it no more, for he was one with it. A quiver began at the bottom of his spine, spreading through his loins, and then it ceased, and he felt rigidity within him—up, up, till he was petrified from loins to head, himself a tower of stone. Even so, he meant to do something, to lift a great marble arm and reach up and pick the stars from heaven and tangle them into a crown—a hard sharp golden crown—for a head such as Nimrod's, perhaps his own. He was setting up a gigantic image of himself for heaven and earth to adore. He was strong and great enough to do what no man had done before, and to stand on the top of some high place which would be stable among the circling lights of the celestial world. And then always, just as he felt his will becoming fixed and strong enough to raise his arm and break the clasp of those cold hands, just as he dreamed of the premonitory prick of the starry spikes upon his head, something within him began to fall. He trembled with giddiness; he would have swayed but could not. There ran a downward rippling through his flesh; his lower jaw dropped; his knees shook; his loins quivered; he was dragged at from within in every direction; he was on the edge of being torn into destruction. Then again slowly he was steadied, and again his long petrifaction proceeded, and so through cycle after cycle of years the making and breaking of his will went on, and slowly after many repetitions his heart failed within him and he assented to the impossibility of success. The stars were beyond his reach; Babel was for ever doomed to fall—at the last minute, when the plains of heaven lay but a few yards beyond its rising structure, confusion invaded it, and spread, and the incoherent workers fled, and the elements of the world roared out each upon its own passage, and came together again in wars and tumults, conflicts and catastrophes. But now, each time that he felt the dreadful ruin go falling through him, he heard also one voice rising among that strange and shattering chorus and saying: "Remember I wanted to love." Out of each overthrow it sounded, and at every overthrow more clearly. This alone of all his past was urgent; this alone had meaning in the void to which his purpose crashed.

It came more quickly; it was repeated again and again; it grew shorter, words dropping away from it. The centuries ended; a quicker rush of years began; vehemently the call reached him, and as he strove to answer it with some single willingness of intention, the hands of the supernatural powers released their hold. He moved and stumbled; times rushed round him; something brushed against his legs; the mist swirled and broke, and as he stepped uncertainly forward he found himself looking into the face of Joanna, and then the golden cloud again swept between them, and parted once more the two most passionate seekers of the Tarots.

Chapter Thirteen

THE CHAPTER OF THE GOING FORTH
BY NIGHT

M r. Coningsby had been lying in bed for some time,
but he was not asleep. He was restless; his mind was
restless. It was all very well, this going to bed, this
being put to bed in case he got a bad cold, but—but—he had
a continual vision of Sybil before his eyes. Sybil, he had rather
dimly gathered, wasn't in bed, and wasn't in the least pro-
posing to go: and if she was up, why was he where he was? Of
course, it showed a very nice spirit, no more than he would
have expected of the old man, who didn't seem to know anything about Henry's indescribable fatuous insolence in hoping,
in rather more than hoping, even expecting, or something like
it, that he should be given a set of cards which were part of
the only memory he himself possessed of an old and dear
friend, a friendship the value of which a young pigeon-stealer
like Henry couldn't possibly know; gipsies never made friends,
or only of their own kind, vagrants and beggars, the kind of
person Nancy had never met—though certainly the grandfather seemed different: probably the mother—the daughter—
had run away, only the name was identical, so it must have
been the father, but they the family would be the same—
however, Aaron Lee was a very different kind of creature, and
had behaved very properly. Still, though in the first shock of
getting back he had allowed himself to be looked after and
waited on and almost cosseted—still, the fact remained that
after an hour or so of solitude he didn't like the idea. He wasn't
so old that he couldn't be out in a snowstorm and laugh at it.

The Chapter of the Going Forth by Night

He did a kind of mocking laugh at the blizzard swirling about the curtained windows, to which the blizzard responded by making such a frantic attack on the house that Mr. Coningsby unintentionally abandoned his laughter and looked uneasily at the curtains. If the infernal thing broke the glass and burst in, a nice sight he'd look, dancing round the room and trying to get dressed in a hurry. He had a momentary glimpse of himself feeling for a stud on a snowy dressing-table and trying to fix a tie which continually, "torn but flying", streamed away upon the wind. Really, there was a lot to be said for getting up. Besides, Sybil was up, and Sybil wasn't a girl any longer, and, though he'd been out in the storm longer than she had, yet he was a man and he had been rather underlining his own active habits, in an only half-conscious comparison of himself with the rest. Aaron, Sybil—he supposed Nancy and Henry were up too—while he was tucked up with a hot-water bottle. A hot-water bottle! That was all that the young thought their parents wanted. "And when," thought Mr. Coningsby, led on by the metaphor, "when they get into hot water, with their jumpings and their jazzings, and their nigger-minstrels and their night-clubs, who do they go to to get them out? To the old fellow tucked up with the bottle." Nothing less likely than any appeal in a crisis by Nancy or Ralph to their father could well have been imagined, but that actual division was hidden from him in his view of the sentimental. They were all up—dining probably. No one so far had brought him any dinner: however, perhaps they weren't dining yet. "I'm a fair-minded man," Mr. Coningsby thought; "I dare say dinner's a bit late. So much the better. I shall get up. If my sister can be about, so can I."

The feeling under the last sentence was, in fact, not so simple as it seemed—and he knew it. There floated in his mind, though he avoided it, a horrible wonder whether in effect he had really saved Sybil quite as much as he thought. Lothair Coningsby was in many things fantastic, but he was not merely stupid. He never insisted on seeing facts wrongly, though he did a busy best to persuade the facts to arrange themselves according to his personal preference. But sometimes a fact refused—Nancy's arrangement with Henry, Ralph's determined departure for Christmas—and then there was nothing to do but to condole with himself over it or to look at it and send it away. The afternoon's experience had been a fact of such a kind. He had meant to be saving Sybil, he had thought he was saving her, he had been very anxious about her, but now, in his warm comfort of repose, he couldn't help seeing that she had been very active about it all; her voice had been very fresh, and she had . . . she certainly had . . . been gently singing to herself while they waited for the door to open. He himself had not been singing, but then he didn't generally sing; he believed in opening his mouth at the proper times, and outside a shut door in a howling snowstorm wasn't one of them. She'd come out to meet him—yes, of course; but which of them—O, good heavens, *which* of them—had really been thankful for the other's presence? Perhaps it didn't matter; perhaps they'd both been thankful? Reciprocal help. Sybil rather believed in reciprocity, so that all was right. So did he, only, in the way the world went, he always seemed having to be more reciprocal than anybody else. But this afternoon?

This was becoming intolerable. The wind banged at the window again and startled him into decision. He would get up. It was Christmas Day—by heaven, so it was! He had never spent Christmas evening in bed. He always took a good-natured part in any fun that there was. Fun perhaps was too much to expect in this house, but there'd be talk, no doubt, and perhaps—Aaron had hinted as much—a rather unusual wine; perhaps a little music or what not. Anyhow, what not or no what not, he wasn't going to lie here like an abandoned log while the other logs were . . . well, were downstairs. Sybil should see that if she had helped him, it was only momentary:

and if he'd helped her, then it was silly for her to be up and him not. And then, if the storm did burst his window, he'd be able to move to another room more easily. So any way and every way it was better to get up. Especially as everyone seemed to have forgotten him: his host, Henry, Nancy, Sybil— everyone. Well, he would go down: he wouldn't complain, but if anyone expressed surprise he might just say a word—"O, well, lying by oneself——"; "Unless one's really ill, one likes to see something of people——"; perhaps, even better, "I thought I'd rather be among you," with just the faintest stress on the "among you"—not enough for them to treat him as an invalid, but just enough to cause a flicker of regret in Sybil's and perhaps Aaron's heart; he didn't much expect to cause even a flicker in Nancy's, and he rather hoped that Henry would be a little annoyed.

While he was dressing, he went on trying over various words to say. Every now and then the English language appeared to Mr. Coningsby almost incapable of expressing his more delicate shades of emotion. But then life—getting other people to understand exactly what you meant and wanted and thought and felt—was a very complex business, and, as he never wanted to push himself on others, he was usually satisfied if he could lightly indicate what he was feeling. One mustn't be selfish— especially on Christmas Day. He abandoned a plaintive, "I thought perhaps you wouldn't *mind* me coming down," in favour of a jocund, "Ha, ha! Well, you see, I didn't need much putting right. Ah, Sybil, you . . . your . . . you don't . . ." Rather peevishly he gave that up. He simply could not think of anything at all jocund to say to Sybil. He finished dressing and went to the door. His hand on it, he switched off the light, opened it, and stepped out. His room was near the top of the staircase, next to Aaron's bedroom. The corridor into which he came ran to his right and left, at each end turning into a short concluding corridor. In the extreme corner to his right was the door of Aaron's study, within which lay that curious inner room, exposed to the wind on almost all sides, where were the absurd little marionettes. He had been rather pleased when he used the word to Henry, and it recurred to him as he stared towards it. For, much to his surprise, he saw a small procession going stealthily along the corridor. It had only just passed his door when he opened it, quietly, as it happened, and had not heard him. Indeed, the tall young masculine back at which he found himself gazing was what had startled him. It wasn't Henry; it wasn't anybody's that he knew. It was wearing a chauffeur's outdoor coat, but as its arms stuck inches out beyond the sleeves and its neck rose high and thick over the collar it probably wasn't the chauffeur. Besides the chauffeur wouldn't be wandering about like that in his master's house. Mr. Coningsby's eyes passed it as he wondered, and lit on someone whom he vividly remembered. There, her eyes on the ground, a blanket clutched round her—"extraordinary dress!" the astonished and already indignant visitor thought—was the old madwoman they had encountered on their journey down. O, it was she undoubtedly: the tangled white hair brought that other evening back in full recognition, and the bent form, and the clutching hand holding the blanket round its neck. She was following something; her head was thrust forward and downwards. Mr. Coningsby instinctively leaned sideways and craned to see what it was, and saw, a yard or so in front of her, a kitten. He stared blankly, as the curious train went on—first the kitten, going gently, pausing now and then with a sudden kittenish crouch, then getting up and going on again, its head turning from side to side; and after it the old woman, with that amazing blanket; and after her the young man in the coat three sizes and more too small for him. Mr. Coningsby's flesh crept at the mere sight of them. Why a kitten? why should even a mad old hag go so softly and carefully after a kitten? Perhaps it was her kitten and she was trying to catch it; she wasn't hurrying it or hurrying after it; if it stopped, she stopped; when it went on, she went on. And so with the third member of the procession, who copied her in all things—moving or staying as she did. It was uncanny; it was rather horrible. His hand still on the door-handle, Mr. Coningsby for a few moments stood gaping after them.

Aaron presumably knew about it—but did he? This wretched woman had seemed to dislike Aaron; supposing he didn't know! It didn't seem very likely he'd let her meander round the house in a blanket after a kitten, nor a young ruffian covered only by a coat that didn't fit him—not anyhow with Nancy and Sybil about. Sybil, it was true, had seemed to get on with them remarkably well, but even so. . . . Suppose Nancy had met them . . . what on earth would a—for all her faults—ordinary nice young girl do? Suppose the old devil dropped the blanket by accident—or purposely? Mr. Coningsby revolted at the idea—revolted against the whole mad fact. He let go of the handle and said in a surprisingly firm voice, "Hallo, there!"

No one took the smallest notice of him. By now he couldn't see the kitten, but the procession was nearing the end of the corridor. At least he ought to see where they went. It was possible that they'd been having baths or something, like himself—no, not like himself. The notion that he and the old woman had shared a bath, that they could have anything at all in common—even the very idea of a bath—was extraordinarily offensive. Besides, the kitten? The kitten might, from the way it was going, have been a maid showing a visitor to her room, but of course it wasn't. Unless it was a new kind of marionette. If any kitten started to show him to his room —— Well, he was going after them, he was going to make quite certain that they didn't run into Nancy. It'd be enough to give her a shock. And he wasn't going to have Sybil kneeling down as if she were in church; she'd been to church once to-day already. Blessing, indeed! Mr. Coningsby went down the corridor after the others with a firm determination to allow no sort of blessing whatever within any reasonable distance of him while he was alive and sane. Except, of course, in a church.

They were outside the door of Aaron's study; he heard the kitten mewing at it. Joanna—if that was her name—opened it. Mr. Coningsby called out again, quite loudly this time, "Hallo, you there!" But the "you there" took no notice; they were going in. Mr. Coningsby broke into a run and then checked—after all, his host *might* have given Joanna the use of the room. He considered the possibility and rejected it; Aaron had apparently had a quite different view of Joanna. No, there was some hanky-panky about.

An awful thought for a moment occurred to him that she might be merely going to let the kitten out into the garden or somewhere; people did let kittens out into gardens, and a nice fool he'd look if that were so. But surely on a night like this— and anyhow not on the first floor—and not into a study. He became shocked at himself; he was almost vulgar. Very much more angry, he reached the study door.

The others, including the kitten, were inside. As Mr. Coningsby came into the room he heard the mewing again, plaintive and insistent; he saw the little beast on its hind legs against the inner door—not that it was so little; it struck him that it was within an inch or so of being a proper cat, and the noise it was making was much louder than feline infancy produces. Joanna was almost beside it, but she had had to go round Aaron's great table while the cat had dashed below it. And a little behind her, just turning the table-corner, was Stephen. Mr. Coningsby remembered that behind that other door were the images of gold. Those were what she was after, of course—gipsies—golden statues—theft. He said loudly, "Now then, now then, what are you doing there?"

She stopped, for this time she heard him, and looked over at him. Her eyes blinked at him from the tanned wrinkled old face under the matted hair, over the blanket fastened together (he now saw) by a strap round her. She said, "Keep away; you're too late."

The Chapter of the Going Forth by Night

"I fancy you'll find I'm just in time," Mr. Coningsby answered, and walked into the room, going round the table on the opposite side to Stephen. "Does Mr. Lee know you're here?"

She chuckled unpleasantly, then nodded at him. "He'll know," she said, "he'll soon know. Wait till I bring him out."

"Out?" Mr. Coningsby said. "What do you mean—out?"

She pointed to the door, and her voice sank to a whisper as she said, "What he has *there*."

"What he has there", Mr. Coningsby said, "is his business. I thought that was what you were after, and it's a good thing for you I happened to be about. I suppose you were going to rob him? Well, you won't this time. Now you get away, and take your damned kitten with you—if it is yours."

She clutched the handle of the door and began to speak, but Mr. Coningsby, in the full tide of satisfaction, swept on.

"Leave go of that door. Come on; we'll go downstairs together. A nice piece of work, upon my word! You ought to know better, at your age."

The cat yowled at the door. Joanna glowered, and then said, "You—*you'll* stop me finding my baby?"

"Your what?" Mr. Coningsby exclaimed. "O, don't be silly; there's no baby there. There's only a set of marionettes— pretty things, but nothing like a baby. And don't try and put me off with that kind of talk. Get you away."

"Ah! ah!" the old creature cried out with extraordinary force, "you're one of them, you're one of the sons of Set."

The cat yowled louder than ever. For a moment Mr. Coningsby felt strangely alone, as the sound went through the room, and he heard and saw the claws tearing at the door. He thought of that continuous movement behind it; he saw the straining beast and the snarling woman; he saw the dull face of the idiot behind her; he heard the noise of the storm without —and he wished very much that someone else was by his side. There was something wrong about the images, the house, the very wind; cat and storm howled together, and the old woman suddenly shrieked, "He's over you, he's over you. Get away before he strikes. All his enemies are close to death. The cats are up; the god's coming."

"Nothing is over me," Mr. Coningsby said in a voice that became high and shrill in spite of himself. "Let that door alone."

"It isn't you that'll stop it," she screeched back, "nor a million like you. They'll take you and cut you in a thousand pieces, they'll embalm you alive in the pyramids of hell, they'll drown you among the crocodiles that are tearing your father, they'll flay you with the burning knives of Anubis, and your heart shall be eaten in the place of justice." She turned towards the door and turned the handle. Mr. Coningsby was on her in a moment, pressing it shut, and incidentally kicking the cat away. As he jumped he almost wished that he'd left her alone; it was all horrible, and he loathed the old voice screaming curses at him. It was of course absolute nonsense, but some minute atom of his mind dragged on the words "embalmed alive". Embalmed alive—he of all people!

"No, you don't!" he said. "Leave the door alone. Ah! ow!"

The cat had leapt back at him and was madly clawing at his legs. Mr. Coningsby kicked at it and missed. It hung on to his trousers, then it fell off and flung itself at his ankles. It was in a state of raging lunacy, almost as wild as Joanna, who dropped the blanket so that it fell back from her shoulders, and herself clutched at him with clawing fingers. Mr. Coningsby avoided her, kicked again at the cat, and desperately held on to the door. But he was suddenly torn from it. Joanna, as she clawed at his throat, had shrieked out a call to her companion, and Stephen, leaping past her, caught Coningsby round the waist, and with a great heave wrenched him away from the door and held him high in the air. Head and feet downwards, he hung, jerking, kicking, choking out anathemas.

"What shall I do with him, grandmother?" Stephen said. "Shall I throw him out into the storm?"

The Chapter of the Going Forth by Night

The old woman turned her eyes to the window, but, alert in hatred, saw that it was too small; to push a struggling full-sized body through it would not easily be done even by Stephen. "Throw him there," she said, pointing across the room, and at once Stephen obeyed. Mr. Coningsby was sent hurtling through the air into the extreme corner of the room, where he hit the walls first and then crashed to the floor. By mere chance his head escaped; he fell bruised, shocked, and dazed, but still in some sort of consciousness. For one fratricidal second fear and pride warred in his heart, and pride won. He lay for some minutes where he had been flung, till rage so bubbled in him that he began painfully to wriggle over, obstinately determined to see what those creatures were doing. He could not see, for the inner door was open and they had disappeared. They were busy then—he had been right—about the golden images; robbery—robbery with violence. A long, long, long sentence for Stephen, and Joanna—Mr. Coningsby's professional knowledge supplied him with a clear view of Joanna's future. But that couldn't happen if they got away, and unless he did something they might get away. He was too confused by his fall to think of the extreme unlikelihood of Joanna's going out into the storm clothed only in a blanket, and carrying in a fold of it a collection of little golden figures; had he thought of it he would have believed Joanna capable of it, and perhaps he would have been right. For when she stood on the threshold of that inner room and peered into the cloud that filled it, when she beheld the rich mystery that enveloped the symbols of our origins, she had cried out once upon the name of the god, and from that moment she lost touch with the actualities of this world. She pressed on: Stephen behind her, made violent movements and noises as if to hold her back, but over her shoulder she turned on him a face of such destructive malignity that he shrank back, and crouched defensively down by the door, only whispering from there, "Don't go, don't go."

The Chapter of the Going Forth by Night

All this was hidden from Mr. Coningsby, who, with a growing determination to stop it, was getting, slowly and gruntingly,
to his feet. "Fortunate," he thought as he did so, "fortunate I
brought my other glasses with me! Losing one pair in the
storm—shouldn't have seen anything of this—didn't someone
say Ralph had called? Get hold of Ralph—not always thought-
ful—couldn't stand seeing his father thrown about the room,
like a . . . like a *quoit*. Just as well he didn't see—soon settle
this nonsense. Ugh! What's that?"

As he came finally to his feet, and adjusted the extra pair
of glasses, the gold chain of which had kept them attached if
not in position, he saw the first wraiths of mist faintly exuding
from the inner room. "What the devil is it?" he thought, staring. " 'Tisn't snow; 'tisn't smoke . . . or is it? Has that infernal
old woman set the place on fire?" He went forward a little,
keeping the big table between himself and the other door, just
in case Joanna and Stephen dashed out at him again, and then
he saw the whole doorway filling with it. He had an impression
that there were a great many people before his eyes, a crowd
of them, just there in the doorway, but that could hardly be
so, unless of course other wanderers had taken refuge in this
house from the storm, but then they wouldn't be here, they'd
be in the kitchen or somewhere. It wasn't people; it was mist
or smoke or something. He remembered suddenly that such
a faint vapour had seemed to enwrap Nancy and the table
when she had her fortune told, but he hadn't taken much
notice, because he had then been, as ostentatiously as possible,
looking another way. If the old woman was asking about *her*
fortune, Mr. Coningsby felt he could tell her exactly what it
would be, only she wasn't there to be told. Nothing was there
but the cloud and . . . again . . . an indefinable sensation of
lots of people, all moving and turning.

"It's those damned figures," Mr. Coningsby thought. "I
expect they shake everything, all that gyrating nonsense.
Good God, it's getting thicker." He turned, ran through the

outer door, and shouted as loudly as he could, "Fire! Fire!"

As he opened his mouth for the third shout, he stopped on the "F——" For there came from below a sudden crash, a crash that was answered from different parts of the house by a noise of smashing and splintering, and then the wind was howling louder and nearer than before. "Great Christ!" Mr. Coningsby cried out, in mere ingenuity of perplexed anxiety, "what the devil's that?" He had guessed even as he spoke; the doors and windows were giving way before the blizzard. "The snow's getting in and the fire's getting out," he thought, distractedly staring back over his shoulder. "O, my Father in heaven, what a Christmas!"

Downstairs, Aaron and Ralph were still gazing at one another in the dining-room when the crash came. At the noise of it they both exclaimed, but Ralph was the first in the hall. He saw there how the front door had given way under the tireless assaults of the storm, which, as if imbued with a conscious knowledge of its aim, had been driving like a battering-ram at the house since the return of Sybil and her brother. It might have been pursuing and hunting him down; the loosened leaves of invocation might have been infused—beyond any intention—with Henry's purpose, and the vague shapes whom Lothair Coningsby had thought he saw in the snow-swept roads might have been hammering with a more terrible intensity at the door which had closed behind him. At last those crashing buffets had torn lock and bolt from the doorpost; the door was flung back, and the invading masses of snow and wind swept in. The floor of the hall was covered before anyone could speak; the wind—if it were not rather the dance of searching shapes—swept into every corner. A picture or two on the walls were torn off and flung down lest they concealed the fugitive; tables were tossed about; an umbrella-stand was kicked to the extreme end of the hall. A howl of disappointment went up, and the snow drove over the first few stairs, as if the pursuit was determined never to stop until its prey had been discovered.

The Chapter of the Going Forth by Night

Ralph gaped for a moment, then plunged for the door. "Come on!" he yelled. "Call everyone! Come and shut it." He pulled it a little forward and was thrown back again along with it. "Come on!" he cried stentorianly to Aaron. "No time to waste! Call the others!"

But Aaron was stupefied. The comfortable reassurances in which he had clothed himself were torn away by the same giant hands that were wrecking his house. This was no unexpected winter storm, but supernaturally contrived death, and, whatever scope it had, this place was its centre. If it were to sweep, eschatological and ultimate, over the world, that destruction was but an accident. The elementals, summoned from their symbols, were still half-obedient to the will that had called them. His brain called to him to give him their desire, to take the stranger and throw him out beyond the threshold, that he might there be beaten and stunned and crushed and stifled and buried, a sacrifice now not to magical knowledge but to the very hope of life. And again his brain answered and told him that he could not, that the storm itself had brought to the stranger a friend and to himself two enemies. There was no one in the house but Henry who would do his bidding, and even if Henry could be found in the darkness where he had hidden himself, what could he and Henry do against Coningsby and his son? A more sinister thought leapt in his mind—what if Henry himself could be made the offering? might not these raging powers be satisfied with the body of the sorcerer who had invoked them? might not Coningsby and his son and he himself manage to make that offering? At least then Aaron Lee would be alive, and now nothing in the whole universe mattered but the safety of Aaron Lee. He looked wildly round, and then Ralph left the door and ran back to him, seizing his arm, and crying, "Call someone! We've got to shut the door and barricade it—then the windows! Hallo, everybody! *Hallo!* Come here! you're wanted! *Come—here— everyone!*"

The Chapter of the Going Forth by Night

The servants—which meant two maids and the cook—had come already, bursting into the hall from their own quarters, and screaming that the back doors were broken down. One of the maids was hysterical with the continued roar of the blizzard, and was screaming and howling continuously. The other, almost equally alarmed, was quieter, and it was on her that Ralph fixed.

"Hallo!" he said, "come along! Look here, we've got to try and get the door held. We'll get a good big table and barge it to with that behind it, and someone else can get some rope or something. The dining-room table's best, don't you think? It's the biggest thing I've seen." He had her by the arm and was rushing her to the dining-room. "O lor', won't anything keep that gramophoning misery behind us quiet? No, don't go back, for God's sake. Here—now smash everything off it— that's right! O, don't stop to pick them up, girl—what's your name? what? Amabel?—all right, Amabel, just pitch them off, so! Now this way—that's it! careful! careful! blast that leg!— sideways, I think—so; yes, so—gently; don't get flustered. Hark at the polish!" as the table-top screeched against the doorpost. They tottered out with it.

"Can I help, Ralph?" his aunt's voice said behind him. Sybil had been half-upstairs when the door had given way, and she had come quickly back to the hall, but her arrival had been unnoticed in the feminine rush that had preceded it.

"Hallo!" said Ralph breathlessly, as they fought to get the table long side on to the storm; it was only the accident of a recess that had enabled them to get it out of the dining-room at all, and at the moment it was being driven steadily towards the stairs, with Ralph and Amabel holding on to it at each end, like the two victims who were dragged prisoners to the power of Set in the Tarot paintings. Sybil caught Amabel's end, and her extra weight brought the other round; Ralph was suddenly spun round in a quarter of a circle, and then they were all pushing towards the door. Ralph, over his shoulder, yelled at Aaron, the cook, and the hysterical maid, "Cord! Miles of cord!"

"Wouldn't it be easier to close the door first, Ralph?" Sybil said, looking back at him.

"Be *better*," Ralph said, "but easier? You try it."

Sybil looked at Amabel. "Can you hold it?" she said. "I think if we shut the wind out first . . ." She let go of the table, went down the hall, took hold of the door, and pushed it gradually shut. "There," she said, "that's what I meant. Don't you think that's simpler, Ralph?"

"Much," said Ralph, a little astonished either at his aunt's suggestion or at her expert dealing with the door, he wasn't sure which: but he assumed there must have been a momentary lull. He and Amabel rushed the heavy table up, and were just setting it with its broad top against the door as Ralph said, "Now we've only got to fix——" when another voice joined in. From high above them—"Fire!" called Mr. Coningsby. "Fire!"

The hall broke into chaos. Amabel, startled, let go her end of the table, which crashed to the ground only an inch from Sybil's foot. The hysterical maid broke into a noise like a whole zoological garden at once. The cook, who had been going steadily, and rather heavily, towards the stairs, stopped, turned to Aaron, and said, "Mr. Lee, sir, did you hear that?" Aaron ran to the stairs, and, checking at the bottom, cried out some incoherent question. Ralph said, in a penetrating shout: "What? What?" then in a much quieter voice he added, "Well, if it's fire, it's not much use barricading the door, is it? Look here, let's wedge it with that chair just for a moment till——"

"Fire!" Mr. Coningsby called out again.

"Go and see, Ralph," Sybil said. "It may be a mistake."

"Probably is," Ralph answered. "Right ho, but let's just push that chair in here. Amabel bright-eyes, give it over here, will you? and then go and smother that fog-horn. There, so; another shove, aunt; so!"

Somehow the table and the heavy hall chair were wedged

across the door. Ralph, letting go, looked at his barricade doubtfully. "It won't hold for more than a second," he said, "but—I'll pop up and see what's biting him now. If there's really anything, I'll tell you."

He shot off, and, overtaking Aaron half up the stairs, arrived with him on the landing where his father was restlessly awaiting them.

"It's that old woman," Mr. Coningsby broke out at once to Aaron. "She's got into your private room, where the marionettes are, and there's a lot of smoke coming out. I don't suppose she's done much damage yet, but you'd better stop her. Come on, Ralph my boy, we may need you; there's a nasty violent ruffian with her, and I'm not strong enough to tackle him alone."

As they ran down the corridor, Ralph heard another splintering crash from one of the rooms. "Window!" he thought. "This is looking nasty! Lord send it isn't a fire! Eh?"

The last syllable was a bewildered question. They had reached the door of Aaron's room, and there the strange apparition billowed—the golden mist swirled and surged before them. Its movement was not rapid, but it had already completely hidden from their sight the opposite wall, with its inner door, and was rolling gently over the large writing-table. It was exquisitely beautiful, and, though Ralph's first thought was that it certainly wasn't smoke, he couldn't think what it really was. He gaped at it; then he heard Aaron at his side give a piteous little squeal of despair. His father at the same time said, "I can't think why she doesn't come *out*. It's such a funny colour."

"Well," Ralph said, "no good staring at it, is it? Look here, this is more important than the door; we'd better have a line of people to the—damn it, father, it can't be *smoke!*"

Mr. Coningsby only said, "Then what is it?"

"Well, if she's inside," Ralph exclaimed, "I'm going in too. Look here, Mr. Lee . . ."

The Chapter of the Going Forth by Night

But Aaron was past speech or attention. He was staring in a paralysed horror, giving little moans, and occasionally putting up his hands as if to ward off the approaching cloud. From within and from without the dangers surrounded him, and Henry was nowhere about, and he was alone. Within that cloud was Joanna—Joanna alone with the golden images of the dance, Joanna who thought he had kept them from her, who knew herself for the Mother of a mystical vengeance, who went calling day and night on her Divine Son to restore the unity of the god. What was happening? what was coming on him? what threat and fulfilment of threat was at hand?

Ralph thought, "The poor old chap's thoroughly upset; no wonder—it's a hectic day," and went forward, turning to go round the table.

"Take care, my boy," Mr. Coningsby said. "I'll come with you—I don't think it can be fire. Only then—— What's the matter?"

Ralph, with an expression of increasing amazement, was moving his arms and legs about in front of the mist, rather as if he were posturing for a dance in front of a mirror. He said in a puzzled tone, "I can't get through. It's too thick."

"Don't be absurd," his father said. "It's quite obviously not *thick*. It's hardly more than a thin veil—of sorts." He added the last two words because, as the rolling wonder approached them, it seemed here and there to open into vast depths of itself. Abysses and mountainous heights revealed themselves— masses of clouds were sweeping up. "Veil" perhaps was hardly the word.

Ralph was being driven back before it; he tried to force his hand through it, and he seemed to be feeling a thick treacle— only it wasn't sticky. It wasn't unpleasant; only it was unpierceable. He gave way a step or two more. "Damned if I understand it," he said.

Mr. Coningsby put up his own hand rather gingerly. He stretched it out—farther; it seemed to touch the mist, but he felt nothing. Farther; he couldn't see his hand or his wrist, still he felt something. Farther, something that felt exactly like another hand took hold of his lightly. He exclaimed, jerked his hand away, and sprang back. "What was that?" he said sharply.

Aaron was watching with growing horror the steady approach of the mist. But it was not merely the approach that troubled him; it was the change in it. The cloud was taking on form— he could not at first distinguish what the form was, and then at one point he suddenly realized he was looking at a moving hand, blocked out of the golden mist, working at something. It was the size of an ordinary man's hand, and then, while he looked, he missed it somehow, as a stain on a wall will be one minute a cat's head and the next but an irregular mark. But as he lifted his eyes he saw another—more like a slender woman's hand—from the wrist grasping upward at . . . at yet another hand that reached downward to it; and then those joining fingers had twisted together and became yet a third that moved up and down as if hammering, and as it moved, was covered and hidden by the back of a fourth. His gaze swept the gathering cloud; everywhere it was made up of hands, whose shape was formed by it, and yet it was not the mist that formed them, for they were the mist. Everywhere those restless hands billowed forward; of all sizes, in all manner of movement, clasping, holding, striking, fighting, smoothing, climbing, thrusting out, drawing back, joining and disjoining, heaving upward, dragging down, appearing and disappearing, a curtain of activity falling over other activity, hands, and everywhere hands. Here and there the golden shimmer dulled into tints of ordinary flesh, then that was lost again, and the aureate splendour everywhere shone. The hands were working in the stuff, yet the stuff which they wrought was also hands, so that their purpose was foiled and thwarted and the workers became a part of that which was worked upon. Over and below and about the table the swelling and sinking curtain of mystery swept—if it were not rather through it, for it did not seem to divide or separate the movement, and the cloud seemed to break from it on the side nearest Aaron, just as it filled all the air around. The room was hidden behind it, nearer and nearer to the door it came, and the three were driven back before it.

Or, rather, Ralph and his father were. Aaron had not moved from the doorway, and now, as he understood the composition of that mist, he cried out in terror. "It's alive!" he shrieked, "it's alive! it's the living cloud! Run, run!" and himself turned and went pattering as fast as he could towards the stairs, sending out an agonized call to Henry as he fled. The cloud of the beginning of things was upon him; in a desperate effort to escape he rushed down the staircase towards the hall. But his limbs were failing him; he went down half a dozen steps and clung to the balustrade, pale, trembling, and overwhelmed.

Mr. Coningsby looked after him, looked back at the mist, which had now almost filled the room, retreated a little farther, and said to Ralph, with more doubt than usual in his voice, "Living cloud? D'you see anything living about it?"

"Damn sight too solid," Ralph said, "at least it's not quite that either—it's more like . . . mortar or thick custard or something. Where does it come from?"

On the point of answering, Mr. Coningsby was again distracted. There was a noise of scampering from within the mist, and out of it suddenly dashed the kitten, or cat, or whatever it was, which tore between them and half-way down the corridor, where it stopped abruptly, looked all round it, mewed wildly, tore back, and hurled itself into the cloud. Before either Mr. Coningsby or Ralph could utter a word, it shot out again more frenziedly than before, and this time rushed to the head of the stairs, where it broke into a fit of mad miauling, ran, jumped, or fell half down them past the step where Aaron clung, and in full sight of the front door crouched for the spring.

Sybil had been doing her best to soothe the hysterical maid, not without some result. Her back being to the stairs, she did not at first see what was happening there, though she heard—as everyone in the house did—the cries of Aaron and the yowling of the cat. She gave the maid a last word of tender encouragement, a last pat of heartening sympathy, and swung round. As she did so, the cat and Aaron both moved. The cat took one terrific leap from the stairs right across the hall, landed on Ralph's barricade, dropped on to the floor, slithered, snarled, and began scratching at the table. Aaron at the same time took another step or two down, slipped, lost his footing, and crashed down. Sybil ran to him. "O, my dear," she cried, but he answered her frantically, "My feet won't take me away. They won't let me escape."

"Are you hurt?" she asked, and would have helped him up, but he shook his head, moaning, "My ankle, my ankle." She kneeled to look at it, soothing him a little, even then, by the mere presence of unterrified and dominating serenity. Equanimity in her was not a compromise but a union, and the elements of that union, which existed separately in others, in her recognized themselves, and something other than themselves, which satisfied them. That round which her brother, exasperated and comforted at once, was always prowling; that to which Nancy had instinctively turned for instruction; that which Henry had seen towering afar over his own urgencies and desires—that made itself felt by Aaron now. In the same moment, by chance a silence fell in the house; the wind sank without, and all things seemed about to be ordered in calm. It was but for a moment. There was, for that second, peace; then again the cat howled by the door, and, as if in answer to the summons, the blizzard struck at it again, and the feeble barriers gave. The chair and table were tossed aside, the door was flung back, the snow poured again into the house, this time with double strength. It swept through the hall; it drove up the stairs; in its vanguard the cat also raced back. And from above, itself rushing forward with increased speed, the cloud of the mysteries drove down to meet it. The two powers intermingled—golden mist with wind and snow; the flakes were aureoled, the mist was whitened. Confusion filled the house; the mortal lives that moved in it were separated each from the rest, and each, blinded and stumbling, ran for what shelter, of whatever kind, it thought it could find. Voices sounded in cries of terror and despair and anger; and the yowling of the cat and the yelling of the storm overbore them; and another sound, the music of the room of the images—but now grown high and loud and passionate—dominated and united all. Dancing feet went by; golden hands were stretched out and withdrawn. The invasion of the Tarots was fulfilled.

Only Sybil, contemplating Aaron's swelling ankle, said, "I think, Mr. Lee, if you *could* manage to hobble up just these few stairs to a room somewhere, perhaps we could deal with it better."

Chapter Fourteen

THE MOON OF THE TAROTS

Nancy found herself alone. The mist round her was thinning; she could see a clear darkness beyond. She had known one pang when she felt Henry's hands slip from around hers; then she had concentrated her will more entirely on doing whatever might be done to save whatever had to be saved from the storm, which now she no longer heard. But the fantastic mission on which she was apparently moving did not weigh upon her; her heart kept its lightness. There had come into her life with the mystery of the Tarots a new sense of delighted amazement; the Tarots themselves were not more marvellous than the ordinary people she had so long unintelligently known. By the slightest vibration of the light in which she saw the world she saw it all differently; holy and beautiful, if sometimes perplexing and bewildering, went the figures of her knowledge. They were all "posters of the sea and land", and she too, in a dance that was happy if it was frightening. Nothing was certain, but everything was safe— that was part of the mystery of Love. She was upon a mission, but whether she succeeded or not didn't matter. Nothing mattered beyond the full moment in which she could live to her utmost in the power and according to the laws of the dance. The dance of the Tarots, the dance of her blood, the dance of her mind, and whatever other measure it was in which Sybil Coningsby trod so high and disposed a movement. Hers couldn't be that *yet*, couldn't ever perhaps, but she could understand and answer it. Her father, Henry, Ralph, they were all stepping their parts, and she also—now, now, as the last shreds of the golden mist faded, and, throbbing and glad, she came into the dark stillness which awaited her.

On the edge of it she paused. The room of the images had been vaguely in her expectation, but if that indeed were where she stood then she could see nothing of it. Complete and cool night was about her. She glanced down; her hands were empty of the cards, but lifted as if she were still holding them, and she was aware that her palms were gently throbbing and tingling. It was something like neuralgia—only it wasn't in the least like neuralgia. But if there could be a happy neuralgia, if some nerve could send to her brain the news of power and joy continually vibrant, then that was how her hands felt. It might so easily have been disagreeable, but it was not disagreeable; it was exquisite. Part of its very exquisiteness, indeed, was the knowledge that if this delight had been overstressed or uncontrolled then it would have been disagreeable. But the energy that thrilled there was exactly right; its tingling messages announced to her a state of easy health as the throbbing messages of diseased mankind proclaim so often a state of suffering. Joy itself was sensuous; she received its communication through the earth of which she was made.

She kept her hands very still, wondering at them. They had been so busy, with one thing and another, in the world, continually shaping something. What many objects had rested against those palms—chair-backs, cups, tennis-rackets, the hands of her friends, birds, books, bag-handles, umbrellas, clothes, bed-clothes, door-handles, ropes, straps, knives and forks, bowls, pictures, shoes, cushions—O, everything! and always she had had some purpose, her hands had been doing something, making something, that had never been before— not just so. They were always advancing on the void of the future, shaping her future. In Henry's—exchanging beauty and truth; in her father's—exchanging . . . the warm blood took her cheeks as she thought ashamedly of him. In Sybil's— not long since, receiving strength, imparting the tidings of her own feebleness. Full of the earth of the Tarots; holding on to Henry's to stay the winds and waters of the Tarots. She stretched them out to either side of her; what could she do now to redeem the misfortune that threatened? what in this moment were her hands meant to shape by the mystical power which was hidden in them? She remembered the old woman's hands waving above Sybil's head; she remembered the priest's hand that very morning raised for the ritual blessing; she remembered hands that she had seen in painting, the *Praying Hands* of Dürer, the hands of Christ on the cross or holding off Saint Mary in some drawing of the garden tryst, the hands of the Divine Mother lifting the Child, the small hand of the Child Himself raised in benediction; she remembered the stretched hand of the Emperor directing the tumults of the world; the hands of the Juggler who tossed the balls, the hand of the Fool as he summoned the last danger from its tomb, the lifted hands of the Juggler and of the Fool as they came together, before the rain of gold had hidden them that evening from her sight.

It was no doubt a thing to wonder at, the significant power of man's hands. She thought of the unknown philosopher who had wrought the Tarot images; his hands had been filled with spiritual knowledge; they perhaps had guided his mind as much as his mind his hands. What would the fortune-telling palmistry with which she had played have discovered in those passive and active palms? the centres of wisdom and energy, which had communicated elemental strength to the images and the paintings, so that other hands could release at their will earth and air and water and fire to go about the world? Release and direct. She stretched out her arms, instinctively passionate to control the storm which she believed, outside her present sense, to be raging over earth; and, as the back of her hands shone lucidly before her in the dark, she felt against them from beyond the first cold touches of the snow.

At the touch she became rigidly attentive. It was time then;

something was about to happen. The darkness round her was changing. She could see below her again a gleam of gold; at first she thought it was the base upon which the images had danced, but it was not that, it was not clear and definite enough. It was rather the golden mist, but it was shaken now by an intrusion of white flakes. The confusion was at first far below her, but presently it was rushing upward, and as it came nearer and became larger she realized that she was indeed still standing in the secret room, in the darkness that had once been curtains; below her expanded the wide open spaces of the Downs. They too were covered with snow, but the tumult was less, and unmingled with that other strange glow: they lay, a winter vision, such as she had seen before in fields or towns. She saw them, white and silent, and then there swept up from the turmoil in the house a giant figure, a dimly defined form waving a huge club from which the snow poured in a continuous torrent. It rose, rushing towards her, and she thrust out her hands towards it, and it struck its club against them— they felt the blow, the blast of an icy wind, and were numbed, but life tingled in them again at once, and the ghostly shape was turned from his course, and sent plunging back into the turmoil from which it came. Others rushed up after it; the invoked elementals were seeking a larger scope. From raging about and in the house they were bursting abroad over the Downs, over the world where men kept Christmas, one way or another, and did not know that everlasting destruction was near. Between that threat and its fulfilment stood the girl's slender figure, and the warm hands of humanity in hers met the invasion and turned it. They moved gently over the storm; they moved as if in dancing ritual they answered the dancing monstrosities that opposed them. It was not a struggle but a harmony, yet a harmony that might at any moment have become a chaos. The column of whirling shapes arose and struck, and were beaten abroad under the influence of those extended palms, and fell in other whirling column; and so the whole of the magical storm was sent pouring back into the place of its origin; and out on the Downs, over villages and roads, over the counties and cities of England, over rivers and mountains, there fell but the natural flakes of a snowy Christmas.

The carols of Christmas, wherever they were sung that night, were sung in ignorance of the salvation which endured among them, or in ignorance at least of the temporal salvation which the maiden-mother of Love preserved. But the snow ceased to fall as the night drew on, and before midnight the moon rode in a clear sky. Yet another moon shone over the house on the Downs, like that which was among the one and twenty illuminations of the Greater Trumps. For there, high between two towers, the moon shines, clear and perfect, and the towers are no longer Babels ever rising and falling, but complete in their degree. Below them again, on either side of a long and lonely road, two handless beasts—two dogs, or perhaps a wolf and a dog—sit howling, as if something which desired attainment but had not entered into the means of attainment cried out unprofitably to the gentle light disseminated from above; and again below, in the painting of mysterious depths, some other creature moves in the sea, in a coat of shell, clawed and armed, shut up in itself, but even itself crawling darkly towards a land which it does not comprehend. The sun is not yet risen, and if the Fool moves there he comes invisibly, or perhaps in widespread union with the light of the moon which is the reflection of the sun. But if the Tarots hold, as has been dreamed, the message which all things in all places and times have also been dreamed to hold, then perhaps there was meaning in the order as in the paintings; the tale of the cards being completed when the mystery of the sun has opened in the place of the moon, and after that the trumpets cry in the design which is called the Judgement, and the tombs are broken, and then in the last mystery of all the single figure of what is called the world goes joyously dancing in a state beyond moon and sun, and the number of the Trumps is done. Save only for that which has no number and is called the Fool, because mankind finds it folly till it is known. It is sovereign or it is nothing, and if it is nothing then man was born dead.

She stood above the world, and her outstretched and down-turned palms felt the shocks, and she laughed aloud to see the confusion of clubs striking upward and failing to break past the small shields that were defending the world from them. She laughed to feel the blows as once she had laughed and mocked at Henry when his fingers struck her palm; danger itself was turned into some delight of love. As if her laughter were a spiritual sword, the last great rush of spectral giants fell back from it: the two-edged weapon of laughter sprang from her mouth, as some such conquering power springs from the mouth of the mystical hero of the Apocalypse. The laughter and the protection that are beyond the world entered her to preserve the world, and, still laughing for mere joy of contact and conflict, she moved forward. The ghostly elementals broke and fled in chaos; a grey swirl of snow received them, and then the golden mist was around her again and she was sinking and moving forward through it. It swirled and shook and con-densed; darkness sprang through it. She stood by the golden base, empty of images, in the room where the dark hangings enclosed her; and then she saw across the table, confronting her, the wild face of Joanna, and her clutching hands, and her mouth gnashing itself together upon incoherent words.

Nancy's hands dropped to her side; the joy that possessed her quietened; she became still. All then was not yet done. The storm had been turned back, but she did not know if it was quenched, and this made personification of storm raged at her a few feet off. Joanna had come to the inner room, when the mist already drawn from its hiding-place among or in the dancing figures by the operation of the lovers had filled the whole chamber; she had entered through the breach which they had made in the constraining power that localized the images, or, to put it another way, she had been received into the vapour which they had loosed from the expanding dance. As Henry had seen her for a moment, so she had seen him; she entering, he returning. His mortal purpose had been overthrown, and his mind had accepted that and submitted. But hers, thwarted long since, had overthrown the mind itself in its collapse. Babel had overwhelmed her being; she walked among the imagined Tarots seeking for the love which she held to be her right, her possession, her living subject. Wild, yet not more wild than most men, she sought to nourish the god in her own way, and that way was by the dream of Horus and vengeance and torments. Full of that hope, tenderness mingled with cruelty, devotion with pride, government with tyranny, maternity with lust, she raged among the symbols of the everlasting dance, and madly believed that, by virtue of her godhead, she ruled it and was more than a part of it. Henry and she had seen each other, then she had rushed on. She rushed into the centre of the room, where now the mist blew in widening circles round the empty base, and saw the void. There, where all restoration should have lain was nothing; there, where the slain god should have lived, the very traces of his blood had vanished; for she had passed the fallen Tarot paintings in her haste, and they lay behind her, hidden and neglected, upon the floor. But she saw Nancy, and at Nancy she now gazed and gibbered. The silence for some seconds was yet unbroken; the old woman mouthed across the empty pedestal, but no sound came from her. Nancy, unafraid but aware of her ignorance before this questing anger, after the pause said, half-faltering: "You're . . . still looking?"

The old woman's face lit up with a ghastly certainty. She nodded vehemently. "Ah," she said, "still looking, kind lady. Kind lady, to hide him there!"

Nancy moved her hands a little. "Indeed," she said, "I haven't hidden him. Tell me what you want and I'll help look."

Joanna went off into a fit of ironical chuckling. "O, yes,

you'll help," she said. "O, you'll help! You've helped all this long time, haven't you? But it was you who ran about the tent and peeped underneath to see if the child was there! Peeping here and peeping there! and wriggling through at last to take him away!"

"What have I taken?" Nancy said, knowing the madness, half-convinced by it, and half-placating it. "What could I take from you? I'll give it back, if you'll tell me, or I'll look for it everywhere with you."

Joanna, up against the table of the Tarots, leaned across it suddenly and caught Nancy's hand in her own. The girl felt the old fingers clutch her and squeeze into her with a numbing strength, so that the free activity in which she had moved during her conflict with visions was now imprisoned and passive. She resisted the impulse to struggle and let her hand lie still.

"I'll look for it," Joanna said. "I know where you keep him. The blood in the blood and the body in the body. I'll let him out of you." She wrenched the girl nearer, and sprawled over the table, leaning her head towards Nancy's breast. "I hear him," she breathed. "It's he that's beating in you. I'll let him out."

Nancy shook suddenly. The laughter that had been in her had died away; a fantastic wonder possessed her whether she might now be paying for her mastery of the storm. Better perhaps to have died with Henry in the snow than . . . but this was nonsense: she wasn't going to die. She was going to live and find Henry, and show him the palms that had taken the snow, and make him kiss them for reward, and lay hers against his, his that had begun and sent the clubbed elementals right into hers, and all ways adore the mystery of Love. The mystery of Love couldn't be that she should die here . . . with only the old woman near. Aunt Sybil would come, or Mr. Lee, or her father. . . . Meanwhile, she must try and love this old woman.

She was jerked forward again. Joanna scrambled upright and dragged Nancy in turn across the table; then, holding her tight-stretched, she bent her head down towards her, and gabbled swiftly: "The hand you took him with, the hand of power, the hand of magic—there, there, that's where we let him out. The middle of the hand—didn't you know? that's where the god goes in and out." She twisted the girl's hand upward and scratched at the palm with the nails of her other hand. "I shall see him," she ran on, "in the first drop of blood, the blood that the cats smell out; that's why the cat brought me here, the cat that lives in the storm, the tiger that runs by the Fool. It'll come"—her nails tore at the hand—"and he'll come out of it. My own, my little one, my sweet chuck! come, come along, come."

The pain struck Nancy as being quite sufficient; it suggested to her that she might scream—scream out—call out. There wouldn't, she thought, be much harm in calling out. But also she must love this old woman—wish her well—understand her—see her goodness. But the old woman was one and she was one—and she couldn't see any clear reason why the old woman should spoil hands that Henry had said were beautiful. She made a final effort to break away, and didn't succeed; almost upside down as she felt she was, that was hardly surprising. So she called, in as steady a voice as possible: "Aunt! Henry! Father! Aunt! Aunt Sybil!"

Her voice ceased abruptly. Instead of any of these appearing out of the golden mist that hid the doorway from her, there was a sudden soft thud, and on the table close up to her stretched arm appeared a cat. Nancy in the few minutes she had spent with Sybil in the hall had heard and seen nothing of the cat, and had had no opportunity since. And she had never heard or seen one in the house. But there it crouched, mewing, turning its head from her to Joanna and back again, unsheathing and sheathing its claws, moving its restless tail. Nancy's first thought as she saw it was, "It's got no hands," and this seemed to her so horrible that she nearly lost control. It had no hands, it had no spiritual instruments of intention, only paws that patted or scratched, soft padded cushions or tearing iron nails—all four, all four, and no hands. The cat put one paw suddenly on her arm, and she almost shrieked at that soft dab. It tried to lift its paw, but its claws were entangled in the light stuff of the afternoon frock she had on, and were caught. After a moment's struggle it ripped them out, and Nancy seemed to hear the sound of the light stuff tearing— absurd, of course, but if it should tear it right away, and her arm lay bare like her wrist and hand, and the cat and Joanna both tore and scratched . . . Love. . . . She must love Joanna. Joanna wanted something, and, though she was afraid Joanna wouldn't find it, she herself must try and love.

Never since the child had died had Joanna been nearer than then to finding the power of whom she told herself fantastic tales, than when the girl's struggling will fixed itself again on that centre. In the place of the images the god offered himself to his seekers, through the effort of his creature. In the depth of Nancy's eyes as she turned them on Joanna, in the sound of her voice as she spoke, he allowed his mystery to expand, as she said, "Indeed, it isn't here. I'd help you if I could. It'll do it if we let it."

The old woman did not meet her eyes; she was looking at the cat. "The cat that lives in the storm," she said. "Go, my dear; go and show me. You brought me here—show me; show me. She's got it in her, hasn't she? go and get it out."

The cat stared at her; then it turned its eyes to Nancy's face, and, keeping them fixed there, seemed to swivel its body slowly round. Nancy had an awful thought, "It's going to spring! it's got no hands and it's going to spring! It'll tear me because it's got no hands!" In the last of the Tarot cards, in the unnumbered illumination, she had seen something like that—a beast rearing against the Fool: in the midst of the images, rigid in the centre of the base, she had seen it, a beast rearing against the Fool. It had not then seemed to be attacking exactly; rather it had seemed as if poised in the very act of a secret measure trodden with its controlling partner among the more general measure trodden by all the shapes. The Fool and the tiger, the combined and single mystery—but it was going to spring. She brought up her other hand from where it had held the edge of the table, to help her keep her footing against Joanna's strong pull; and she slipped a little more forward as she did so, bringing her face too near to that crouched energy that was gathering itself . . . too near, too near. Her hand came up, clutched, missed, for the cat slithered aside snarling, and then, as her hand came down on the golden table, crouched again, and was unexpectedly caught by its neck. A high, peevish voice said, "Good God! what *is* all this? Let go at once, you wretched creature! Do you hear me? Let my daughter alone. *Damn you, woman, let my daughter alone!*"

Chapter Fifteen

THE WANDERERS IN THE BEGINNING

The descent of the golden mist separated the inhabitants of the house from the sight of each other, with the single exception of Sybil and Aaron. The servants, caught in the hall, clung together, not daring to move yet frightened to remain where they were. They felt in the closeness of hands and bodies the only suggestion of safety, as, long since, our scarcely human ancestors crowded together against night and the perils of the night. The cook gasped continuously; her hysterical companion was reduced to a shaking misery of moans; even the silent Amabel quivered spasmodically as she clutched the arms of her unseen colleagues. Between them the mist rolled and stayed.

In the corridor above, ignoring social divisions, reducing humanity to an equality of bewildered atoms, it had swept between Ralph and his father. Ralph, frankly defeated by this inexplicable amazement, fell back against the wall in a similar stupor to the cook's. A world upon which he had all his life relied had simply ceased to exist. Mist on mountains, fogs in towns, he had heard of; sea-fogs and river-mists. But here was neither sea nor river, neither mountain nor town. Existence as he knew it had just gone out. In a minute or two he would pull himself together and do something. But this stuff, as he leaned against the wall, was damned unpleasant: the wall gave to his back, and he came hastily upright, feeling gingerly for it. He couldn't feel it; he couldn't feel any difference between anything.

He brought his hand towards his thigh, trying to touch himself, and couldn't: where he ought to be was nothing but this thick consistence. He closed his hand upon itself, and what felt like fingers pressed more deeply into the same shifting and resisting matter. He could feel himself all right, so long as he didn't definitely try to find himself. But when he did, he wasn't there. That was silly: he was there. He put up both hands to his head—at least to where his head ought to have been, and still, if his head was there, he couldn't get it. This porridge-like substance oozed between his fingers and clung to them—porridge or thin mud. He had had a tooth out once, and afterwards felt as if the tooth was still there. Suppose his whole body had been pulled out, and he were only feeling as if it were there. But the rest of the world? That was gone too. Suppose everything had just been pulled out—leaving only the place where it had been, and himself feeling the place, seeming sometimes full and sometimes empty? For a moment he visualized a hole in the air, out of which the round world had been neatly and painlessly extracted, but his mind, unused to metaphysical visions, refused to pursue this thought, and restored him to the simple view that he was feeling very funny, probably a bit overtired with all this snow. Nevertheless, he couldn't forget that never in his life, fresh, tired, or overtired, had he searched for himself and not found himself. His hold on sanity depended on the fact that the fingers of either hand did sometimes rub together as he moved them, though the two hands never quite met each other. If they only could, he would be getting back to normal; something would have joined. There would have been a kind of shape, a point of new beginning, a definite fixture, in this horrible mess, where at present were only two wandering feelers, antennae moving about in a muddy mass. He wondered abruptly what his father was feeling like, but no sound—yes, but there was a sound, four sounds. Four separate notes of music, in an ascending scale, came to him, faint and monotonously repeated—la, la, la, la; la, la, la, la; la, la, la, la. Well, sooner or later perhaps this incredible nightmare would *stop*.

The Wanderers in the Beginning

Mr. Coningsby had found himself cut off from Ralph with as much sudden expedition as Ralph had experienced. But, unlike his son, he did not feel the cloud that so surrounded and deprived him as being thickly material. It was an offence, certainly, but an offence of shocked bewilderment. It removed his world from him as it had removed Ralph's and, like Ralph and the servants, he instinctively put out his hand to find companionship. He found—not companionship certainly, but what he had found before, another hand that laid hold of his, a strong, gentle, cold, strange hand. He pulled his own hastily back, and the other let it go. It had rather invited than constrained him, and it did not attempt to control. He rubbed his fingers together distastefully, and pretended that it might have been Joanna's hand or Stephen's. Anything else—it couldn't be anything else. It might be Henry's or Aaron's—it might even have been Ralph's. Only he was, in spite of himself, certain that it hadn't been Ralph's or Aaron's or Henry's, and, in spite of himself, he didn't believe it to be Stephen's or Joanna's; it had been too cold and strong for any mortal hand. It was then—it wasn't; certainly it wasn't. Or if it was, then the only thing to be done was to keep out of the way of these released marionettes. "Robots!" Mr. Coningsby indignantly thought, though how the Robots had got from their table to the corridor he didn't attempt to explain. He would get right out of the house—but the storm was outside. It cut him off from his home, from London, from trains and taxis; it shut him in and he must stay in. And within was the mist. There was, Mr. Coningsby realized, absolutely nowhere in the universe he could get to. He was *there*, and *there* he was going to stop.

Blundering along what he supposed to be the corridor, he exclaimed aloud, "Lunacy!" At the word all sorts of dim memories of his work awoke, only he seemed to be on the wrong side of them. He had never heard of a lunatic whose delusion was that a whirling snowstorm shut him up in a golden cloud, where cold hands touched his. Some lunatics were violent and had to be held down by others' hands. What if he, struggling in his horror, became violent, and those hands held him? suppose his mind was, by their judgements, mad? Lunacy—lunacy—what was lunacy? what was the mad mind wrestling with contemptuous and powerful enemies? what was he doing at the moment? If he should be caught and carried away for ever into the depths and distances which opened now and then before him—the mist falling away on either side and making a league-long valley of itself, or heaving up and leaving a great abyss round which it swirled and then covered it again. Borne into it . . . taking precedence, O, for ever and ever taking desolate and lunatic preference of the elder sons of younger sons of peers. They would always be behind him; they could never catch him up. As if bound upon a great wheel, spinning round, with lives bound to it—no wonder he was giddy; the mist or the wheel had made him so. That was why he saw the depths—as the wheel turned; it didn't go quickly, but it was always revolving, and he had been on it for so long, so many years, and now he was old and sinking deeper and deeper down. But the elder sons would never catch him up; they were tied to it too.

His head was aching with the dizziness of the revolutions all the same; wheels within wheels—he had heard that phrase before. The mists were revolving round him or he in them: which—what—was it? Wheels within wheels—there had been some phrase of glory, angels or something, wheels full of eyes, cycles in cycles all vigilant and intelligent, revolving. These weren't eyes; these were hands. Perhaps hands were eyes; if the eye of the body was dark, if the hand had no power—a vague wheel of innumerable hands all intertwined and clasped and turning, turning faster and faster, turning out of mud and into the mist, hands falling from it, helplessly clutching. . . .

It was at this moment that Mr. Coningsby, blindly edging along the corridor, his own hands feeling nervously along the wall, touched a door-handle; he turned it, went in, found himself in his own room, still miraculously and mercifully free from mist, and slammed the door behind him. It was at the same moment that a voice within him said in tones of startled concern, "Nancy? Sybil?" If they were out there, as of course they were—he had seen Sybil in the hall when he was calling "Fire!" down the stairs. But Sybil—he knew it and admitted it at last—didn't matter. In any unusual variation of normal things—snowstorms or shipwrecks or burning houses—he could have regarded himself as Sybil's superior. But this was entire subversion of normal things, a new world, a world of lunacy, and he was not superior to her there. Confronted with any utterly new experience, he was her inferior, for he existed only in his relationships, and she—she existed in herself. There was certainly no point in his looking for Sybil.

All this he understood in a swift revelation; but he understood also that Nancy was different. Nancy was not merely his daughter—she was much more likely to find him useful than Sybil was. And he didn't trust Henry to look after her; he had always thought that Henry was more concerned with himself than with Nancy. Poised three steps within the room, Mr. Coningsby turned round and looked unhappily at the closed door. Must he really go back into that mist on the chance of being useful to her? It seemed he must. "Blast!" Mr. Coningsby said aloud, in a rare explosion of disgust. Sybil, Ralph, Henry—any of these might be looking after her; yes, but he didn't *know* they were. Besides, there was Joanna. His altruism excited into action by this opportune dislike (as so often happens: even love often owing more to hate than perfection of love could altogether approve), he went back to the door, and observed disagreeably that the golden cloud was beginning to ooze through it. He was past surprise by now; he didn't even try to see that it was coming through the keyhole or anywhere except straight through the wood. There it was, growing thicker. In that case it was just as well that he'd

already determined to leave the room, since things would soon
be as bad within as without. Very well; only this time he must
keep his head; he wouldn't be any use to Nancy if he lost it.
No nonsense about wheels or hands that were eyes or distances.
This was a house; it had a fog in it; he was Lothair Coningsby,
and he was going to find his daughter in case she was frightened
by an ugly old woman. Very well. He opened the door.

Actually, when he had gone a little distance down the
corridor, he thought the mist wasn't too bad. He even ventured
to open his mouth, and say in a curiously subdued voice,
"Nancy!" He didn't quite admit that he didn't want any—
anybody—anybody with inhuman hands to hear him, but he
knew it would be very inconvenient if they did. But nothing
at all happened, blessedly. So he took a few more steps and
said "Nancy" again. This time another form stepped against
his own—very nearly crashed into him—and a voice said, "She
hasn't come back then?"

Mr. Coningsby, recovering from a spasmodic fear that the
new appearance might be one of the presences of the cloud,
peering closer, saw that it was Henry, and his fear spoke
angrily: "What d'ye mean—come back? Why aren't you with
her?"

"Because I can't get there," Henry said. "God only knows
where she is, and if He does He knows why I'm not there."

"Don't stand there talking about God," Mr. Coningsby
snapped. "Tell me what devil's trick you've played on her."

"When I tried to kill you," Henry began in a low, mono-
tonous voice, as if he had often said it over to himself, "because
I thought you stood in the way of the entrance into the——"

"When you what?" Mr. Coningsby cried out, "tried to kill
me? Are you mad? When did you try to kill me?" The nightmare was getting worse; he couldn't really be standing in this
accursed welter of golden cloud talking to his daughter's lover
of his own plotted murder. Had there been any trying to kill
him? or had he been killed? and was this mist the ghostly

consequence of death? He checked in time to hear Henry say:

"When I brought the storm out of the Tarots. I poured the waters on you out of their vessels and I beat the winds against you with the staffs because you wouldn't give up the cards. But she went away to stop it."

"Stop it!" Mr. Coningsby said, clutching at the first words he really understood. "I should think she would stop it! What under heaven are you talking about?" He peered closely at Henry's face, and was struck silent by what he saw in eyes of which the brightness had been dulled. Pallid and fixed, the face looked back at him; mild and awful, the voice answered him, "I meant to use her, and now I can't find her. She's gone beyond me, and I can't catch her up. You may."

"I certainly will," Mr. Coningsby said. "I—I—— Where *is* she?"

"She's gone into the dance," Henry said, "and I don't know whether even she can hold her past there. I was a fool once and dreamed, and I tried to kill you because you were in the way of my dreams."

"You were a fool all right," Mr. Coningsby said, "and if this utterly detestable nonsense you're talking means anything, you were a great deal worse than a fool. Pull yourself . . ."

Henry looked at him, and he stopped. No man with a face of that colour and of that agony would be talking nonsense— not if he knew it. If the storm had been—but storms *weren't*! Nor, of course, was mist. Nancy was trying to stop the storm— he'd got that much—and she'd gone into the dance. That, whatever else it meant, meant those damned silly marionettes in their infernal black magic of a room—where Joanna had been going. He had known all the time that Joanna would be in it somehow.

He pushed past Henry, rather thankful even in his angry distraction to feel Henry's undoubted body as he shoved it away, and said, "I'll deal with you after. If you can't find her, I will."

The Wanderers in the Beginning

Unexpectedly docile, Henry said: "You may. That may be the judgement. Do it; do it, if only you can."

Mr. Coningsby had gone on several paces when he, without quite knowing why, looked back over his shoulder. It was a silly thing to do, he knew, with this God-forsaken mist all round him and when he had done it he knew it all the more. For looking back was like seeing things reversed; he was looking back in two ways at once. He saw Henry, but he saw him upside down—a horrible idea. Nevertheless, there it was: Henry was, in the ridiculous reflections of the mist, hanging in the void, his head downwards; his hands out of sight behind him somewhere, his leg—one leg—drawn up across the other— it was the other he was hanging by. For a full minute Mr. Coningsby stood gaping over his shoulder at that vision seen in one of the opening hollows of the cloud, then a driving gold as of storm swept across it, and he could see no more. He turned his head again, but now he stood still. He was feeling sick and ill; he was feeling very old; he wished Sybil were with him. But she wasn't, and however sick and ill and old he was, still Nancy was somewhere about, in danger of being frightened, if nothing worse, by that loathsome hag of a Joanna. He went on, and for the first time since his childhood prayed, prayed that he mightn't look round again, prayed that Nancy at least when he found her might be whole and sane, prayed that if Sybil was any good, Sybil might pretty soon turn up, prayed that he might keep his mind steady and do for the best whatever he had to do. The mist opened in front of him in one of its sweeping unfoldings, and he was aware of figures moving in it, tall figures emerging and disappearing, and it covered them again, and again those cold fingers closed round his own. Mr. Coningsby said, in a voice that shook despite his efforts, "Who are you?" The fingers warmed suddenly to his, and became a grasp; a voice in answer to his exclaimed, "Hallo, father!" and he realized that it was Ralph's, though he would have sworn that the touch hadn't been Ralph's when it first caught him. But he must have been mistaken. He said in enormous relief: "Hallo, my boy! glad to find you."

"I'm damned glad," Ralph answered, and his head appeared close to his father's. "You're solid, anyhow."

"Whereabouts are we?" Mr. Coningsby asked.

"Where we were, I suppose," Ralph said. "By that doorway into the study or whatever it was. I've not done much moving since, I can tell you. Funny business this."

"It's a wicked and dangerous business," Mr. Coningsby cried out. "I'm looking for Nancy. That fiend's left her alone, after trying to kill me."

"What fiend?" Ralph asked, even more bewildered. "Who's been trying to kill you?"

"That devil's bastard Henry," Mr. Coningsby said, unwontedly moved as he came to speak of it. "He said so. He said he raised the storm so as to kill me."

"Henry!" Ralph exclaimed. "Raised a storm. But I mean—O, come, a storm!"

"He said so," Mr. Coningsby repeated. "And he's left Nancy in that room there with that gibbering hag of an aunt of his. Come on with me; we've got to get her out."

"I see," said Ralph. "Yes; O, well, let's. I don't mind anything so long as it's firm. But raised a storm, you know! He must be a bit touched. I always thought he was a trifle gibbery himself."

"O, everyone's mad in this damned house," Mr. Coningsby said. "I suppose we're going right?"

"Well, I can't see much," Ralph answered, "but perhaps we are. I mean—if we're not we shall find out. What's that?"

They had both bumped into something. Mr. Coningsby, his language becoming less restrained every time he spoke, cursed and felt for it. But it was Ralph's less maddened brain which found the explanation. "It's the table," he said suddenly. "The big table we saw from the doorway."

The Wanderers in the Beginning

"Then we'd better get round it," Mr. Coningsby said. "The room where those gargoyles are is on the other side. I wish I could smash every one of them into fragments and cram them down his gulping throat."

Hand still in hand, they groped round the table, and, when they judged they were almost opposite the inner door, struck out towards it. After two or three cautious steps, "It's getting thinner," Mr. Coningsby said.

Ralph was more doubtful, but, dutifully encouraging, he had just answered, "Perhaps you're right," when he was startled by his father nearly falling. Mr. Coningsby's raised foot had come down on something that jerked and heaved under it. He cried out, staggered, recovered himself, and came to a halt as the thing rose in their pathway. It was in the shape of a man; it was a man; it was the fellow that had been with the witch; it was Stephen. He must have been lying across the threshold of the inner room. He looked at them with dull hostility.

"Get back," he said. "You can't come here. She's there."

"She is, is she?" Mr. Coningsby said. "Here, Ralph, move him."

Ralph started to obey. He put a hand on Stephen and began to say, "Look here, you must let us by," when Stephen leapt at him, and the two were locked in a wild struggle. Mr. Coningsby just avoided their first collision, and slipped past them as they swayed. Both of them, clutching and wrestling, went, under the impulse of Stephen's rush, back into the outer room; all the emotions of fear and anger that had been restrained in their separate solitudes now broke into activity through the means of that hostile embrace. In the mysterious liquefaction of everything which had distressed Ralph, in the outbreak of the mysteries of the vagrant goddess which had terrified Stephen, each of them found something recognizable, natural, and human, and attacked it. The beings who possessed the cloud were veiled by it from both of them; like primeval men of undeveloped capacities, they strove with whatever was near. So had dim tribe battled with tribe—and earlier yet, before tribes were, before the beasts that grew into tribes, when the stuff that is the origin of all of us had brought forth only half-conscious shapes, such struggles had gone on. The nature of the battles of all the world was in them; to pass or not to pass—neither knowing clearly why, except that great command intensely swayed their spirits—was the centre of their conflicting wills. The gateway was taboo, for the goddess had entered; mystical age, nourishing wisdom, had gone into the sanctuary and must be inviolate. The gateway must be forced, for kinship was in danger; mystical womanhood, unprotected helplessness, was abandoned within and must be saved. Religion had commanded, and the household: the unknowing champions of either domination panted and fought in the outer courts of the mystery. The mist rolled into and over them; it possessed and maddened them. Life strove with life, and life poured itself into them to maintain the struggle. In such unseeing obedience, at that very moment, in the wider world, armies poured to battle, for causes as obscurely known. They battered and struck; they had no hope but destruction and no place but war. Ignorant of all but simple laws, they closed and broke and struck and closed again, and the strength of earth fought in them for mastery.

But of that manifestation of primitive violence Mr. Coningsby saw nothing: he had glimpsed the inner doorway and went hurriedly through it. Within, all was clear: clear so that he could know, unknowing, another mystery of mankind. For there, in the room with the dark hangings, through or in which had appeared to the initiate the vision of the painted world, he saw the solemn intention of sacrifice, the attempted immolation of the victim to the god. Fate had fallen on deity, and only by bursting the doors of human life could deity be relieved. Humanity, caught up into dooms and agonies greater even than its own, was madly attempting to relieve them, and itself with them. Over the golden altar of blood the body of the girl lay stretched; on one side the hierophant clutched her wrist and tore at the mystery of the hand, which means so much in its gentle and terrible power; and on the altar itself, as if some god had descended to aid and quicken the sacrifice, the cat lay crouched in a beautiful and horrible suspense before its spring. As far as the struggling bodies without from the holy striving of joyous imaginations, so far within was the grotesque group from the sacred and necessary offering which (the testimony of the myths declares) releases, after some spiritual manner, the energies of the gods. But it was not wholly alien; and that which is common to all was the purpose of death.

Mr. Coningsby, as he broke into the charmed circle, saw the priestess, the cat, and the body of the sacrifice. It was on the last that his attention was concentrated, and he cried out in a voice rather of objection than of protest, but that was the result of fifty years of objection to life rather than of protest against it. He ran forward, grabbed the cat, lifted it, and flung it with violence at the doorway, much as Stephen had flung him away not long before. Joanna screeched at him, and he swore back at her. Dominant for the first time in his life, moved for the first time by those two great virtues, strength and justice, he commanded her, and for a moment she flinched. She was distracted from the hand she held by the hand that gripped her shoulder—before its owner had time to realize how offensive to his normal habits such a grip was. Nancy at the same moment twisted her wrist and jerked her own scratched hand away, standing once more upright on the other side of the table. Mr. Coningsby ran round the table to her. She put her arm round him and realized suddenly how much she owed to him—owed because she was a blundering servant of Love to this other blundering servant of Love, owed from her struggling goodwill to his struggling goodwill: and how full of goodwill his labouring spirit was. He was a companion upon the Way, and how difficult she had made the Way to him! She hugged his arm, not so much in gratitude for this single service as in remorse for her impatient past.

"O, thank you, darling," she said. "You did come just at the right time."

"Are you all right?" Mr. Coningsby said. "Are you all right? Has she hurt you? What was she doing?"

"She was looking for something," Nancy said, "and she thought I'd got it. But I haven't. If I only knew exactly what it was! Perhaps Aunt Sybil could find out if we could get them together. Ask her to come downstairs, won't you, father?"

"I'll ask her to come downstairs," Mr. Coningsby said. "I'll ask her to come down into the cellars, and I'll ask her if she minds the doors being locked on her, and if she'd very much mind if we tied her up for the dancing, raving monstrosity of ugly hell that she is. Looking for something!"

At any rate, Nancy thought, that would give them a chance of finding Sybil on the way, and perhaps something more satisfactory than cellars would open. She couldn't feel, for all her smarting hand, that locking Joanna in a cellar would do any real good. Nothing but giving Joanna what she wanted or getting Joanna to change her wants would be any real good. She pressed her hand to her heart; it was smarting dreadfully; the blood stood along the scratches. She didn't want to show it in case her father became more annoyed with Joanna, but the sooner she could find Henry or (if needs must) bathe it herself the better. She began gently to edge Mr. Coningsby round the table. She said, "Let's go with her at least. I'm sure Aunt Sybil could help. She knows what the lost thing is."

Mr. Coningsby felt a shock of truth. Sybil did seem to know —Sybil had quietened this old hag—the lost thing—he took an automatic step or two forward. Joanna had already re- treated a little, and was darting angry eyes round the room She went back yet farther, and, as Nancy also moved, the golden cloud which hung behind the old woman rolled back, disclosing on the ground at her feet the paintings of the Tarots which had fallen from the hands of the lovers that evening. They lay there, throbbing and vibrating. With a scream of rage and delight she dropped to her knees and scraped them together in her hands.

"What——" Mr. Coningsby began, surprised, and ended in a different voice. "Are those my cards? What under heaven are my cards doing there?" He rushed round the table, and Nancy ran with him.

But they were too late. Joanna was on her feet again, had turned, was running off into the mist, clutching the paintings. The other two ran also, and, as if their movement was itself a wind, the mist rolled back from before them, driven to either side and about their feet and floating over their heads. But, as Joanna ran, her hands fingered the cards, and she cried out in ecstasy.

They broke into the outer room, and at the sound of that shrill rapturous voice the two combatants ceased to struggle. She was upon them, and both of them, startled at the coming of such a hierophant in such exaltation, released the other and fell back. But Stephen sent a word to her, and she answered: "I'm finding him, I'm finding him. I'll burn them first and then he'll come. He'll come in the fire: the fire is for Horus, Horus in the fire."

She was by him and out of the room, and still she worked the magic in her hands, and by now, so swift and effective was her insanity, she had separated the suit of the swords from the rest, and was setting them in some strange order. She made of them a mass of little pointed triangles, three living symbols to each triangle, and the King of the Swords, whose weapon quivered and glowed as if in flame, she thrust on top of them all, and laid her own hand over it, warming it into life. And as she came into the longer corridor, already the sparks went about her, and she was calling, "Little one, little one! I'm coming. They shan't hurt you any more. I'll drive them away —your mother'll save you. I can hear you—I'm coming."

The Wanderers in the Beginning

Behind her those who pressed were parted. At the door of the outer room Mr. Coningsby's strength went from him. He staggered, and would have fallen had not Nancy held him, and Ralph, by whom they paused, sprang to her help. Nancy gave her brother one swift, delightful smile and exclaimed to him, "Look after him, there's a dear. I must go."

"Right ho!" Ralph said, and took his father's arm as Nancy released it. Stephen uncertainly looked at them, then he left them and followed Nancy. She came into the longer corridor and saw before her Henry leaning on the balustrade at the top of the stairs. Joanna, checking as she went, had lifted the swords that were beginning to shoot from between her hands in little flames, and was thrusting them continually forward towards him in sharp spasms of motion. And about them the cloud gathered into shapes and forms, and through all the translucent house Nancy was aware of golden figures unceasingly intertwining in the steps of the fatal dance.

Chapter Sixteen

"SUN, STAND THOU STILL UPON GIBEON"

Sybil, with a great deal of difficulty, although it did not occur to her to call it that, had managed to get Aaron downstairs and into the drawing-room. She had wanted him to be helped to his bedroom, but this he had altogether refused. He wouldn't go up those stairs; he wouldn't go back into the thicker mist; he would go down; he would get away if he could. She wasn't to leave him—everyone else had left him—and they would be on him.

"They?" Sybil asked as she helped him cautiously along. "Splendid, Mr. Lee. You *could* get upstairs almost as well, you know. Easier, in fact. No, all right—if you'd rather. They?"

"They," Aaron babbled. "They're all round us. They always are, but we shall see them. I daren't see them. I daren't. I can't see anything: it's too bright."

"It *is* very bright," Sybil said. "If it wasn't so late, I should think the sun was shining. But I never heard of the sun shining at ten o'clock on Christmas night. Gently; that's perfect."

"The sun!" Aaron said. "The sun's gone out for ever; we're all blind. Lame and blind, so that we can't escape them."

Sybil smiled at him. "Well, then," she said, "I wouldn't worry about escaping. Leave that to Nancy and Henry, unless they're sensible enough not to worry either. I wasn't at their age. I tried to insist on escaping; fortunately, I didn't. That's the bottom."

"How can you tell?" Aaron exclaimed. "Can you see? can you see through the mist and the snow?"

"Sun, stand thou still upon Gibeon"

"Fairly well," Sybil said. "I wonder if Amabel—Amabel, could you give Mr. Lee your arm on the other side?"

The words reached Amabel where she was clasped with her companions. They reached her out of the bright cloud; she raised her head, felt it against her eyes, and promptly shut them again. Sybil looking across the hall at them—the hall that in this curiously golden-tinted snow looked more lovely, though more ruinous, than she had thought any mortal thing could look—considered a moment, and then in a firmer voice called again, "Amabel!" Snowstorms were all very well, but it was silly to get into a state of crouching hysterics over a snowstorm; Amabel's immediate job was to be of use. Normally one wouldn't order other people's servants about, and she said to Aaron between two calls: "Will you forgive me, Mr. Lee? Perhaps if you called her . . .?"

Aaron, however, it was clear, had no notion of doing anything of the sort; the words didn't seem to mean anything to him. Sybil called for the third time, with an imperious certainty: "Amabel! will you come here?"

Amabel heard the voice and looked up again. In the awful vagueness of the hall, tumultuous with cloud and storm, she saw figures moving. A mingled sense of her duty and of wild adventure filled her. She released the cook and the other maid; she said, faintly but definitely, "I'm coming."

"Well, come, then," Sybil said, still slightly imperious. "My dear girl, do hurry. I know it's very unusual, but we may as well be useful."

Amabel dashed through the mist, terrified but exultant. It swirled round her; it carried her along; she was swept, deliriously panting, to the side of the strange lady who walked in the cloud as others did by day, and laughed at the storm as others did at spring, and closed doors that the whole power of the world dashed open, and carried an old man safely through chaos to—

"Where to, madam?" she asked, an attentive executant once more.

"Sun, stand thou still upon Gibeon"

Serenely Miss Coningsby smiled at her—a smile that Amabel felt to be even brighter than the golden glow about them: so much brighter that for a moment the glow was only the reflection of the smile.

"How dear of you!" Miss Coningsby said. "So—yes. I thought the drawing-room. You and my nephew made rather a mess of the drawing-room, didn't you?"

Amabel smiled back, a thing she didn't much believe in doing as a rule, having been for some months with a lady who held that if you smiled at your servants they would do everything for you, and also held that you had a right to see that they did. The company proceeded slowly to the drawing-room, and Aaron was made as comfortable as possible on a divan. Sybil, kneeling by him, bared his ankle and looked at it.

"It doesn't", she said, "seem very bad." She laid her hand over it; thinking how charming Aaron Lee's courtesy had been, very willing to be courteous in her turn. He looked up at her and met her eyes, and his anxious babblings stopped.

Her hand closed round the ankle; her mind went inwards into the consciousness of the Power which contained them both; she loved it and adored it: with her own thought of Aaron in his immediate need, his fear, his pain, she adored. Her own ankle ached and throbbed in sympathy, not the sympathy of an easy proffer of mild regret, but that of a life habituated to such intercession. She interceded; she in him and he in her, they grew acquainted; the republican element of all created things welled up in them both. Their eyes exchanged news. She throbbed for an instant not with pain but with fear as his own fear passed through her being. It did but pass through; it was dispelled within her, dying away in the unnourishing atmosphere of her soul, and with the fear went the pain. Her hand had fastened on him; she smiled at him, and then with the passing of that smile before her recovered serenity her hand was released. She sank back on to her heels, and said, her voice full of a deep delight: "O, no, not very bad."

Of what exactly she spoke she hardly knew, but he answered her in the greater sense. "Let them come then," he said. "I was a fool ever to think I knew."

"Why, no," she said. "Only perhaps you sprained your ankle—hurrying."

Negligent of his supposed hurt, he put his feet to the floor and stood up; then, as if from the weight he put on them, he flinched. "But the cloud! the living cloud!" he cried. "And Joanna's there!"

She came, in a complex movement of harmony, to her feet. "Yes," she said thoughtfully, "Joanna might perhaps be a little carried away. Ought we to go and see if we can find her?"

"Must we find her?" he said irresolutely. "Let her fight them if she wants to. Must we go back into the mist?"

"What is this mist you see?" Sybil asked. "Why do you call it a living cloud?"

"It's the cloud from which the images were first made," he said, almost whispering. "It hides in everything; it's the golden hands that shape us and our lives. It's death to see them; no one can bear it."

"Are our hands so different?" Sybil said.

"So many degrees less", he answered, "in life and power. There have been those whose palms were touched, when they were born, by figures leaning over the cradles: some by one and some by another." His words came faster, as if he would keep her where she stood, keep her by his talk in forgetfulness of the dangers without. "Napoleon . . . Caesar. There was one who came to Olympias on the night when Alexander was conceived, and to the mother of Samson. Great priests—the hierophant touched their hands when they were tiny. Death sometimes—Joanna's child—and the innocents of Bethlehem. And others that we can't see, others beyond the seventy-eight degrees."

"Yet all this time", Sybil said, "Joanna cries for her child."

"Sun, stand thou still upon Gibeon"

He caught her arm. "Leave her alone," he cried. "Perhaps she'll turn the magic against the princes, then she'll die, she'll be blasted. Keep your hands from her."

"Why, she blessed me once with hers," Sybil answered. "And I can't see this mist of yours, though I agree there's a new loveliness in things. Let's go."

"If you enter the cloud, you'll never come out," he cried again. "The hands'll drag you down, the hands of the beginning."

"Let's go and see," she said. "There are the others, and there's always a way through all mists." She looked at Amabel, who was listening in puzzled and fearful silence. "Thank you, my dear," she said. "Shall we go back now?"

She moved forward and out into the hall. Aaron, half-willing, half-unwilling, followed her, hobbling either from his hurt or his fear, if indeed the two were separate. Amabel, in the mere growing certainty that to be near Miss Coningsby was to be as near safety as possible, followed; but she took care to follow her master. Somehow she didn't think Miss Coningsby, if she should look round, would like to see her pushing on out of her place. So, biting her lips a trifle nervously, and as nervously settling her sleeves at her wrists, she controlled her impulse to thrust right up against the strange lady and contented herself with keeping her eyes fixed on the tall assured figure which passed through the drawing-room door and came out among . . .

Among the powers and princes of the dance. For Amabel, as she in turn came into the hall, had the most bewildering vision of a multitude of invaders. She couldn't at once grasp it, but as she gazed and panted she saw that the whole house had changed. The walls, the stairs, the doors, the ceiling, were all alive. They were formed—all that she could see of them through snow and mist—of innumerable shapes, continuously shifting, sliding over and between each other. They were in masses of colour—black mostly, she seemed to see, but with ripples of grey and silver and fiery-red passing over them. Dark pillars of earth stood in the walls, and through them burning swords pierced, and huge old cups of pouring waters were emptied, and grey clubs were beaten. She screamed once despairingly, and Miss Coningsby looked round over her shoulder. But the very movement, though in a way reassuring, was immediately more terrifying; for it seemed to divide even that solitary figure of comfort, and there were two shapes before her: one was the strange lady and one was a man, in a great white cloak and a golden helmet with a crown round it. As if treading a dance together, the two went forward—and the king or emperor or whatever he was also looked back over his shoulder. Amabel was near fainting, but as she met the awful eyes that shone at her she was gathered together and strengthened. She had her duty to do, she reminded herself; if the storm stopped, they'd want the hall tidied up. She must be there in case the hall wanted tidying up. She forgot, in that necessity, the eyes that called to her, and the lord of secular labour vanished from her sight, for she was herself part of the hierarchy that is he. She stood still, concentrated on that thought: "If the storm stops, they'll want the hall tidied up— tidied up—tidied." She wished spasmodically that those sudden shining figures wouldn't come between her and Miss Coningsby, and determined, early in the New Year, to have her eyes seen to. Meanwhile, if the storm stopped . . .

High above them, at the top of the stairs, Nancy looked down. She saw below her Sybil standing in the middle of the hall: she saw the storm in its elemental shapes of wind and water dancing about her. The sight kept her gaze momentarily even from Joanna in front of her, and in that moment she saw Sybil imperiously put out her left hand.

She remembered that movement: once, not so long ago, her father had come home tired and with a bad chill, and she and Ralph had been making rather a row dancing to the gramophone or something—she remembered the exact gesture with which Sybil had flung a hand out towards them while going on some errand. She hadn't needed to speak; the hand had somehow tossed them into subjection. Ralph and she had rather awkwardly broken off and begun chatting—quite quietly chatting—instead. Nancy smiled as the memory touched her in the recognition of the gesture, and smiled again to see the flagging of the white whirlwind. Sybil stood there, one hand flung out, looking up, and Nancy's eyes went back to the two in front of her, to Henry and Joanna facing each other now.

They went back to meet Henry's. He was looking past Joanna and the burning threat which was leaping and darting from the agile, hateful hands; he was looking, as he had never looked before, at the girl who had come again from among the mystery of the images. She looked back at him and laughed, and beckoned him by throwing out her hands towards him; and in simultaneous movement both she and Henry took a few running steps and came together on Joanna's left.

"You're safe," he said abruptly, holding her.

"And you, darling?" she breathed anxiously.

"I?" he said. "O, yes, I'm safe"; and then, as if realizing the new danger. "But run, run quickly; she's got the magic in her hands and she may do anything. Get away, dearest and best; leave me to deal with her."

"You do it so well, don't you, sweetheart?" she mocked. "O darling, you never ought to be let deal with anyone but me."

The throbbing voice caught him away from the danger near them. He said: "And you then?"

"Ah! me," she said, "that was given to you alone: that's your only gift. Do you want more?"

"Haven't you that also—you who have all the rest?" he said.

She answered, smiling, "If you give it me. But don't give it me too soon. Love isn't all that easy—even with you.

223

Darling, your aunt's very angry: let's talk to her together."

Obedient to her initiative, he turned with her. Between them and the top of the stairs the half-naked creature stood, sparks flying off from those spasmodically thrusting hands and little flames breaking from them. The paintings between those hands were thrusting of their own volition as nights before they had slid and rubbed in Nancy's. But the old woman was not facing them; she did not seem even to have noticed Henry's movement. She glared round her, unseeing, or rather seeing everywhere hostility; she cried out accusing and cursing the whole world of things that had caught away her victim, who was also the casket of the hidden god, and had left her but this solitary weapon of magical fire. At the top of that height, between the lovers on one side and Sybil below her on the other, she broke into a paroxysm of despair and desire, supplicating and reassuring the lost child, denouncing the enemies that held him apart. Between the young lovers hand in hand on one side, and on the other the solitary figure of Sybil, whose hand was still stretched out over shapes that might, as Nancy saw them, have been blown heaps of snow or might have been such forms as had come rioting up from the centre of the storm but were now still and crouching—between those reconciled minds the distracted voice of Joanna pealed on. Nancy had meant to speak, to try to soothe or satisfy, but she dared not. If she did, if she asked and was answered, it would not be an answer that she could comprehend. Witches at the stake, with the fire already about them, might have been shrieking so, with as little chance that the stricken hearers would know the names they adjured. But it was not of witches that Nancy thought, for all the screams and the flames; she heard a more human cry. She heard the wail that rang through the curses, and it was a wail that went up from the depths of the world. Her hand clasped Henry's passionately, for the sound of that universal distress terrified her young soul. On the edge of a descent an antique misery was poised, and from the descent, from the house, from the earth, misery beyond telling lamented and complained—to men who could not aid, to gods who made no signs, for it was the gods themselves that had been lost. "Ah! ah! ah!"—something final was gone, something beyond description precious: "ah! ah! ah!"—the little child was dead. They were weeping for it everywhere, as they had been always. She who stood there screamed and stabbed for torment of hate and loss, and from marshes and cities all desire that had not learnt its own futility rose and swelled in hers. The litany of anguish poured out as if it were the sound of the earth itself rushing through space, and comfortless for ever the spinning globe swept on, turning upon itself, crying to itself; and space was the echo of its lament, and time was the measure of its sobs. But more than mere awe of such unavailing grief and desire awoke in Nancy then: cold at her heart, a personal fear touched her and stayed. It was a fear of that actual moment, but futurity lived in it. One hand was in Henry's, but the other was torn by Joanna's nails. Joanna stood in the way; beyond her the way led on to Sybil. She could see Sybil— ever so far off, in that descent upon which the great stairs opened. But Joanna stood in her way, overarching the way, pouring out her voice like the way itself. She wanted to go to Sybil, and that voice was in the way—O folly of cowardice! that voice was the way. Why didn't Sybil move? why didn't Sybil come? Around her, before her, glimmering in the red glow that was uncertainly breaking from those ever-busy hands, she saw the mighty golden shapes looming. They were looming out of the cloud which was at once their background and yet they. It was difficult to see, but she caught the form of the designs she had studied—the one and twenty revelations of the Greater Trumps. The red glow leapt and faded; but the crown of the Emperor, but the front of the sphinx-drawn Chariot, but the stretched sickle of the image of Death, but the sandals of the two children playing together under an unshaped sun, themselves shedding the light by which they played, but the girdle

of the woman who danced alone—all these and other frag-
mentary visions struck on her straining eyes. The glow faded;
her dazzled eyes refused to see more distinction in those walls
of mist. But as she shut them she heard Sybil call, and then
she heard a sudden rush close by her. She opened her eyes
hastily, in time to see—of all mad things—the cat that had
crouched on the altar dash down the stairs towards Sybil.
That wild and alien thing which Sybil had found in the
magical storm, which had followed Joanna to her room and
led her thence to the room of the images, which had almost
made a way for the snow to break into the house, which had
dashed from snow to mist and from mist to snow as if it were
the living secret of uncontrolled power, which had instinctively
assisted at the attempted sacrifice to uncontrolled desire, itself
unshaping since lacking the instruments of shape, now rushed
to the foot of the stairs, and absurdly checked itself, and then
with high feline grace stepped across the hall to Sybil's feet.

Sybil dropped her hand towards it and dropped it a soft
word; it jumped delicately towards her hand and played round
her foot, and jumped again. As it rushed, as it stayed, Joanna's
cry also ceased. The power of it was withdrawn; all power, all
utterance, was withdrawn. The unexpected silence was more
awful than even the wailing, for it was not a silence of relief
but of impotence. The cry of the world was choked; the ball,
tossed from the Juggler's hand, revolved in unspoken anguish.
The mad-woman reeled once, as if she had been struck on the
mouth; then, recovering, turned darting eyes to Sybil in the
hall below. Through the silence Sybil called to her: "The
child's found, Joanna; the child's alive and lovely. All's well;
the child's found." Joanna tried to speak and could not. She
shuffled towards the stair; she turned her pointing hands,
bearing their fiery weapon, as if she herself carried the sword
of the crowned chieftain of fire, downward towards that other
confronting form. Sybil took a step forward, the cat leaping up
against her, and called again: "He's here. Come and adore."

"Sun, stand thou still upon Gibeon"

In a forced and horrible croak, as if speech broke through against commandment and against control, Joanna said: "It's you all the time. I shall see him when you're dead. When you're dead and the world's destroyed, I'll see my desire."

Amabel, crouching by the drawing-room door, saw the strange lady, her left hand rising and falling in a dance with the leaping cat, stretch out the right as if in invitation. The open palm, the curved fingers, the arching thumb, took on a reflection of the cloud that hung over all things: it seemed to Amabel that Miss Coningsby held out a golden hand towards the staircase down which Joanna was beginning to creep. The hand which had helped Lothair and comforted Nancy and healed Aaron, which had picked up the kitten and closed the door and controlled the storm, was stretched to gather in this last reverted madness of man. It lay there, very still, the centre of all things, the power and the glory, the palm glowing with a ruddy passion veiled by the aureate flesh—the hand of all martyrs, enduring; of all lovers, welcoming; of all rulers, summoning. And, as if indeed it summoned, the cloud of gold rushed down towards it, but it moved in shapes and figures, the hands of all the symbols stretched towards the hand that, being human, was so much more than symbol. Nancy and Henry from above beheld them, hands imperial and sacerdotal, single and joined, the working hands that built the Tower, the helpless hands that formed the Wheel, white hands stretching from the snow, fiery hands thrusting from between Joanna's that burned downwards and vanished, all activities rushing towards that repose through which activity beat in the blood that infused it. So the hand of the Juggler had been stretched to cast and catch the tossed balls of existence; so the hand of the Fool had at last fulfilled the everlasting promise and yielded its secrets to the expected hour. The cloud swirled once around that open palm, as the intermingling shapes trod out a last circling measure, hiding all other forms, so that the hand itself was all that could be seen as the rapturous powers wheeled inwards to it. For an infinitesimal fraction of time the immortal dance stood still to receive the recollection of that ever-moving and never-broken repose of sovereign being. Then suddenly they were gone, and the cloud was gone, and everywhere, breaking from Sybil's erect figure, shone a golden light, as of the fullness of the sun in his glory, expanding in a rich fruition. Over the snow spread and heaped around, over Aaron and the others by him, over the stairs and the landing and those who were on it, and so over and through the whole house, the light shone, exquisite and full of promise, radiant and full of perfection. The chaos of the hall was a marvel of new shape and colour; the faces of those who stood around were illumined from within. It was Christmas night, but in the sunlight, between Sybil and Joanna, seriously engrossed, two small strange children played. The mystery which that ancient seer had worked in the Greater Trumps had fulfilled itself, at that time and in that place, to so high a point of knowledge. Sybil stood there, and from her the sun of the Tarots ruled, and the holy children of the sun, the company of the blessed, were seen at least by some of the eyes that watched. For Amabel saw them and was ignorantly at peace; and Aaron saw them and was ashamed; and Nancy and Henry saw them, and Nancy laughed for mere joy of seeing, and when he heard it Henry felt his heart labour as it had never done before with the summons and the power; and Sybil saw them and adored, and saw beyond them, running down the stairs between herself and Nancy as if he were their union, and poised behind Joanna as if he supported and protected her, the vivid figure of the Fool. He had come from all sides at once, yet he was but one. All-reconciling and perfect, he was there, running down the stairs as he had run down the storm. And as he passed, receiving and bestowing light, Nancy, on an impulse, turned and kissed Henry—before the light should vanish, so that she might have done it, might have done it if in days to come she should ever find herself a part of that dreadful cry which had gone up from the world. But even in the kiss she felt her smarting hand throbbing an answer, an answer and an oath that years should see valiantly kept. When she looked back, the figure of the Fool was gone; she heard Joanna cry out in a natural voice, and she saw the children cease from their play and look up, and then Joanna ran down the rest of the stairs, and, as she reached the bottom, cried out once more as if in pain, and stumbled and fell.

The cry shook the golden light; it vanished. Amabel, gazing, saw Miss Coningsby in the hall and the old woman lying in a heap at the foot of the stairs, and before she had time to move she saw the other visitors coming flying down them. They came very swiftly, but as if they also came in order; the lovers first, still hand in hand, and after them Mr. Coningsby, still anxiously watching Nancy, and thinking as fast as he could that he must keep in touch with her, whatever happened. And after him again came Ralph and Stephen, distracted from their mutual hostility, but with all their strength ready and vigilant. The three great orders of grace and intellect and corporeal strength, in those immature servants of their separate degrees, gathered round the place where Sybil kneeled by Joanna, and the search within and the search without were joined.

Mr. Coningsby peered over Henry's shoulder. "Has she collapsed?" he said hopefully.

Nancy kneeled down also, and Sybil's hands and hers were busy with easing and helping. Amabel, released at last from what she felt must have been a deliciously thrilling nightmare, ran of her own accord to get some water. Aaron came over to the rest. Joanna opened her eyes, and they fell on Nancy. She looked, uncertainly and then eagerly, at the grave young face bending over her, then a great gladness shone in her own. She put out a trembling hand, and Nancy clasped it. She murmured something, and Nancy in similar indistinguishable words answered. Sybil stood up, and Mr. Coningsby edged round to her.

"What's she doing?" he asked, not quite knowing why he was speaking in a whisper. "Is she apologizing or what?"

Sybil did not immediately answer. She looked at him with a smile; then with the same smile she looked round the hall, and her eyes lingered on a little heap that lay where she had been standing just before, a little heap of golden dust, strewn with charred and flimsy scraps, so light that already one or two were floating away in the mere stir of the air. The presentation of the dance was for ever done. She looked at them tenderly; then she turned back to her brother, and said, "She has found her child."

"Has she?" Mr. Coningsby said. "Where?" And he also looked round the hall, as if he suspected that Joanna's child was likely to be a fresh nuisance.

"She thinks Nancy is her child," Sybil said.

Mr. Coningsby stared, tried to grasp it, moved a little, was gently pushed out of the way by Amabel with an "Excuse me, sir," glowered after her, and said: "Nancy?"

"She thinks so," Sybil answered.

"But... but, I mean... what about the age?" her brother protested. "She can't think a girl of twenty—forty, perhaps, if she thought she'd grown up, or four if she hadn't. But not twenty."

"She's looking at something immortal," Sybil said. "Age . . ." She delicately shrugged it away.

Mr. Coningsby stared at her, and then realized that he was a little frightened of her, though he couldn't think why. "But," he began again, and suddenly remembered a single simple fact, "but I thought her child was a *boy*. I'm sure someone told me it was a boy. She doesn't think Nancy's a boy, does she? Don't you mean Henry?"

"No," Sybil said, "I mean Nancy. I don't think it much matters about girl or boy. She thought her child was Messias."

"O!" Mr. Coningsby said. "And is Nancy Messias?"

"Near enough," Sybil answered. "There'll be pain and heart-burning yet, but, for the moment, near enough."